Also by Alissa Grosso

Popular

Ferocity Summer

W9-BFK-106

SHALLOW POND

To my sister Emily, who will appreciate a family
that's even weirder than ours.

Secrets run deep in . . .

SHALLOW
POND

Alissa Grosso

flux
™
Woodbury, Minnesota

First Edition
First Printing, 2013

Book design by Bob Gaul
Cover design by Adrienne Zimiga
Cover images: Woman © JPagetRMphotos/Alamy
         Winter tree reflection © cyberstock/Alamy

Flux, an imprint of Llewellyn Worldwide Ltd.

This is a work of fiction. Names, characters, places, and incidents are either the product of the author's imagination or are used fictitiously, and any resemblance to actual persons living or dead, business establishments, events, or locales is entirely coincidental. Cover model used for illustrative purposes only and may not endorse or represent the book's subject.

Library of Congress Cataloging-in-Publication Data
Grosso, Alissa.
  Shallow Pond/Alissa Grosso.—First edition.
     pages cm
  Summary: "High school senior 'Babie' Bunting is constantly mistaken for her two older sisters, and when her oldest sister comes down with a mysterious illness, Babie and fellow orphan Zach Faraday discover the unimaginable truth about her family"—Provided by publisher.
  ISBN 978-0-7387-3071-4
  [1. Sisters—Fiction. 2. Identity—Fiction. 3. Family life—Fiction. 4. Dating (Social customs)—Fiction. 5. Sick—Fiction. 6. Genetic disorders—Fiction. 7. Orphans—Fiction.] I. Title.
  PZ7.G9088Sh 2013
  [Fic]—dc23

                                              2013005028

                              Flux
                     Llewellyn Worldwide Ltd.
                       2143 Wooddale Drive
                     Woodbury, MN 55125-2989
                         www.fluxnow.com

                Printed in the United States of America

Acknowledgments

I am grateful to everyone at Flux for all their work in turning my words into a real, live book. Special thanks to Brian Farrey-Latz who picked my first novel out of the slush pile and whose continued support and encouragement are very much appreciated. Sandy Sullivan has a sharp eye, a far better grasp of time than I, and very valid concerns about hospital logistics, and this book is much better for it.

Many thanks to Jim McCarthy, who has been there from those early drafts to this finished product.

I am so fortunate to count so many kind, talented writers among my friends. It's always nice to talk to someone who speaks my language. The moral support, words of wisdom, and rock-throwing abilities of The Graduates have been invaluable and have helped to keep me more or less sane, as has the companionship and tireless enthusiasm of my fellow KACers.

I would not be here if it were not for the encouragement and support of my family, in particular my parents, who if you happen to run into them on an elevator or on line at the grocery store will likely hand you a bookmark and tell you all about their daughter's books. Special thanks to my other family, the Grosses, who may have lost an "o" along the way but more than make up for it in their warmth and love.

Ron's support knows no end. Filming book trailers, dog-walking when book promotion keeps me away from home, and supporting me in countless ways, he is always there for me and for this I am eternally grateful.

ONE

Zach Faraday and Cameron Schaeffer showed up in Shallow Pond on the same day. In terms of excitement, it was sort of like Christmas, the Fourth of July, and the annual winter carnival all rolled into one. Yeah, not a lot usually happened in Shallow Pond. That's why my exit strategy was already planned out.

I didn't know, when I got that text message from Jenelle after fourth period, that my exit strategy was already in jeopardy, but I guess I should have seen it coming. History has a tendency to repeat itself, and the Buntings had already shown themselves pretty much incapable of getting out of Shallow Pond. I don't know why I thought I should be any different.

As I headed down the hallway toward my locker, I read Jenelle's message: *Just met your date for winter carn. He is hawt!* I made an attempt to text back that "hawt" was not actually a word, but texting and walking was not yet something I was skilled at. The phone was a recently won concession, a

Christmas gift from my older sisters after years of begging and pleading.

I had only just gotten my locker opened when Jenelle and Shawna showed up, breathless from sprinting down the hall-way. Like I said, not a lot happened in Shallow Pond. A new guy in town was certainly worth a full-out hallway sprint. I glanced down at Shawna's not entirely practical choice of foot-wear.

"In kitten heels, no less," I said. "I'm impressed."

Shawna winced. "I think I twisted an ankle," she said.

After that followed a frenzied string of oh-my-gods and he-is-so-hawts. Somehow in there I was able to gather that his name was Zach Faraday, that he had for reasons no one understood moved to Shallow Pond from someplace far more cosmopolitan, and, oh yes, he was the top contender to be my date for the winter carnival.

"I thought I made it clear that I don't need a date for the carnival," I said.

"But it would be perfect," Jenelle said. "Shawna and I are going with our men. It would be great if you had someone too."

I refrained from pointing out that calling Dave and Frank "men" might have been something of an exaggeration. My two best friends had both paired off in the fall. Somewhere along the way they'd stopped thinking of Dave and Franky as the dorky boys we'd known our whole lives and suddenly saw them as attractive members of the opposite sex. It all boggled my mind. It also left me playing the role of fifth wheel, and as a result Jenelle and Shawna were determined to find me a suitable guy. They'd gotten it in their heads that the winter carnival was going to be the event for which they found me a partner.

"I've been going to the winter carnival my whole life," I said. "I never needed a date before."

"But Zach's not going to have a date," Shawna said. "He just moved to town. You don't want him to have to go by himself."

"He probably isn't going at all," I said.

"Which is why you need to go with him," Jenelle said.

"Just give it a rest," I said.

"He's perfect for you, Bunting," Jenelle said. "He's an orphan, like you."

"Seriously," I said, meaning she had gone too far with that one, but she took it as more of an oh-my-god-no-way sort of "seriously."

"It's like you guys were made for each other," Jenelle gushed.

"That's enough," I said through gritted teeth. I slammed my locker shut. "I don't care if this guy is the best-looking guy to ever set food in Shallow Pond. I'm not interested."

I thought the silent reaction from Jenelle and Shawna meant that they were finally listening to me. They weren't. They were ignoring me completely. There was something else far more interesting at the other end of the hallway. Make that some*one*. I turned to see what was going on, and realized that Zach Faraday was in fact the best-looking guy to ever set foot in Shallow Pond.

I didn't know where exactly Zach Faraday had come

from, but it looked like he'd stepped straight out of a magazine, and not *Sportsman's Quarterly* like the rest of the Shallow Pond population, but *Gentleman's Quarterly*. His clothes made even Shawna in her kitten heels look underdressed. His hair was golden-brown and seemed to glow, as if it was actual molten gold, beneath the fluorescent lighting. His eyes were an intense icy blue, and his smile had the ability to melt knees in a single flash. And you could tell just by the way he walked, by the look in his eyes, that he knew how good he looked. So, naturally, I was determined to have nothing to do with him.

"Still opposed to taking a date to the winter carnival?" Shawna asked.

"Yes," I said. I stormed down the hallway, careful to not even glance in Zach's direction as I passed him.

In a town as bland and drab as Shallow Pond, it didn't take much to stand out. Despite living there my whole life, I'd never really felt like I belonged. Perhaps part of it was the fact that, unlike most of the people in town, I wanted to get the hell away as soon as I possibly could. I knew that my oldest sister, Annie, had once felt the same way; hell, maybe even Gracie had wanted to cut and run at some point. All I knew was that both of them were still there, and I was determined not to suffer the same fate. My hopes were riding on the half-a-dozen college applications I'd mailed out two-and-a-half months earlier, right after Halloween.

I was glad Zach Faraday was around. It meant there was actually someone who would do an even worse job of fitting in than I did. I hoped that his freakishness wouldn't wear off, but I had a feeling that come next week, he'd be sporting the same crappy relaxed-fit jeans and Penn State sweatshirts as the rest of my male classmates. Probably he would crop that thick golden hair of his to a length and style that would blend in nicely with the rest of the men in town.

I didn't care what sort of clothes Zach Faraday wore. I didn't care what he did with his hair. No matter what, I wasn't going to pay him the slightest bit of attention. I had a plan for getting out of this place, and I wasn't going to let some boy come along and ruin all that.

"Wait up!" I heard Shawna shout as she shuffled after me, favoring her twisted ankle. I didn't wait.

"Babie!" Jenelle yelled. She might have been about to say something else, but I spun around and glared at her.

"Don't call me that," I said.

"You need to chill out," Jenelle said. "What's wrong with you?"

"I'm hungry," I said, and I resumed my brisk walk into the cafeteria. But I wasn't hungry. Not really.

The problem with Jenelle and Shawna was that they thought this stuff really mattered. They thought the winter carnival was a big deal. They thought some new guy in town was earth-shattering news. I think they actually sort of liked living in Shallow Pond.

I bought myself a sandwich and an iced tea and headed toward our table in the far back corner. The cafeteria was filled with the kids I'd known my whole life. Dave and Frank were already at our table, their trays overloaded with food.

"You see the new guy?" Dave asked as soon as I sat down,

and that pretty much set the tone for the whole lunch period. In between fawning over their boyfriends, Jenelle and Shawna repeated the same bits of gossip about Zach over and over again. Pretty much the same conversation was going on at every other table in the cafeteria. I almost felt bad for Zach. Then I noticed him at the other end of the cafeteria, at a table mobbed with people—the most popular guy in the school, at least for the day.

"I wonder what he makes of all this?" I said.

"He's going to like it here," Shawna said. "People are probably a lot nicer here than where he's from."

"You don't even know where he's from," I pointed out.

"But people are nice here in Shallow Pond," Shawna said. I wondered if that's what my parents were thinking when they'd picked this unlikely town to settle down in.

"We think Barbara should go with Zach to the winter carnival," Jenelle told the boys.

"Yeah, that would be cool," Dave said.

"Maybe you guys should talk to him," Jenelle said. "You know, get him to ask Barbara to the carnival."

"We don't even know him," Frank said. Shawna nudged him hard in the ribs.

"Just talk to him," she said.

"No, don't," I said. "I don't want a date for the carnival."

"No, we can ask him. It's all right," Dave said.

"I don't even know if I feel like going this year," I said. That's when the four of them looked at me as if I'd just said I was planning on jumping off the Empire State Building or something equally outrageous, but then I noticed them all turning to look at something else. I was afraid to look. I did so, slowly, and I saw Zach and his confident-cool-guy walk headed right toward our table. Crap.

I grabbed up all my stuff and my half-eaten lunch and started heading for the door.

"I just remembered I have to go to the library to look up that thing for class," I called over my shoulder.

"Babie," Jenelle said. I didn't even bother turning to glare at her. I bolted from the cafeteria.

For the record, I'm not afraid of guys. I even technically had a boyfriend once, if you count the three-and-a-half weeks that me and Rob O'Dell were "going out" sophomore year. What I was afraid of was becoming my oldest sister. It's a well-known fact in my family that when she was in high school, Annie was head-over-heels in love with one of her classmates, Cameron Schaeffer.

Annie had been accepted at a decent college and had the opportunity to leave Shallow Pond forever, but she didn't go. She never really explained why, but I always assumed it was because of Cameron. Yes, it's true that he went away to school, but it seemed she figured that if she stayed in Shallow Pond, she could at least see him when he came home on breaks or whatever. Only that never really happened, because it wasn't long after he went off to college that Cameron ditched her. She became mopey and unhappy for an impossibly long time. I doubted that she'd ever really gotten over Cameron.

I never really thought I was in danger of following in Annie's footsteps. I knew every single guy in Shallow Pond, and there wasn't one of them I was in any danger of falling head-over-heels in love with. At least there never used to be—but then I got a good look at Zach Faraday, enough of a look to know that if I wanted to follow through on my plan to bid farewell to Shallow Pond, it would be best to avoid those cold blue eyes, that completely captivating smile, at all costs.

I went into the nearest girls' room and locked myself in one of the stalls until the first bell rang, and then I waited until the hallways were nearly deserted before racing to English class. I stepped through the door just as the bell was ringing.

I hadn't even sat down yet when I heard a voice behind me say, "Sorry I'm late. I got lost on the way here."

I didn't have to turn around to know who it was. How completely unfair was it that a guy who had it all in the looks department also had a smooth, velvety voice? I took my seat and refused to even glance in Zach's direction.

"You must be Zach," said Mrs. Grimes, who was approximately two hundred years old. "Let's see, there's a seat over there next to Gracie Bunting."

"Barbara," I corrected automatically.

"Hmm, yes, I'm sorry," Mrs. Grimes said. "You do look just like your sister."

Zach sat down beside me, and I could hear all around me a twitter of gossiping going on.

"So, you're Barbara," Zach said. I didn't look at him. "I've heard about you."

"It's a small town," I said, still without so much as glancing in his direction. "My guess is that within a week you'll know the complete biography of every resident in this back-water burg."

"Even that of the mysterious Buntings?" Zach asked.

"What's that supposed to mean?" I asked, but unfortunately Mrs. Grimes was suddenly looking right in my direction.

"Gracie, since you feel like talking, why don't you read the passage on page fifty-two for us," she said. I didn't even bother correcting her.

TWO

Jenelle's text messages had reached such a furious intensity, I had no choice but to turn my phone off completely before last period. I ran to my locker after class, pausing only long enough to grab my coat and run. I figured that if I ignored them, then there'd be no way they would be able to arrange for Zach Faraday to be my date for the winter carnival. I suppose I was something of an optimist.

The Bunting residence, a two-story house with peeling-paint siding, had a shabby, dilapidated look to it. Or, to put it another way, it looked like just about every other house in Shallow Pond. Our small side yard was coated with a thin layer of dirty brown snow, what remained from the pre-Christmas storm we'd gotten. It didn't really add very much to the ambiance of the place. I climbed up the four steps to the front door, fumbled for the key in my pocket, unlocked the door, and stepped into the living room—startling Annie, who had apparently dozed off on the couch.

"You're home early," she said. She sat up, sending the

afghan and a book she must have been reading crashing to the floor. "What time is it?"

"Almost three," I said. "You must have fallen asleep."

She glanced at her watch to confirm this fact, then shook her head.

"Unbelievable," she said. "I don't know where the day went. I'm still exhausted from that cold."

Annie got sick right before Christmas, but it seemed to be taking her forever to recover. I don't think it helped that she didn't really do anything besides read and take care of the house.

"Maybe you should go to a real doctor," I said. She laughed at my suggestion. She'd seen Dr. Warrell, Shallow Pond's one and only physician. Let's just say he made my ancient English teacher look young. His initial prescription was bed rest and plenty of fluids. Annie had always balked at the idea of leaving Shallow Pond to see another doctor, but in my opinion she could have benefited from seeing someone whose medical license was obtained sometime *after* the close of the second World War.

"How was school?" she asked.

"Changing the subject?" I watched as Annie got up to fold the afghan and pick up her book. Her movements were stiff and slow, like she was an old lady and not someone in her twenties.

"All the parenting books say that you should have a healthy dialogue with your teenager. It's called a conversation. It works like this: I ask a question and you answer it. Care to try it?"

"You're not my parent," I pointed out. I couldn't help but glance at the mantel where all the pictures were, dated school pictures of the three of us. We looked so much alike—same strawberry-blond hair, same crooked smiles—that it was only the style of clothes that gave us away. On the end of the mantel was my parents' wedding portrait. I used to spend hours just gazing at my mother when I was a kid; I even remember having imaginary conversations with her, as if she could hear me in heaven or wherever I imagined her to be. She was beautiful in her flowing white gown, her strawberry-blond hair in perfect round curls. The man beside her was sharp and good-looking, but it wasn't hard to see who the three of us took after.

"I am, however, your legal guardian," Annie was saying, "and it's my job to make sure you don't run away to Mexico or get a hideously ugly tattoo or get brainwashed by some cult who worships umbrellas and is in secret conversation with space-faring aliens."

"Would a cool-looking tattoo be okay?" I asked. "School was fine."

"See, that wasn't so hard, was it?" Annie sat back down on the couch, as if the effort of folding the afghan and picking up the book had taken all of her energy.

"There's a new guy in school," I said. I'm not sure why I told her. She would have found out sooner or later anyway, I suppose.

"Oh, what's he like?"

"I'm not sure," I said, which wasn't a lie. I wasn't really sure what Zach Faraday was like. The only thing I knew about him was that he was incredibly attractive, but I didn't really know anything about who he was. Well, there was one thing. "I heard he's an orphan too."

"Huh," Annie said. "Well, that's unusual."

"I guess maybe his parents died and he came here to live with some relative or something."

My mother died when I was born. Annie says it wasn't due to complications from childbirth, that it wasn't my fault my mother was dead. She said it was something else that killed her, a disease, but I had to figure that if she was sick, having a child couldn't have been good for her. It probably weakened her, wore her out. The fact that she died right after I was born made it pretty clear to me that I probably *did* have something to do with her dying. Even if the disease would have killed her anyway, my arrival probably killed her quicker. Annie was always saying this wasn't true, but I knew that it was only to make me feel better. Annie's like that. She's always thinking about everyone else's feelings.

Gracie was only three-and-a-half when I was born, so she doesn't remember my mother either. Annie's the only one who remembers her, and the whole time we were growing up she always told us happy stories about how Mom was so sweet and loving, and how she probably still watches over us and takes care of us.

My father almost never talked about my mother. Annie said it was because he loved her so much that it hurt him to talk about her. Maybe this was true, or maybe this was just another one of those things that Annie said to make us feel better. Growing up, I was always scared of my father. He seemed like he was a million miles away; he spent most of his time in his office with the door closed. He would get mad easily and yell at us for things like talking too loud or giggling or other little things that we couldn't really help. I liked to imagine that he was a different person before my mother died, that he was happy and sweet, but then when she died he became so upset that he turned into this nasty man.

He died when I was twelve, a heart attack. I don't know if the heart attack was brought on by him always being angry or because he'd gotten so fat and out of shape. By the time he died he didn't look anything like the slim, sharp-dressed man in that wedding photo. It's weird, but even though I knew my father and never knew my mother, I missed my mother more. Anyway, when Dad died, Annie was twenty years old and old enough to be our legal guardian, so it wasn't as if all that much changed, except now we didn't feel like we had to tiptoe around the house and speak in whispers. Now it was okay to laugh once in a while. It was actually sort of a relief when my father died, which I know sounds awful, but it's true.

Annie must have gathered up enough strength to make dinner, because when I came downstairs a couple of hours later I could smell potatoes and pot roast cooking in the kitchen. My stomach remembered that I'd deprived it of half its lunch and growled angrily.

"Need help with anything?" I asked as I stepped into the kitchen.

"Do you want to set the table?" Annie said. "Gracie should be home any minute."

As if she'd been waiting to be announced, Gracie stepped in the back door, shaking a few snow flurries from her hair. The phone began to ring and Gracie pounced on it. She didn't say much on her end besides "Hello," and a few "yeahs" and "I knows" and such. I assumed she was talking to one of her friends until about five minutes later, when she held the phone out to me and said, "Babie, it's for you."

I sighed loudly through my teeth and snatched the phone from her hands. We'd talked about this before. Gracie had been expressly forbidden from pretending to be me on the phone.

"What?" Gracie said. "She didn't even give me a chance to say who it was—she just started talking."

"Sorry about that," Jenelle said. "I thought it was you. Hey, what's wrong with your phone? I tried calling you."

"I turned it off. What did you tell her?"

"Nothing, really, only that Dave talked to Zach about you and the carnival and Zach thinks you are like totally cute, but he thinks maybe you don't really like him or something. What's that about? What did you say to him?"

"Nothing really, but I already told you I don't want to go to the carnival with him."

"Why not? It would be so much fun! Dave says Zach really wants to go with you."

I could feel both of my sisters watching me. It probably would have been more convenient to just have left my phone on and talked to Jenelle privately, not in the middle of our kitchen.

"I've got to go. We're about to eat dinner," I said, and hung up.

"So, who's this new guy?" Gracie asked. "Jenelle says he's got the hots for you."

"Jenelle is prone to exaggeration," I said. "He's just some guy."

"An orphan," Annie added, not especially helpfully. "Sit down, let's start with some salad."

I thought maybe the spotlight would be off me once Gracie's mouth was full of salad, but I'd underestimated my sister.

"Is he cute?" she asked around a mouthful of lettuce.

"He's all right," I said.

"Let me explain something about the opposite sex," Gracie said. "You have to practically beat them over the head to get them to notice you. So, it wouldn't hurt to show a little interest."

"Let her be," Annie said.

"Thank you," I said.

"I'm just saying," Gracie said, "it's about time this one got herself a boyfriend."

"Enough," Annie said, and amazingly Gracie actually listened. We got through the rest of our salad in silence. As it turned out, she was just biding her time before dropping her bomb.

I had only stuck the first forkful of pot roast into my mouth when Gracie said, "Guess who I ran into today at Mr. K's?" Mr. K's was Shallow Pond's one and only grocery store. Like the town itself, it was small and pathetic. It was also where Gracie worked as one of the cashiers.

She had an eager look on her face, like she actually expected Annie and me to make guesses. We didn't. Then she couldn't hold it in any longer: "Cameron Schaeffer!"

I looked over at Annie. I thought she was going to choke on her food, but she swallowed it down and chased it with half a glass of water. It had been seven years since Cameron Schaeffer was a subject of conversation in our house. After he dumped Annie, we'd pretty much stopped speaking about him, as if he'd ceased to exist.

"How's he doing?" Annie said. I could tell she was trying very hard to make her voice sound light and casual.

"Oh, all right, I suppose," Gracie said.

"Home visiting his mother for a bit, I guess," Annie said.

"Actually, he's moved back in with her," Gracie said.

"What?" Annie and I asked the question in unison. It seemed unthinkable to me that anyone who had successfully moved out of Shallow Pond would move back.

"Is his mother sick or something?" I asked, thinking that maybe Cameron had come back to take care of her.

"I don't think so," Gracie said. "Yeah, it was so funny. I was out on the floor, helping Wanda with a bakery display, and this guy who I didn't even recognize came over to me and goes 'Annie?' and I go, 'No, I'm Gracie.' And then I realized it was Cameron Schaeffer. I mean it's been so long since I've seen him, and he looked a little different and everything."

Out of the corner of my eye, I could see that Annie had gone quiet. She was still eating, but she was chewing as if she couldn't taste the food, staring off at something in the distance. I tried to get Gracie's attention, to indicate that she should shut the hell up, but she was worse than Jenelle sometimes.

"Yeah, so he and I started talking about things and stuff, and of course he was asking how you were doing, Annie, and you too, Babie, and I told him Dad had died. He said he'd heard something about that, and that he was sorry, but I don't think he really was sorry, you know, because of how Dad was to him and all, and, well, I said since he was back living here, he really should come over and visit with us one day."

Annie reached for her glass of water but managed to knock it over instead. As she scrambled to grab it up, it slipped off the table and shattered into a thousand pieces on the floor.

"Oh," she said.

"I'll get it," I said, jumping up from the table to grab the broom and dustpan. I began sweeping up the broken glass before Annie could protest. I tried making eye contact with Gracie while I did so, but she was oblivious.

"Anyway, he said he would love to come by," Gracie said. "He's going to stop by this week some time."

"I'll be right back," Annie said. She nearly ran out of the room, and I heard her feet pounding up the stairs. The bathroom was directly above the kitchen, and the sounds of Annie throwing up in the toilet were unmistakable.

"Well, that's completely unappetizing," Gracie said as she put her fork down.

"What's wrong with you?" I said.

"What are you talking about?" Gracie asked.

"This guy completely broke her heart seven years ago,

and now you're talking about him la-la-la and inviting him over to our house like nothing ever happened. Did it ever occur to you that she may not want to see him?"

"Don't you see, this is the perfect opportunity for a second chance. We throw them together and it'll be like nothing ever happened. They can start all over again."

"Why would she want to do that?"

"She's been mooning over this guy for the past seven years. Believe me, I'm doing us all a favor."

"He broke up with her," I pointed out. "What if he doesn't want to get back together with her? What if he's not interested in her? How do you think that's going to make her feel?"

I heard the toilet flush upstairs and wondered if I should go up and see if Annie was okay, or if she would prefer to be left alone.

"You're so negative, Babie. Maybe if you actually gave something a chance, you wouldn't be so miserable. You should go to the carnival with Zach what's-his-name."

I dumped the cleaned-up glass in the trash, and stormed out of the kitchen.

THREE

When I woke up there was a coating of snow on the ground. It wasn't much, just enough to make things look pretty and wintry. I was hoping for a two-hour delay but no such luck. I didn't feel up to trudging to school in the slush, so I called Jenelle.

"Hey, can I get a ride with you?" I asked.

"That depends," she said. "Are you sure you're okay being in the same car with me?"

"What's that supposed to mean?"

"You don't take my calls, you never called me back last night, I'm not sure if you're still interested in being my friend."

"Oh, relax. We're still friends. Anyway, things got kind of tense here last night. I'll explain in the car."

Jenelle's parents had given her an old Honda for her six-teenth birthday. It was small, belched blue smoke, the speed-ometer was broken, and one of the doors was the wrong color, but it ran and it was hers. All I had was occasional use of the family minivan. When the Honda pulled up to get me, Shawna was in the front seat with her shoes up on the dashboard. She'd ditched the kitten heels and had on a pair of pretty but completely impractical-looking canvas boots.

"I'm trying to dry them on the defroster," she said when she saw me looking at them. "They got wet in the snow."

"That's sort of the idea behind boots," I said.

"So, you've decided you're not mad at me anymore, or you just want a ride?" Jenelle asked.

"I'm not mad at you," I said. "But did you really have to say all that stuff to Gracie?"

"Oh, come on, I can't tell you two apart on the phone, and she was totally going along with it like she was you, so how was I supposed to know?"

"Yeah, I guess you're right," I said. "Gracie's a bitch."

"Wow, I so did not say that at all," Jenelle said.

"No, she is," I insisted. There was enough snow on the road to make things slippery and the little car slid about some, but Jenelle was keeping things under control. "She ran into Annie's old flame at Mr. K's and told him to stop by the house sometime."

"Wait," Shawna said. "By Annie's old flame, do you mean *the* guy? The guy who like broke her heart and made her into this depressed, lovesick, jilted spinster chick?"

"Um, I think spinster is kind of a dated term," I said. "And besides, she's only twenty-six. She's not exactly an old maid. But, yeah, him."

"So, wait, what was the fight about?" Jenelle said.

"She invited this guy—who dumped Annie and pretty much completely ruined her life—over to our house."

"I think it's sort of romantic," Jenelle said. If I didn't look so much like Gracie, I would think Jenelle and Gracie were sisters.

"It's not," I said.

"Speaking of romance," Shawna said, "what's going on with Zach? Is he going to ask you to the carnival?"

"I told you I don't want to go with him."

"But do you really not want to go with him?" Shawna asked, "or are you just saying that so you don't seem over-eager if he doesn't ask you? Because, I mean, I can understand not wanting to look too eager and all, but I can't understand why you don't want to go with Zach to the carnival."

Jenelle must have noticed the look of annoyance rapidly turning to rage on my face because she suddenly said, "So, today's the volunteer assembly. Have you guys figured out what you're doing for your project?"

One of our graduation requirements was that we had to do a service project of some sort. Which basically boiled down to logging twenty hours of community service. Technically we had four years to get this work done, but just about everyone waited until sometime in senior year to get their hours in, and to that end we had a special assembly where we could pick out a volunteer project to do.

"I'm just going to use my assistant Sunday school teaching hours," Shawna said.

"I thought you just did that to get out of having to sit through church service," Jenelle said.

"Yeah," Shawna agreed, "but it still counts as volunteering."

"I was thinking of maybe doing the animal shelter," I said. "That way I don't have to deal with people."

"I was thinking that too, but my neighbor told me she did that her senior year and it was basically just cleaning up shit. So, I don't know, maybe I could do the candy striper thing at the hospital."

The nearest hospital was fifteen miles away, which meant the hospital was out for me. Annie would never agree to drive me there; I couldn't even get her to go there when she was actually sick. Unless I got the same schedule as Jenelle and we could commute together, I wouldn't be able to do it.

"How do you know that's not emptying out bed pans?" Shawna asked.

"No, they just, like, deliver the meals and stuff," Jenelle said.

"But what if someone coughs on you or something and you catch some nasty disease?" Shawna asked.

"Look, just because you got your volunteer hours in doing your stupid Sunday School thing doesn't mean you need to rub it in my face," Jenelle said.

I was kind of glad the two of them were arguing. It took the pressure off of me.

Jenelle's car did a little fishtail as she pulled into the school parking lot, and she had to swerve to avoid hitting a black shiny car driving a little too fast through the lot. We couldn't help it; we all turned to look.

"Who was that?" Shawna asked.

Closer inspection revealed that the car was a Mustang, an old one, though it was so sleek-looking it had either been recently restored or was very well maintained. The vibration from the engine actually made the Honda's windows rattle. We watched as the car pulled into a spot and the engine's roar was silenced. The driver's side door opened, and out stepped, who else, Zach Faraday.

"Wow," Jenelle said.

———————

I spent the day doing my best to avoid Zach Faraday. I skipped lunch, making up some excuse about having to get extra help in Physics. In English class I pretended to be so engrossed in the free-writing exercise we were assigned that I didn't even notice him next to me. When we got to the volunteer assembly, I was prepared to go straight to the animal shelter booth and sign up, then beat a hasty retreat to the girls' room, but as I marched across the room, I noticed a familiar figure milling about in the vicinity of the animal shelter booth. I could probably have just run over, signed up, and run off again before he even noticed me, but what if he signed up for the shelter? I could wind up doing my volunteer time right alongside Zach Faraday.

I looked around at the bright-colored banners displayed in the media center. I was hoping to find something so unappealing that Zach wouldn't even consider signing up for it, but I noticed something else, a little sign taped to the front of one of the tables that read, *Sorry, boys, this opportunity is for girls only*. I made a beeline straight toward it.

"Hi," said the cheery woman behind the counter. "Are

you interested in signing up to volunteer for the women's support hotline?" She was ready to launch into a spiel about the hotline and how I would be able to help others by generously volunteering my time, but I cut her off.

"Yes," I said, "I am."

I wrote my name and contact information down on her clipboard, thanked her for the magnet she handed me, and all but ran out of the room. I was still moving at a pretty fast clip down the hallway when I rounded a corner and plowed straight into Zach Faraday. Smooth, I silently told myself. Also, nice work on avoiding Zach.

"Hey," Zach said in that friendly, laid-back, perfect voice of his.

"Oh," I said, and then, proving that I was skilled in the art of conversation, added, "hey."

He flashed me one of those smiles and held out his hand. "Zach Faraday. I don't think I've ever properly introduced myself."

He obviously expected me to shake his hand. I hesitated.

"Barbara Bunting," I said. I shook his hand quickly.

"See, I feel better now."

I certainly didn't. I felt nervous and weird, and I prayed that someone, anyone, would walk through the deserted hallway and interrupt our meeting, but no one was in the hallway. They were busy scoping out the volunteer opportunities and eating the free chocolate chip cookies.

"I have to go," I said.

"Okay, I'm starting to get paranoid. Was it something I said?"

Yes, it was everything you said. It was also everything you didn't say, just the way you can look through me with those cold blue eyes or set me instantly on fire with that perfect smile. How could I explain to him that I knew I needed to avoid him at all costs, at the risk of throwing away everything I'd always wanted.

"I need to go to the bathroom," I said. It was the best excuse I could think of on short notice. I hated it.

"Oh, okay, um," Zach stammered. I knew he wanted to say something but I didn't want to hear him say it.

I speed-walked in the direction of the nearest girls' room, doing my best impersonation of someone who desperately needed to pee even though I think he knew I was faking it.

I locked myself in a stall and just stood there trying to remember how to breathe. What was wrong with me? Why was I allowing myself to get so freaked out over some random guy? I told myself that he was just a guy, that he wasn't really special, but like my excuse about needing to pee, it was a complete lie. Zach was not just some guy, and if being the best-looking guy to ever set foot in Shallow Pond's high school qualified as special (and how couldn't it?) then Zach Faraday had specialness oozing out his ears. So I tried a different tactic. I tried telling myself that someone who looked like that and dressed in those sort of clothes and drove a car like that must be a stuck-up snob. I told myself that he was probably a complete asshole. The only problem there was that, so far, he seemed more like a nice guy than an asshole. I clung to the flimsy excuse that the nice-guy thing was just an act to hide his true asshole nature.

As for why I clung to this excuse, the answer was once again simple. If I allowed myself to start seeing Zach as a sweet, gorgeous guy who had the ability to turn me into mush with a single glance, then it was only a matter of time before we started dating, before I became head-over-heels in love with him, before I made him the sum total of my existence, only to have my heart smashed to smithereens when he dumped me. Maybe it was a lot to infer from a few encounters, but I'd seen the scenario play itself out with Annie and I had no desire to follow in her footsteps.

Four

I cleared the plates from the dinner table. Annie had barely eaten anything. The previous night's unpleasant dinner atmosphere still hung heavy in the air. Gracie had been good, had not even mentioned Cameron's name, but it didn't matter. The damage was done. I'm sure Annie hadn't been able to put Cameron's return out of her mind. When Gracie went upstairs to watch some TV show in her bedroom, I loaded the dishwasher while Annie remained at the table staring into space. She looked awful. Her skin was too pale. Her face was drawn.

"Do you feel okay?" I asked.

"I'm fine," she said.

"Maybe you should go to a real doctor, at the hospital," I said. "Jenelle's probably going to be volunteering there. I could ask her to find out which doctor is good."

"I'm fine," Annie said again. This time her tone was a bit more clipped and angry. I let the matter drop.

"What about you? Have you figured out what you're doing for your volunteer project?" she asked.

I thought about the women's support line I'd signed up for on a whim. Did I even want to do that? I imagined the hopeless sort of women who called a support line for help. These were women who didn't have the wits or the strength to get by, women who were intimidated by the big scary world. They were, I realized as I pictured these helpless waifs, women very much like Annie. I felt sorry for these women, but what sort of help could I give them?

The advice I would give would be to quit whining about their problems and do something about them instead. To quit being so scared of life and just start living it already. They probably wouldn't let me anywhere near a telephone, though. In fact, they would probably tell me I wasn't the right sort of person for helping out with the support line. I would have to find a different volunteer job. It seemed pretty obvious—I was going to end up at the animal shelter cleaning up shit, and probably, with my luck, I would be working right alongside Zach.

I was about to tell Annie I hadn't yet made up my mind about a volunteer job when our doorbell rang. The sound made me jump. Our doorbell almost never rang.

"Who is that?" I said, before realizing who it probably was. Annie pushed back her chair and started to stand up, but she looked shaky and fragile. She seemed like she could collapse at any moment. "I can get it," I said, and I ran to the front door.

I opened the front door expecting to see the Cameron

I remembered, the lanky eighteen-year-old with the shaggy hair, but, of course, the guy standing on our stoop bore only a passing resemblance to that Cameron. He had filled out some. His hair was cropped close and was even starting to thin out a bit. His face had stubble on it, like either he had forgotten to bring his razor back home with him or he was trying to go for that casual sort of look that only a handful of movie stars are actually capable of pulling off. The liberal cologne application made me think that his aim was to impress, and that the stubble was part of some sort of look from a magazine he was going for. This is what would happen if any of my Shallow Pond classmates tried to emulate the effortless cool of Zach Faraday. After all, Cameron was nothing but a Shallow Pond boy all grown up.

He looked surprised to see me. Well, he wasn't the only one who'd changed since we last met. Last time Cameron had laid eyes on me I was still a kid, ten years old.

"Babie," he finally said when the shock had worn off. "Wow, look at you."

"It's Barbara now," I said.

My mom's name was Susie, and Annie and Gracie had just seemed like cute nicknames for Anne and Grace that echoed my mother's cute nickname. Then I was named Barbara, and no one wanted to give me a nickname that would forever be associated with a voluptuous doll, and besides, my last name was Bunting. So, naturally, I became Babie. When I was thirteen, I decided I really didn't want to be Babie anymore. I grudgingly let my sisters get away with it, since I didn't see any way to break them of the habit, but for everyone else I decided I would be Barbara.

"Barbara," Cameron repeated. He'd been gone a long time. I could forgive him for not knowing about my nickname change, but I couldn't forgive him for everything.

"What are you doing here?" I asked. I stared hard at him, hoping he would come to his senses and crawl away back home, but, though he shrank away from me a bit, he did not attempt to run.

"Cameron!" Gracie's happy squeal was followed by her dashing down the stairs. She nearly pushed me to the ground in her run to the door. "Babie, what's wrong with you? Cameron's freezing his butt off out in this cold." Cameron gave me the slightest of smirks as he stepped into the house. Was it because Gracie had called me Babie? Was it because he'd won this little showdown? "Annie, come out here!" Gracie yelled.

"Hi, Cameron," Annie said, surprising Gracie and me. We hadn't realized she'd come in from the kitchen.

"Hey," Cameron said.

No one knew what to do. The four of us stood there; I assumed everyone felt as awkward as I did. I kept looking from Annie to Cameron, trying to figure out what they were thinking, what it must be like to see each other after all this time, but I couldn't tell what was going through their heads.

Several seconds passed and no one said anything, no one moved. Then Annie and Cameron both started to say something at the same time, so both stopped talking, and then again at the same time they tried to tell each other to go ahead. I thought it was uncomfortable, but Annie actually started laughing—not a polite chuckle, but a real laugh. When was the last time I'd heard Annie laugh like that?

"Sorry," Cameron said. His face had gone somewhat pink with embarrassment, and that made him look a lot more like the boy I remembered. "Did I catch you at a bad time? I should have called first. I was just driving around, and then I thought I would stop by."

"It's fine," Annie said. "We just finished eating a little while ago."

"Let me take your jacket," Gracie said. "Sit down."

With a significant amount of awkwardness we found places to sit in our living room. It made me realize how small and cramped the room was. Gracie and Cameron sat on the couch, and me on the little bench no one ever sat on by the window. Annie lowered herself gently into the armchair.

"So, the prodigal son returns," Annie said. She seemed so relaxed about this whole thing. I wondered if she was in shock.

"Something like that," Cameron said. He played absently with the fringe on the pillow.

"You're living with your mother?" Annie asked.

"For a while, yes," Cameron said. "Until I can get back on my feet."

How bad did things have to be for a grown man who had escaped from Shallow Pond to come back and move into his mother's house? I figured Cameron Schaeffer had hit rock bottom.

"I'm sorry about your father," Annie said. I had a vague

memory of Mr. Schaeffer dying a few years back. I wondered if that was the last time Cameron had been in town.

"Thanks," Cameron said. "I mean, I'm sorry about your father as well."

Once again, an awkward silence filled the room. I knew my father never really liked Cameron, but the details were hazy in my mind. Was it just the stereotypical dad-not-liking-the-guy-who-is-dating-his-daughter sort of thing, or was it something more than that? Did my father have a good reason for hating Cameron? Maybe it was the fact that it was Cameron's fault Annie had stuck around this town instead of getting out while she had the chance. I wondered about my father letting her do that. Could he really have been that apathetic about her future? Unless he let her stay for selfish reasons, not wanting to have to handle taking care of me and Gracie on his own.

"It must be so weird to be back home in little Shallow Pond again," Gracie said. "You were living in New York, weren't you?"

"New Jersey, actually," Cameron said. "The wilds of suburbia."

Annie laughed at this, and this time it was a fake laugh. I cringed at the sound of it.

"It probably beat this place," I said.

"I kind of like being back," Cameron said. "It's nice the way nothing changes here." I thought he was right about nothing ever changing, but I didn't see what was so nice about that.

"Well, some things change," Annie said in a quiet voice.

"Yeah," Cameron agreed with a fake laugh of his own. "Look at Babie. You're practically all grown up." He shook his head. "I remember when you were just a little kid."

And I remember when you were just some stupid guy my sister was madly in love with, I thought but didn't say. *Some stupid guy who didn't think twice about breaking her heart.*

"Babie's got an admirer," Gracie announced.

"I don't," I said.

"The new boy in town is sweet on her," Gracie said.

"Gracie, that's enough," Annie said.

"What?" Gracie protested. "It's true. I thought you were going to the winter carnival with him."

I shook my head. What *didn't* Jenelle say on the phone last night?

"The winter carnival," Cameron said. "I forgot all about that. It must be coming up soon."

"It's Saturday night," Gracie said. "You are going, aren't you?"

"I don't think—it's been so long since I've been back here. It would probably just feel strange."

Cameron was trying to politely say he would be bored out of his mind spending his Saturday at the ridiculously lame Shallow Pond winter carnival, but Gracie was oblivious.

"You have to go to the winter carnival!" she shrieked. "Annie, tell him he has to go to the carnival. Nobody misses the carnival."

"Well, I think I'm probably going to sit this one out," Annie said. Walking across a room seemed to tire her out, so of course she couldn't be outside traipsing around the park in the cold.

"I'm sure if I go, every person I meet is going to want to know what I've been up to and what I'm doing back here," Cameron said. "I pretty much got sick of answering those questions about a half hour after I got back."

"You could go with Gracie," Annie suggested. "She could run interference."

"Oh, no, I couldn't make her do that," Cameron said. "She's young. She doesn't want to hang around with an old has-been like me. I'm sure she wants to go with her friends and have fun."

"What friends," Gracie said with a snort. "All my loser friends ran off to college and they hardly ever come home anymore, not even for the carnival."

I thought to myself that Gracie had it backward. She was the loser who didn't go to college and instead stayed in this backwater town operating under the delusion that the carnival was some sort of important social event. I glanced over at Annie. She looked uncomfortable. Her face was pinched. I thought it might be some sort of physical discomfort, but it could also have been what Gracie just said. That bit about her loser friends running away and never coming back—just like a certain young man who'd left town with Annie's heart all those years ago.

"We *should* go together," Gracie said to Cameron. Didn't she realize he didn't want to go? How dense could she be? "We could have so much fun. We could even make up some wild story to tell people when they ask what you've been doing all this time."

Cameron smiled at this. "It would be interesting to go to the carnival again," he said. Wait, what? Was he serious? "Annie, you sure you couldn't be persuaded? Does Ben still make those ice sculptures with his chain saw?"

"If you mean the unidentifiable misshapen lumps of ice, then yes, every year," Annie replied. "I think he considers it his civic duty. So you'll excuse me if I pass. I'm just getting over a bad cold, and don't feel one hundred percent yet." I figured she was maybe twenty percent at most. "You and Gracie should go, though." She smiled at Cameron, but it was a forced smile that almost looked like a grimace.

"This will be so much fun," Gracie gushed. "Babie, you could come along with us, you and—what's the new guy's name?"

"I'm not even sure if I'm going," I said.

"Of course you are," Gracie said. "Only a complete loser would miss the carnival."

I wished Gracie would learn to use her brain before she opened up her mouth. I tried to send a look of sympathy in Annie's direction, but Annie was in some sort of daze, staring off into space.

"That's different," Gracie said, seeing my expression. "Annie's not going because she's still sick. Right, Annie?"

"What?" Annie asked, snapping out of her daze.

"You're not going to the carnival because you don't feel well," Gracie said.

"Yes," Annie said, but she sounded distracted.

Sitting there in the armchair, Annie looked old. She looked a lot older than twenty-six. She did look a bit like the spinster Shawna had accused her of being. The weird thing was that Annie was the same age as Cameron, and even though he'd clearly matured some, he still looked pretty young—a lot younger than Annie looked, anyway. Maybe it was just the light in the room, and maybe it was because she'd been sick—was *still* sick—but it scared me a little seeing her looking old like that. I'd already lost two parents. I didn't even want to think about losing a sister as well. Still, it was hard not to think about that when I saw how awful she looked.

FIVE

I remember there used to be a picture in Annie's room of her and Cameron taken at the winter carnival back when they were in high school. The two of them were bundled up in hats and coats, his arm around her. They both wore big huge grins on their faces. It was hard to imagine that my sister had ever been that happy, and yet vaguely I could remember she used to be a different person. It made me realize what a complete shit Cameron Schaeffer was.

Did he have any idea what he'd done to her? Did he even care? When he saw her the other night, didn't he notice how different she was from the girl he used to know? If he had a shred of humanity, he might have at least wondered whether he was the cause of that radical transformation.

I couldn't remember the last time I'd seen that picture of Annie and Cameron. Probably she'd taken the thing down and burned it. That would be the sensible thing to do. Who needed to be reminded about the way things used to be? Annie used to have a bunch of pictures in her room—not just of Cameron but of everyone she knew, including some of our parents. They were all gone now, tucked away in a box somewhere, I supposed, or maybe burned up. If she had it to do over again, I'm sure she would do it differently.

"Is Jenelle picking you up?" Annie's voice startled me. I'd been lying on my bed thinking of her, and then suddenly she was there.

"I told her I'd meet her there," I said. "I don't even know if I'm going to go."

"Don't be silly," Annie said. "You can't miss the carnival."

"I feel bad leaving you here all by yourself," I said. It wasn't really true, but I couldn't tell her the real reason I didn't want to go.

"Well, I was planning on taking a hot bath and then turning in early. So I'm afraid I won't be much company."

This is what happened if you let yourself get tripped up by some stupid romance. The next thing you knew, you were someone whose youth was vanishing before her very eyes, someone who spent Saturday nights taking baths and going to bed early, someone so sad and depressed that it seemed to be making her physically ill.

"It's not easy having him back here, is it?" I asked.

"Cameron?" she asked, like there was some other mysterious guy who had returned to Shallow Pond. "That was all a long time ago, another lifetime."

The lifetime where she'd been happy and full of hope. The lifetime where she had a chance to get out of Shallow Pond and do something, anything, with her life.

"It's not too late," I said.

"What? Me and Cameron?"

"No!" I yelled the word, startling both of us. A reunion with Cameron was the last thing I had in mind for her. "I meant it's not too late to go to school or travel the world, or do whatever you need to do to get out of here. It's not like you have to stay here to take care of me."

"Ah, the self-centered musings of a teenager," Annie said. She sat down next to me on the bed and began to play with my hair. "You do realize it's entirely possibly that I might be here in Shallow Pond because I actually like it here."

"It seems highly unlikely," I said.

"You have her hair," Annie said. "It's the same exact shade."

We all had her hair, that same strawberry-blond that was actually a spectrum of shades from light blond right through to fiery red. They mixed together in a reddish blond that sparkled in the sunlight. Photographs could never quite do it justice, not managing to get the sparkling sort of quality, making it look darker.

"Did I ever tell you that it was the winter carnival that convinced her to move to this town?" Annie added. "At least, that's what I was always told."

She looked out the window, where day was fading rapidly to night. It had been a chilly day and once the sun set, it would be bitter out. Not the sort of night any sane person would want to be wandering around outside. If all else failed, maybe I would be able to use the weather as an excuse.

"She saw the winter carnival and the way everyone in town knew each other, the way everyone was laughing and talking to one another, and she decided that this was the town she wanted to live in and raise her family in. I know you find this hard to believe, but there are some people who think that Shallow Pond is a charming little town."

I tried to imagine what it must have been like, my mother and father visiting Shallow Pond for the first time. I imagined her appreciating the quaintness of the place. She would have found the winter carnival cute. It's always easy to think of such things as cute when you don't actually live there. She would have imagined what it would be like to settle down there, to raise a family in a town where everyone knew everyone else, where there could be no secrets. Perhaps she thought about growing old in this town, dreamed of someday becoming a grandmother. Not all dreams come true. Surely she never dreamed that her life would come to a sudden early end after the birth of her third child. I could feel a lump forming in my throat as I tried to imagine the mother I never knew. The woman whose hair was the same as mine.

"Did she go with you to the carnival when you were growing up?" I asked.

"Oh," Annie said. "Sure, we all went." When I was growing up, I'd always gone to the carnival with Annie and Gracie. I don't remember my father going; maybe that was one of those things that reminded him too much of her. When I was younger, any opportunity I had to make a wish, I always wished that my mother was still alive. Things would have been so different if she'd been there. I think I might have even felt like I belonged in Shallow Pond, that I wasn't just some outcast freak who didn't fit in.

"It's not really my kind of thing," I said, about the carnival.

"You should go," Annie said. "Next year, you'll be away at college somewhere and won't be able to go."

"Something tells me I won't be all that crushed."

"Just go," Annie said. "And bring back some of those roasted chestnuts for me."

I was about to ask her if that was her ulterior motive behind insisting I go, but my phone began to ring. It was Jenelle. She wanted to know where I was. I told her I was just about to leave the house, which was only a small lie.

———————

Jenelle told me to meet her and Shawna by the food stands. That worked out well. I would be able to pick up Annie's roasted chestnuts first thing, before I had a chance to forget about them. Memorial Park was only about a half mile from our house. I was dressed warm enough, so the walk down there wasn't too bad. Part of the way, I walked behind a family with two young kids. It reminded me of what Annie had said about my mother moving to Shallow Pond because of the carnival. This would have been what she envisioned for her life, walking to the carnival as a family, and that's how it had been before my arrival had messed everything up.

At the park I threaded my way past the kiddie area, with its face-painting and bouncy castle, to get to the food stands. The air was rich with the smell of roasted chestnuts, and even though I thought they tasted disgusting, the smell made me hungry.

"Finally," Jenelle said. "We thought you were never going to get here."

"My feet are numb," Shawna told me, but I decided that wasn't really my fault. She was wearing the impractical kitten heels again.

"Didn't you realize you'd be walking around on the frozen ground?" I asked.

"Yeah, but nothing else matched," Shawna said.

"You can tell the doctors that when they have to saw off your frostbitten feet."

"The guys just went off to get us some hot chocolate," Jenelle said. "Let's grab a table."

The park's pavilion was decorated and lit up for the occasion. It almost made you forget that it was late January and bitter cold outside. Almost. Half-frozen people huddled at the tables warming themselves with paper cups full of steaming beverages. Shawna spotted a table off to the side and moved toward it as fast as her kitten-heeled feet could go. We sat down, and a few seconds later Dave and Frank showed up with six cups of hot chocolate and Zach Faraday.

"Look who we ran into," Frank said, in a wooden voice that sounded completely fake.

"Seriously, Shawna?" I asked. "You couldn't have coached him any better than that?"

"I don't know what you're talking about," Shawna said, in a voice that was only slightly more believable than her boyfriend's.

"This was just an impromptu meeting," Dave said. "It didn't seem right to make Zach spend his first winter carnival all alone."

I'd known Dave my entire life, and I knew for a fact that he had never before used the word "impromptu." This whole thing had been staged for my benefit, and I felt like an idiot. I should have known they'd do something like this.

"If you want me to leave, it's okay," Zach said.

I did want him to leave, but it wasn't like I could say that out loud, not without sounding like the biggest bitch in the world.

"It's fine," I said without looking at him. Instead I stared at Jenelle, who was clearly the brains behind the operation. "I'm just annoyed that the people I thought were my friends feel compelled to pull stunts like this."

So we all sat there at the chilly picnic table sipping our hot chocolate in silence. No one seemed to know quite what to say. I almost felt bad for Zach, but then I glanced over at him and saw how cool and calm he looked and changed my mind. No one had the right to be that unflappable.

"Hey, the bonfire starts in like ten minutes or so," Dave said. "Then after that we could go skating."

The bonfire, where Shallow Pond ceremoniously burns each year's discarded Christmas trees, is pretty much the head-lining event of the winter carnival. You know how people use the term "watching paint dry" to describe something really boring? Well, watching Christmas trees burn is sort of like that, only less exciting.

As we walked from the pavilion over to the bonfire, Jenelle and Dave and Shawna and Frank paired off. Normally I felt a little awkward walking on my own, usually trailing them by a few steps, but tonight I wasn't alone. By default, I found myself walking alongside Zach. Still, there was a good three feet between us. There was little chance anyone would mistake us for a couple.

"So," Zach said, "they have this thing every year."

"Every year," I agreed. "And sadly, this is what passes for excitement around here."

"I think it's kind of cool," Zach said. "It feels sort of friendly and homey."

"Apparently, that's a pretty common reaction. It's what convinced my mother to move to Shallow Pond."

"Is she here tonight?"

"She's dead."

"Oh. Sorry."

"It's fine," I said. "I never even knew her."

I quickened my pace just enough that I wouldn't have to walk right alongside Zach, and he had enough sense to not try to keep up with me. It was weird, but I'd never needed to explain my family situation to anyone before. Everyone in Shallow Pond knew about the Buntings. We were those poor girls who everyone pitied. It would be awesome to go somewhere where no one knew about my dead parents or me and my sisters, where I was just some normal, average girl.

"Gracie!" someone called. I turned around, but I didn't see my sister. Instead I saw Mrs. Mullen, who worked with

Gracie at the grocery store, headed in my direction. She stopped short and squinted at me through the Coke-bottle lenses of her glasses, apparently realizing her mistake. "Sorry, you're Gracie's sister, aren't you? You don't know where she is, do you?"

"She's here somewhere," I said. This seemed to satisfy Mrs. Mullen, who wandered off in the direction of the frozen pond.

"You have a twin?" Zach asked.

"No," I said. "Just two older sisters. People are always mistaking us because we have the same color hair."

"That must be a pain," Zach said.

"It is."

"But it would be cool to have sisters."

I remembered what Jenelle said about Zach being an orphan. I wasn't even sure if it was true, and I wasn't about to ask him. Still, I wondered what things had been like for him. Had he grown up all alone? Did he live with grandparents or relatives or something?

"What's that supposed to be?" Zach asked.

We were walking past one of the ice sculptures. Ben Roberts, who had a tree-cutting business, carved the ice sculptures for the carnival every year. The problem was, he didn't really have any artistic talent, so his carvings never really looked like much of anything.

"Ice sculpture," I said.

"Yeah, but of what?"

This one was sort of egg-shaped; well, a lumpy sort of egg with something kind of spiky protruding from one side.

Perhaps it was supposed to be some sort of face in profile, or maybe a furry woodland creature. It was hard to say.

"It's sort of like a guessing game," I said. "You have to use your imagination."

"Oh," Zach said. He squinted and tilted his head as if that might bring the lumpy statue into focus.

Standing there looking at Zach looking at the ice sculpture, I felt a bit of my resolve evaporating. It wasn't that I was overwhelmed by his good looks or his charm, though God knew he had both in abundance. I felt something else. I couldn't explain it, but it was almost like Zach and I had known each other for a long time. He had that comfortable sort of feel, like an old pair of jeans that fits just right. I wondered if that's the way it always feels when you meet that someone who you're supposed to be with, your soulmate.

The idea freaked me out, and I took a few steps away from Zach as if physical proximity alone could bind the two of us together. I didn't need a soulmate. I didn't want a boyfriend, let alone a soulmate.

Zach turned away from the ice sculpture and smiled at me. It was a friendly sort of smile, as if he was completely oblivious to that weird connection between us. Maybe he was. All I knew was that Zach had a smile capable of melting ice sculptures, and if I wanted to keep my wits about me, I had to stay as far away from that smile as I could.

The bonfire was as lackluster as ever. We were so far back from it that we could barely feel the heat it gave off. Shawna started to complain about her frozen feet, and Jenelle suggested we all go over and rent some skates, which might be a good way for Shawna to warm up her feet.

When we got to the stand where they rent the skates, Dave and Frank paid for the rentals for each of their girl-friends. I was on line behind them, but before I had a chance to get my skates, Zach asked me what size I took. I started to answer, but stopped when I realized he was planning on paying. I didn't want to give him the wrong idea. I had no idea what Zach had been told about me, but perhaps it was time to set the record straight.

"I can pay for my own skates," I said in an icy tone.

"It's no big deal," Zach said. "I have the money."

"So do I," I said. "Look, I don't know what Jenelle or Shawna or anyone told you, but let me make something very clear. I'm not interested in you."

Zach held up his hands defensively, like I'd just attacked him, which I suppose in a way I had. I could feel myself shaking with anger. Dave and Frank had already gone off to bring the skates to Jenelle and Shawna, and I realized how it was going to be. It was going to be another one of those couple things, where I would automatically get paired off with Zach. Not only that, but I could already see that this could easily become a weekly tradition—the six of us hanging out together, and by default Zach and I would always wind up together. It would be pretty much inevitable we would wind up together unless I did something to radically alter the course of events. Or maybe I could just let things take what seemed to be their natural course.

I glanced over at Zach and again felt that energy between

us. What would happen if I *did* go skating with Zach, and if next weekend we all went to the movies together, and on and on until, well, when exactly? Until the point when Zach found someone new and ditched me? I thought of Annie at home, taking her hot bath and going to bed early. I thought of the way she'd looked when Cameron showed up at our house. I didn't want my future to look like that, and if there was anyone who could make me lose myself so completely that I ended up following in my jilted sister's footsteps, it would be Zach Faraday and his stupid smile.

"Look, I'm sorry they conned you into coming to this carnival," I said. "That was wrong, and I had nothing to do with that. In fact, if I had known that's what was going on, I would have stayed home. I think I've changed my mind about skating. I don't really feel up to it."

"Okay, you're right. I was being presumptuous. Let's try this again." He gave me a puppy dog look that I guess was supposed to make me melt. Why did he have to be so damn good-looking?

"Go skate," I said. I waved in the direction of the frozen pond where a bunch of folks were skating around. "Go enjoy Shallow Pond in all its shallowness." I stalked off.

"Let me at least give you a lift home," Zach said.

"I'm fine," I said. I walked faster.

"Hey, where are you going?" Shawna asked.

"Home," I said. "It was a mistake to come here tonight."

"What are you talking about?" Jenelle said. "We're having a great time."

"You're having a great time," I said. "I'm not. Good night."

I broke into a run as soon as I got away from the pond. I felt hot and angry and I just wanted to get away from everyone. I glanced back at the pond as I ran, but I couldn't see them anymore. No one had tried to follow me. Then I looked where I was going and saw something big and brown.

I was so startled that it took me a second or two to realize I needed to stop running to avoid a collision. I did, but just barely.

"Whoa," someone said. "Look out."

It was a horse-drawn sleigh, and I'd nearly run into the horse. The sleighs are one of those cozy romantic things that couples pay extra for at the carnival. It would probably be the next stop for my group after they finished skating. I'd gotten away just in time. This sleigh had a couple in it, curled up together in the back seat.

"You can't come through this way," the driver said. "This is the sleigh track through here."

"Sorry," I said.

"Babie?" Looking up, I saw Cameron Schaeffer. He disentangled himself from Gracie and stood up. "Are you okay?" he asked.

"I'm fine," I said.

"Why aren't you with your friends?" Gracie asked.

"I just decided to head home. I thought I would cut through this way."

"You can't walk home by yourself," Cameron said.

"I'm not a little kid."

"I know," Cameron said. "It's not safe to be walking around by yourself in the dark."

"This is Shallow Pond," I reminded him.

"I'll give you a ride," Cameron said.

"Why don't you get Jenelle to drive you?" Gracie said. "Cameron and I weren't planning on leaving yet. We haven't finished our sleigh ride, and then we want to go skating."

"Actually, I'm getting tired of having to explain to everyone what I'm doing back in town," Cameron said.

"I'm fine," I told them again, but Cameron insisted on driving me home. I think he was just looking for any excuse he could to leave the carnival early. He may have been a complete shit, but I felt bad for him. The Shallow Pond winter carnival was sheer torture.

Gracie, on the other hand, was clearly pissed to be leaving early. She glared at me as we got into Cameron's car. It was old and came to life with a very reluctant shudder. As we pulled out of the parking lot, Gracie waved to someone she recognized. She rolled down the window to shout something at them, and cold air blew on me.

"You're freezing out your sister in the back seat," Cameron told her. She sighed, gave one last wave, and rolled the window back up.

"Oh, it was so funny," she said. "Everyone kept thinking I was Annie, you know, because I was with Cameron. Right, Cameron? Wasn't it funny?"

"Yeah," Cameron said.

"Yeah, Mrs. Mullen thought I was you," I said.

"She has bad eyesight," Gracie said. "Did that new guy show up? The one who likes you?"

"I don't want to talk about it," I said.

"She's going through her moody teenager phase," Gracie told Cameron, in a voice loud enough for me to hear her clearly.

Cameron glanced at me in the rearview mirror, and I'm not sure, but I think he was trying to offer me a sympathetic smile. Perhaps he wasn't so bad after all. Hell, between the winter carnival and having to spend the evening with Gracie, I figured he'd certainly done his penance.

It wasn't until we'd pulled up in front of the house that I realized I forgot to get Annie her roasted chestnuts.

Six

I woke up Sunday morning to my cell phone ringing. It was Jenelle. I'd ignored all her calls and texts the night before. I wanted to ignore this one as well, but I knew from experience that she would try calling the house line instead.

"That was total bullshit yesterday," I said.

"Well, I'm glad you can admit your mistakes," she said in a snotty voice.

"No, I meant what you did to me was shit. My behavior was completely reasonable."

"Storming off like a spoiled kid?"

"I told you I didn't want to go to the carnival with Zach."

"What? It's not my fault he was there and Dave and Frank felt bad for him being all alone."

"Cut the crap," I said. I didn't hear anything for a few seconds and wondered if she'd hung up on me. "You still there?"

"I don't like seeing you all miserable and depressed, and I just thought if you met a nice guy, maybe you would come out of your funk."

"I don't need a guy to make me happy," I said.

"What? Are you saying I do?"

"I'm saying that the only thing that will make me happy is getting the hell out of this piece-of-crap town."

"I guess we're not good enough for you, is that it? We're just small-town folk and not all cosmopolitan like you are, because you're from—wait, where are you from again? Oh, that's right, Shallow Pond, just like the rest of us."

"Look, I just woke up," I said. "Can I call you back later?" My head hurt, and I didn't really want to have this conversation right now.

"Just forget it," Jenelle said, and this time the silence signaled the end of our conversation.

Odds were, only a handful of kids from my class would actually stick around Shallow Pond after high school. Most kids went off to college or whatever, and few of them ever returned except for the occasional holiday or funeral. I knew Jenelle probably wouldn't be spending the rest of her life in Shallow Pond, but the difference between her and me was that she wouldn't have minded spending the rest of her days there, whereas I couldn't imagine a worse fate. Of course, part of the reason I was so desperate to leave, so hung up on getting out of that place, was our own family legacy. The Buntings seemed to have a difficult time getting away from Shallow Pond.

I waited a few seconds to see if Jenelle was going to call back or perhaps send an angry text, but the phone remained silent. I climbed out of bed and headed downstairs. The kitchen was empty, and I wondered if I really could be the first one up. I poured myself a bowl of cereal and was just about to start eating when the back door swung open and Gracie stepped in with a bag of groceries. I couldn't believe that my sister would actually go into Mr. K's on her day off to go shopping.

"I ran into Shawna at Mr. K's," Gracie said. "She told me you totally ditched them last night."

"Well, that's her version of the story. It's actually a bit more complicated than that."

"Oh, I don't think it's complicated at all. I think you're a selfish, miserable little girl who can't stand to see anyone else happy."

"Yeah, that must be it," I said. I pretended to be completely engrossed in reading the facts about whole wheat on the back of the cereal box.

Gracie put away the groceries she'd bought, muttering to herself as she did so. She sounded like a bit of a crazy person. Finally she shoved the milk into the fridge and turned around to face me. "Cameron and I were having a good time last night until you came along and spoiled everything."

"Cameron wasn't having a good time," I said.

"What are you talking about?"

"He was miserable. You know, once you've lived in places where things actually happen occasionally, it's hard to return to a world where the winter carnival is about as exciting as it gets."

"Just because it's not your sort of thing doesn't mean other people don't enjoy it, and, FYI, it's not always the event itself that makes things fun, it's who you're with."

I thought about this. There had been something bothering me ever since I saw Gracie and Cameron cuddled up together in that sleigh, and Gracie's words seemed to drive this home for me.

"What the hell are you doing?" I asked.

"Putting away the groceries. What does it look like?"

"No, I mean with Cameron."

"I don't know what you're talking about."

"I saw the two of you together. Gracie, are you two like a couple or something?" She didn't answer right away, but she didn't have to. I could see the look on her face—she liked him. "Oh, this is so wrong."

"It's not wrong at all," Gracie said. "We're two grown-ups. Cameron's only a few years older than me. I don't see what the big deal is."

"But this is Cameron Schaeffer. I mean, what about Annie?"

"What about her? She told us to go to the carnival together."

"Yeah, but she didn't mean it like that."

I realized I had lost my appetite. I dumped the rest of my cereal bowl into the sink.

"That was all a long time ago," Gracie said.

"You can't do this to her," I said.

"Can't do what to whom?" Annie asked. She was standing in the kitchen doorway. I don't know how long she'd been there. I looked at Gracie, hoping she knew better than to say anything out loud. She looked flustered and nervous.

"Nothing," Gracie said.

Annie raised a skeptical eyebrow. "How was the carnival?" she asked.

"Fine," Gracie and I said in perfect unison. Annie gave us another curious look.

"I forgot your chestnuts," I said. "I'm sorry."

"It's all right," Annie said. "They always smell better than they taste anyway."

Gracie finished putting away the rest of the groceries and all but ran off, saying she had something she needed to do upstairs. I didn't want to be alone with Annie. I knew she'd start asking me questions about the carnival, and it would only be a matter of time before I blurted out something about Gracie and Cameron. So I said I was going to take a shower and abandoned Annie in the kitchen.

———

Jenelle made a point of not speaking to me at school on Monday. I couldn't tell if Shawna was in on the silent treatment campaign also, but I figured it would be just as well to avoid the awkwardness of the lunch table. So I spent my lunch in the library instead, trying to read my history book but not having much luck. It was true that Shallow Pond wasn't exactly awash in eligible bachelors, but there were at least a few of them. Surely Gracie could have hitched her star to one of their wagons. Did she really have to pick Cameron Schaeffer, of all the available men in town? It wasn't like he was that good-looking.

"Hey." It was like he was reading my thoughts or something. Unbelievable. Zach Faraday stood beside the study carrel. "I didn't see you at lunch, so I thought I might find you here."

"Perhaps I'm not at lunch because I needed to get some studying done," I said.

"Oh, sorry. I'll let you get back to your work." He started to walk away, and I was thinking it had gone incredibly smoothly, but then he stopped and turned back toward me. "I feel like we kind of got off on the wrong foot."

"We haven't gotten off," I pointed out. I was careful not to look at Zach. It was easier that way. If I looked at him—those eyes, that smile—it might have just melted me. I assured myself that as long as I kept my distance, I would be fine.

"What I mean is, your friends. I mean, they were all trying to play matchmaker or whatever, and I guess I should have realized you weren't really involved in any of that. That they were kind of doing it behind your back and all. I thought maybe you were just kind of shy."

"It's cool," I said. "I forgive you." I turned away and read the same paragraph in my history book that I'd been reading for the past twenty minutes with no success. I thought he would take a hint and walk away. He didn't. I could feel him standing there. I finally spun around and glared at him. "What?"

Why did he have to be so damn good-looking? I wondered if he stood for hours in front of his mirror practicing looking cool. His clothes must have cost a small fortune.

If he really was an orphan, perhaps he was one of those orphans who'd been left a big fat trust fund.

"You hate me," he said.

"I don't hate you." I didn't. I didn't like him, either. I couldn't afford to like him. I wanted to avoid having to feel anything about him.

"Well, it seems like you hate me."

"Look, I'm sorry you got stuck moving to this shithole town halfway through your senior year of high school. It's a fate I wouldn't wish on my worst enemy, but I'm sorry if I don't feel like it's my job to play angel and try and rescue you or something."

"I don't think I'm really looking for an angel. I would settle for a friend."

"I have enough of those," I said.

"You're talking about those flighty, giggly girls who tried to fix you up with some guy against your will? The girls who aren't even speaking to you at the moment?"

Damn you, Zach Faraday and your incredible powers of observation. "Jenelle and Shawna have their flaws, but we've been friends a long time," I said.

"I suppose one more friend would push you over your limit then?" He smiled at me like this was all some big joke, and it was one of those million-watt smiles. I could feel my defenses weakening.

"In August, I'm leaving for college and never looking back."

"I don't think spending the rest of my natural-born life in Shallow Pond was exactly what I had in mind either, but August is, like, eight months away. So, what do you say? Truce?"

"Sure, whatever."

"Friends?" he asked.

I sighed. "Fine, friends."

He held out his hand and I shook it. It was ridiculous and formal, and I couldn't help but laugh at it.

"Ha, I knew you could smile."

I snatched my hand away and shook my head. "Don't push your luck," I said.

"Right, well, I'll let you get back to your studying."

He walked away and I watched him leave. Of all the people in this school, why did he feel compelled to be friends with me?

I returned my attention to the history book, but my brain was even more useless than it had been before. I couldn't make any sense of the words on the page. I kept thinking about the way Zach's hand had felt so warm and soft and perfect. I kept thinking about that smile. I kept thinking about the way he'd gone out of his way to be friends with me. Was this how it all began? I felt dangerously close to the precipice, like at any moment I would stumble off and into the waiting arms of Zach Faraday. It seemed like only a thin thread was holding me back from becoming the sort of girl who could throw away her whole life for some stupid guy.

I forced myself to read the history book, trying to drill each word into my head and chase away those ridiculous thoughts that had taken up residence there.

SEVEN

"I hate to tell you this, but that television isn't even turned on."

I looked up, and Annie was standing next to the couch smiling at me. I'm not sure how long I'd been sitting on the couch staring off into space.

Nearly a week had passed since the carnival, and it had been a strange week. Jenelle and Shawna were finally speaking to me again, but things weren't back to how they used to be. It felt like something had changed forever between us. I wasn't sure that things could ever go back to the way they used to be. Maybe it was because we were growing up and changing.

"I was planning on making some biscuits from Mom's recipe to go with dinner. Why don't you come help me?"

It sounded like a question, but what Annie was really saying was get your lazy ass off that couch before you grow roots. I followed her into the kitchen.

It looked like she had finally kicked that cold. She was up and about and acting like her old self again. It was good to have her back to normal. At least something in my life was normal.

Annie flipped through the little tin box that held all of our mother's recipes. Some were worn-out pieces of paper clipped from magazines, but the best recipes were the ones on dirty, stained index cards that had been written in her own hand. Annie pulled out the biscuit recipe and placed it on the counter. I stared at the familiar card with its looping handwriting and tried to conjure up an image of my mother.

"Did you used to help her make biscuits when you were younger?" I asked.

"Well, I was pretty young," Annie said. "She would let me help her measure the flour, though."

That was the reason Annie was such a good cook. She'd actually had someone to teach her. I helped her get the ingredients out, trying to imagine that there was a third person in the kitchen with us. But there was no third person, just an old recipe card and an empty place.

"Gracie said you had some sort of fight with your friends."

"I don't want to talk about it," I said.

"Sometimes it helps to talk about things."

"We're not fighting anymore," I said. It was true, but it almost felt like a lie. It was like the fight between us would never quite go away. "When you were getting ready to graduate, were you excited about college and moving away?" I asked.

"I had mixed thoughts on that," she said. "Shallow Pond was my home. It was the only place I'd ever lived. I was scared about going away."

"Really?" I didn't feel that at all.

"You're not scared at all?" she asked.

I thought about it. The only thing I was scared about was getting stuck in Shallow Pond, or having to come back.

"I'm scared of things not working out," I said. "I'm scared of failure."

"Well, so you are human after all." I ignored the derisive tone in Annie's voice. If it were anyone else I might have snapped at them, but I couldn't snap at Annie.

"So, you didn't go to school because you were scared?"

"Well, yeah, that's a big part of it. It's complicated."

I watched her as she stirred the biscuit ingredients together with a wooden spoon. She stared off into space as if she was seeing the future she'd given up on.

"Complicated, how?" I asked.

"Well, for one thing, there was you and Gracie," she said. *And Cameron*, I thought but didn't say.

"So, you're saying it's our fault you didn't go to school."

"Not at all, but somebody needed to take care of you."

"But Daddy was still alive then."

"That he was." Her voice trailed off as she said the words. She stared into the bowl of batter. "Come here and help me roll this out."

I helped Annie to get the batter rolled out, and then we began to cut out biscuits using a glass to make perfect little circles. I didn't for a second buy the idea that fear of the big bad world and the need to help take care of me and Gracie were the only reasons she didn't leave home. Those were excuses, not real reasons. Maybe that's what she'd told herself, and maybe after years and years of telling herself this she actually believed it, but it sounded like a load of crap to me. The reason my sister was still stuck in Shallow Pond was Cameron Schaeffer. Yes, she may have been scared to leave town, but that's because she was scared it would also mean losing Cameron. I wanted to ask her a thousand different questions about Cameron, but I couldn't.

Instead I said, "Our parents were really in love, weren't they?"

"Yes." Annie said. "Yes, I suppose they were. What makes you say that?"

"I was just thinking about the way Daddy was. How he always was so unhappy and upset about things, but he probably wasn't always like that. It was probably just because he was really in love with Mom and he missed her so much."

"He was very much in love with her," Annie said. "Sometimes, when someone is so in love, they lose all sight of everything else. They can think of nothing else." Was she talking about our father, or was she talking about herself?

"I don't know why anyone wants to fall in love," I said.

"Because love can be a beautiful and magical thing."

"Yeah, until it comes to an end. Then it's ugly and painful." Annie nodded in agreement with this observation. "I'm not going to fall in love," I said. Annie began to laugh. "I'm not," I repeated, angry that she thought I was making some sort of joke.

"It's not like you have much say in the matter," Annie said. "Love is one of those things that just sort of happens."

"Yeah, but you can prevent it from happening," I said.

"Well, that doesn't sound like much fun."

We lined the biscuits up on the cookie sheet and put them into the oven. There were way too many of them. Annie said every time we made the recipe that we should cut it in half, but then she always forgot when it came to actually making the biscuits.

There was an old, faded picture of our mother in one of those magnetic frames on the refrigerator. It was taken wherever our parents had lived before they'd moved to Shallow Pond. There were three dogs in the picture, golden retrievers, family pets who'd died before I was born. They were all girls from the same litter, and Annie said our parents had trouble keeping them straight so they had the dogs wear different-colored collars. Rose, Tulip, and Crocus—those were the names of the dogs.

My mother had a big huge grin on her face as she sat on the ground with the three of them. The picture was so faded that her hair and the dogs' fur were about the same drab peach color. I wished I'd known her. It was not hard to see why my father had been in love with her. She looked like such a happy, free-spirited person.

The back door opened with a bang and I jumped, but it was only Gracie home from work, rushing into the house.

"Smells good in here," she said. "Hope you didn't make any for me."

"Of course there's some for you," Annie said.

"Not eating with you," Gracie said as she walked past, grabbing up a lump of leftover biscuit dough and sticking it in her mouth. "I've got a date tonight, and I'm late. I've got to go get ready."

"With whom?" Annie asked. I looked at Gracie in alarm.

"Just, um, some guy, from, um, work." Gracie didn't bother to elaborate and headed upstairs, taking the steps two at a time.

"We're going to have way too many biscuits," Annie said.

"We could eat some for breakfast," I said. Annie didn't know that Gracie was going out with Cameron, and it was better that she didn't find out. Why did Gracie have to be such an idiot? What was she doing going out with Cameron anyway?

"And perhaps lunch as well," Annie added. "We're going to have a lot of leftover chicken too. You know anything about this guy she's going out with?"

"Like she would tell me anything." I forced a laugh. Maybe it would be possible to keep Annie in the dark for however long it took for this stupid romance to run its course. I prayed that it was as short-lived as nearly every other relationship Gracie had ever had.

Then the doorbell rang.

"That must be her date," Annie said.

"I'll get it!" I yelled, but Annie was closer to the door.

"I'd like to get a look at this guy," she said.

No you don't, I thought.

Annie opened the door and stared at Cameron standing there. She seemed to have forgotten how to speak.

"Hi, Cameron," she finally managed. "How are you doing?"

"About as good as a down-on-his-luck guy who's back living with his mother can be, I suppose."

"What can I do for you?" she asked. If Cameron had any brains at all he would make up some excuse that would set her mind at ease, but he was an idiot.

"Is Gracie not ready yet?" he asked. "I guess I'm a few minutes early."

There was a second or two of dead silence as Annie finally realized what Cameron was doing at our house. She waved him into the living room graciously.

"Gracie's upstairs getting ready," she said. "I'm sure she'll be down in a couple of minutes. So, did you get a job at Mr. K's?"

"Mr. K's? No, why?"

Annie gave a phony laugh that made me cringe. "Oh, just something Gracie said." Then she called up the stairs in a completely false sing-songy voice, "Gracie, your date is here."

I heard something drop on the bathroom floor and Gracie swore.

"Hey, Babie," Cameron said to me. "How's it going?"

"Barbara," I corrected automatically. "I'm fine."

Gracie came running down the stairs. She smiled at each of us in turn. "Cameron!" she said, as if surprised to see him in our living room. "What an unexpected surprise."

"I'm sorry," he said. "I guess I'm a few minutes early."

"Oh, I…" Gracie stammered, aware that her cover had been blown.

"I better go check on the biscuits," Annie said, and she escaped into the kitchen.

"Let me just grab my jacket," Gracie said to Cameron, her voice so quiet it was practically a whisper. She sprinted up the stairs and was back down again in record time. She grabbed Cameron's arm and dragged him out the front door. He waved over his shoulder at me as the door closed, and I waved back.

Annie came out of the kitchen. She didn't say anything to me, just walked over to the window and watched Gracie and Cameron get into his car and drive away. She kept standing there long after they left. The air became thick and unpleasant, and it took me a few seconds to realize that it was the biscuits burning. I ran into the kitchen and rescued them from the oven. I began removing the biscuits from the cookie sheet. Their bottoms were charred black.

EIGHT

Shallow Pond seldom got rain in the winter, but it began raining sometime between second and third period and kept up all day. I hadn't brought an umbrella with me, and I wasn't looking forward to getting soaked walking home. Normally I would ask Jenelle, but she and Shawna and Dave and Frank were going to drive to the mall after school. I'd been invited, but declined. It would have been one of those weird fifth-wheel situations for me, and extra awkward as I'd have to share the back seat with Shawna and Frank. Last time that happened, I found myself with my face pressed against the window trying unsuccessfully to ignore the two of them sucking face and groping each other beside me.

I tried calling home, but I only got the voicemail. Where could Annie be? Was she asleep? Maybe she was vacuuming or watching television or doing something else that prevented her from hearing the phone. I tried two more times before giving up.

I pulled my jacket's hood up before stepping outside into

the miserable afternoon. I slipped on the sidewalk and nearly did a faceplant into the concrete. Apparently the rain had turned to sleet. It was going to take forever to get home, and I was going to look like an icicle when I got there. I trudged along, my hands in my pockets, my head down so that the ice pellets didn't sting my face.

It had been a weird weekend at my house, and I'd been relieved that morning to go to school. Annie claimed that she was fine with Gracie dating Cameron, but she didn't act fine. Instead she spent pretty much the entire weekend lost in daydreams, barely aware of what was going on around her, and trying to cover for this weird behavior by laughing at things that weren't funny and saying things that she thought sounded bright and cheerful but just made her sound like she was trying too hard. Gracie acted like the cat who'd eaten the canary and kept making defensive comments like, "Well, it's not like it was my idea," or "Well, he's going to date someone, right? I don't see how it matters who he dates," even though no one was criticizing her. It was almost like she was asking Annie to make some critical remark. I just tried to avoid both of them, but our house wasn't that big.

I heard a car pull up beside me and assumed it was Jenelle, yet even as I thought that I realized the engine was too deep and rumbly for her car. I looked over and there he was, that smile turned up full blast. The car, even in this weather, glistened and shone the way no car that old had any right to.

"Need a lift?" Zach asked.

"I'm fine," I said. I kept walking. Zach just rolled along

beside me. The car looked warm and inviting and I wanted more than anything to get in there, but I knew that I shouldn't.

"There's ice raining from the sky," Zach pointed out.

"It's called winter," I said. I tried to add a bit of chipper to my tone, but I feared I sounded creepy and slightly demented, like Annie and her forced happiness.

"Get in the car," he said. "I really don't want your death from pneumonia on my conscience."

"It's not that far," I said.

"Good, then I won't have to charge you for gas. Now would you get in already?"

At that a big gust of wind tore up the road and bit right through my jacket. Zach stopped and popped open the passenger-side door. I sat down, relieved to be someplace dry and reasonably warm.

"Thanks," I said.

"Are you always this stubborn?"

"I'd been planning on walking."

The car looked as perfect inside as it did outside. Either the thing had spent the first thirty-some years of its life locked up in a museum somewhere or somebody had spent a lot of time and money meticulously restoring it to its former glory. I wondered how someone like Zach Faraday got his hands on it.

"Nice car," I said.

"Thanks," he said. "It was a gift."

"Kind of puts the sweater I got for Christmas to shame."

"It's a long story," he said.

"You need to make a right here," I told him.

"I got a better idea. Let's go to the diner. They have great pie and spectacularly awful coffee."

"I'm not hungry," I said.

"Well, you can at least keep me company then. I hate eating alone."

I reasoned that it would be rude to demand that he take me home, but honestly? I wanted to go to the diner with him. I wanted to go anywhere and everywhere with him.

We got a booth in the back. Zach ordered a slice of apple pie à la mode for himself and a coffee. I tried to beg off from ordering anything, but Zach told me I should at least try a slice of pie. I relented and ordered the cherry pie and a glass of water.

"I don't blame you," he said when the waitress walked away. "The coffee's atrocious."

"Then why did you order it?"

"I'm a glutton for punishment," he said.

"Speaking of which, what brought you to Shallow Pond?"

He laughed at this, then scratched at his temple as if deciding whether or not he felt like telling me, or maybe just figuring out which lie to spin.

"It's a long story," he said. Apparently he had a few of those.

The waitress returned. She set down a gigantic slice of pie in front of each of us along with my water and Zach's atrocious coffee. The pie was pretty good. The filling had just the right amount of sweetness. The crust was perfectly flaky.

"So," I said, "you were going to tell me how the fates of the universe brought you here."

His hair was already perfect, but he ran a hand through it and made it even more perfect.

"It's almost absurd," he said. "Very nineteenth-century."

"You weren't kidding about it being a long story," I said.

"I mean, it has the feel of something from a nineteenth-century story or play or something. Like the *Importance of Being Ernest*, but not as funny and without the cucumber sandwiches." He'd lost me on that one. "The play," he clarified. "Oscar Wilde." I shrugged, to let him know it was fine to continue. "Right, well, the thing is, I was raised by a bunch of nuns. I was left in a basket on their front step. There was a blanket wrapped around me with a note clipped to it. It told them my name and thanked them for taking care of me."

I laughed. He sat back and waited patiently for me to finish laughing.

"You think it's a joke. You think that what I know about my origins is a tale to amuse you." I thought this might be more of the joke, but there was something about his look that told me I might have jumped to conclusions.

"Seriously?" I asked. "You were abandoned on the front step of a convent?" He nodded. "That almost makes my family look normal."

"If it's any consolation, mostly people have a hard time believing my story."

I thought about this. It all did seem highly improbable, and then there was the matter of his nice clothes and nice car. Orphans raised by nuns did not drive cars like that.

"What about the Mustang?" I asked, "And all your clothes?"

"Ah, well, if the whole left-in-a-basket thing isn't enough to strain your credulity..." He shoveled another forkful of pie into his mouth and chewed it all before he continued. "I have a wealthy benefactor."

"A wealthy benefactor?" I repeated.

"Yeah, I know. It's very Dickensian, isn't it?"

"Who is this benefactor?"

"Well, that's the ten-thousand-dollar question. He or she has supported me over the years with gifts of money and material goods sent to the convent. Sometimes there are notes with the gifts, but they're never signed."

"And you're not at all curious that you have this mysterious sponsor?" I asked. I wasn't sure if I believed him or not. It all seemed a bit far-fetched. There was a good possibility that he wasn't even an orphan at all, just some ordinary guy who was especially good at making up stories.

"I was pretty much obsessed with the idea of finding out when I was younger," Zach said. "I would read my benefactor's notes over and over, again hunting for clues. I would try and make sense of the different postmarks on things. The truth is, it's probably either my mother or my father, who feels a terrific amount of guilt for abandoning me like that and thinks this is the way to pay their penance. Maybe I was some inconvenient love child, or maybe my parents were dirt poor and then through some twist of fate became suddenly wealthy after abandoning me or something. Anyway, I guess I've come to terms with the fact that whoever he or she is, they don't really want to be found out, and I guess I can live with that."

I shook my head. I didn't feel there was anything I could

say. The story was ridiculous. It couldn't possibly be true, but the ho-hum way in which Zach told it made me wonder. If he was making up the whole thing in order to get attention or create an air of mystery or whatever, I would think he would work a bit on his delivery. I ate my pie, stealing glances at Zach while I did so. I waited for him to break, for a smile to creep over his face or for him to add one last completely ridiculous detail to the story that would push everything over the edge—an alien abduction, perhaps, or the curious fact that he had no reflection when he looked in mirrors.

"Okay," I said. "What percentage of that story is true?"

"All of it," Zach said. He scraped the remaining pie residue from his plate, avoiding looking in my direction while he did so. I kept staring at him, waiting for him to come clean. He didn't. Then he looked back up and said, "I don't normally tell people the whole story. I learned early on that it's easier to just keep my mouth shut."

"Then why did you tell me?"

"Because we're friends."

"Cut the crap," I said.

"Okay, the truth is, because I thought of all people, you might be able to understand."

"What's that supposed to mean?" I asked, but Zach didn't get a chance to answer.

"Babie! Hey, how's it going?"

I looked up to see Cameron Schaeffer standing there.

"Hi," I said, because *please leave me the hell alone and don't call me Babie again unless you want to lose a testicle* might have come out sounding kind of rude.

"This must be your cousin," Cameron said, giving Zach a nod of hello. "Hey, sorry I can't stay and chat, but I've got to go pick my mother up from the beauty parlor, and I'm running late."

I watched him walk away. I hated to admit it, but he was sort of a good-looking guy. I mean, don't get me wrong, he was a complete jerk, but I could understand what my sisters saw in him, sort of.

"Cousin?" Zach asked. I shrugged.

"I have no idea. Probably some sort of weird Cameron Schaeffer version of a joke," I said.

"And Cameron Schaeffer is?"

"My one sister's old flame and my other sister's new flame."

"Well, that is seriously fucked up."

"Yeah," I agreed. "It is."

The thing was, if Zach, a complete stranger, could see how seriously wrong it was, how could Cameron Schaeffer *not* have known how weird it all was? Basically, he'd traded in Annie for a newer model. Hey, if I was unfortunate enough to get stuck in Shallow Pond for the rest of my natural-born days, I could be Cameron Schaeffer's next girlfriend. Well, as if I didn't have enough incentives, there was one more reason to get the hell out of this town as soon as I possibly could.

"Well, at least I know it isn't me," Zach said.

"What?"

"I'm guessing for a Bunting girl to show any interest in me, I'd have to be named Cameron Schaeffer."

"I'm not interested in Cameron Schaeffer," I said, and

even as I said it I could feel myself blushing. What was wrong with me? "I'm not my sisters."

My pie plate was empty. So was my glass of water. I had nothing to distract me. I looked out the window, only to find myself staring at Cameron walking across the parking lot. I quickly looked away and found myself looking at Zach. He smiled at me, and I forgot about Cameron.

"So, then, you aren't a coven of witches?" he said, still smiling. "Or let's see, what were some of the other rumors I heard? Oh, right, that the three of you were vampires or succubi or something."

"Shut up," I said.

"I'm just saying the Buntings have quite the reputation."

"Shallow Pond's the sort of town where they like you to fit in and not do anything to rock the boat."

"So I gather," Zach said.

He wasn't so bad. I mean, with his good looks and excessive confidence I thought he'd be kind of a stuck-up jerk, but he wasn't. He was a nice guy and super attractive, which didn't really seem fair, or possible, for that matter. Like his life story, it was just a little bit too much to believe. There had to be something wrong with this guy. Nobody was perfect, unless maybe he was a robot.

"Why are you here?" I asked.

"Because I like pie, and I saw it as an opportunity to spend some time with the prettiest girl at Shallow Pond High."

I rolled my eyes and shook my head. "I meant, why are you in Shallow Pond?"

"Oh," he said. "That would be because of my benefactor."

"You tracked your benefactor down?" Already I was coming up with possible suspects from Shallow Pond's residents.

"No, nothing like that," Zach said. "I received a letter. There was an apartment waiting for me here, and arrangements had been made for me to finish my senior year of high school here."

"Why?"

"Couldn't tell you." Zach glanced out the window, and it was the first time I'd seen him look anything but supremely confident. For the briefest second he looked a little bit like the lost boy he must still have been inside.

He turned back to face me, and he was all cool and confident again. "I wasn't going to come here, but then I decided it was time to get on with my life, see the world, that sort of thing."

"I'm going to assume that's nothing but a lame joke," I said. "No one gets on with their life here, and no one comes to Shallow Pond to see the world."

"I'm not disappointed I came," he said. His icy blue eyes met mine, and I felt them burrowing into me, weakening my resolve. I looked away.

"We should get home," I said. I felt hot, like I was blushing again. "The roads are going to get bad."

There was a thin layer of ice on Zach's windshield. Some of the other cars had been sitting there longer and had a thicker coating. It was going to start sticking to the roads. I'd walked out of the diner ahead of Zach when he'd insisted on paying for my pie; I was annoyed or confused or a little bit of both.

"Friends let friends buy pie for each other," he said as he came down the steps. He wobbled a bit on a slick spot on the last step. Well, look at that, Zach Faraday was human after all. He quickly recovered and, in that confident swagger of his, walked over to unlock the passenger-side door.

A car pulling into the parking lot did a little bit of a fishtail, and I looked up and saw a familiar-looking Honda. Jenelle must have decided the weather was too iffy to drive all the way to the mall. I hoped she was totally focused on controlling her car in the slick parking lot, but no such luck. She'd seen us, and she pulled into the handicapped space beside us.

"Babie?" she asked, like maybe I might be someone else.

"Don't call me that," I corrected. It was pure reflex. "You can't park here," I said, pointing at the handicapped sign.

"Hey guys," Zach said. "How are the roads?"

"The highway was a mess," Dave said. "We turned around and headed back."

"What are you two doing here?" Jenelle asked.

"Zach was just giving me a ride home," I said.

"We stopped to get some pie," Zach said.

"Do they have cherry pie?" Shawna asked from the back seat.

"Yeah," Zach said, "but the apple's the best."

"I just didn't know you two were…" Jenelle didn't finish her sentence. She probably considered herself some master of subtlety.

"We're not," I said. "And we've really got to go. The ice."

I opened the passenger door of Zach's Mustang and quickly slid in, pulling the door closed after me. Zach waved goodbye to everyone, then got in on the other side. He started the car and the big loud engine roared to life. He cranked up the defroster to melt the ice on the windshield. I could feel Jenelle staring at me from her car but I didn't look over, and after a few seconds she pulled out of the handicapped spot to find another parking space.

"So, what was that about?" he asked.

"What was what about?" I asked.

"I thought you two were friends. You're having some kind of fight again?"

"We're not having a fight," I said. We weren't having a fight, at the moment anyway. It was just that I could already see how this was going to play out. Jenelle and her big mouth would turn me and Zach eating pie at the diner into some sort of whirlwind romance or something. Within a week, people would be convinced I was carrying his love child. A part of me was thrilled at the prospect of a Barbara-and-Zach rumor making the rounds at school, and that part of me scared the hell out of me.

Zach ran the wipers to clear the ice from the windshield, then backed out of the spot. He pulled out of the lot a little too quickly and we skidded slightly on the ice. My hand tightened on the door handle, but he quickly righted the car. He drove slowly and cautiously toward my house.

"How come people call you Babie?" he asked.

"It's just some stupid nickname," I said. "If you use it, I'll probably have to kill you."

He nodded, as if he took this pronouncement very seriously. I was impressed.

"I agree," he said. "It's a stupid name. I mean, it's like people are calling you a little kid or something."

"It's why I have to leave Shallow Pond," I said. "Around here, I'll always be the littlest of the Buntings, the Babie of the family."

————————

When I stepped through the front door, Gracie nearly tackled me.

"Who was that?" she asked. She'd seen me get out of Zach's car. It was possible she'd been lying in wait by the window, but probably she had heard the Mustang a half mile away. Unless Cameron had tipped her off. I didn't know if they were at the I'm-calling-you-because-I-saw-your-sister-eating-pie-with-some-teenage-hearthrob stage of the relationship yet.

"Just someone from school," I said. I decided it would be best to be as vague as possible.

"A boy from school?"

"Yeah, a boy, and he only gave me a ride home because it was nasty out." I left out the part about the diner, hoping she hadn't been in communication with Cameron.

"It's that new guy, isn't it? Chip in produce was saying he had some fancy car."

"If you already know all this, why are you asking me so many questions?"

"He's sweet on you, isn't he?"

"I don't know and I don't care," I said. "Where's Annie?"

"She wasn't feeling well, so she turned in early. Is he cute? I heard he's really cute."

"What do you mean, turned in early? It's four in the afternoon." I started up the stairs. I still had my coat on and my wet shoes, and I was sure I was leaving a trail behind me, but I didn't care.

"Just let her rest," Gracie called.

I peeked in on Annie. She was sound asleep beneath her blankets, snoring lightly. She'd been feeling so good lately, it was hard to believe she was sick again. Maybe she was faking it to avoid having to spend time with Gracie. I listened carefully, but the snores sounded real.

My phone rang, shattering the silence, and I ran down the hall hoping it hadn't woken Annie.

I didn't pull the phone out until I was in my room with the door closed. I looked down at the screen. I already knew who it would be. Jenelle. She was going to want details. She was going to want an explanation. I debated answering. On the one hand, it would feel better to get this all over with, to get everything out in the open. On the other hand, I didn't know exactly what to say to Jenelle. I mean, there wasn't anything to say. All that happened was that Zach had given me a lift home and we had stopped along the way for pie. That was it. End of story.

So why did I feel like I was hiding something from Jenelle? Why did telling Jenelle that Zach and I were just friends feel like a half truth at best, and at worst a bald-faced lie? I didn't answer the phone. I wasn't sure what would come out of my mouth if I started talking to Jenelle.

NINE

I could ignore all the phone calls and text messages, but there was no way to ignore the Honda surrounded by a cloud of blue smoke parked outside our house the next morning. I guess I should have considered myself lucky. I would have been late for school if I hadn't gotten a ride, but I knew it wasn't going to be a pleasant ride.

"I can't believe you blew us off to have some sort of secret date with Zach Faraday," Jenelle said when I got in the car.

"Good morning to you too," I said.

"Good morning," Shawna said. Jenelle just glared at me in the rearview mirror.

I fastened my seat belt. "Well, (a) I didn't blow you off. I was walking home in the middle of an ice storm, about to succumb to hypothermia, when Zach graciously offered to drive me home. But then he wanted to stop off to grab something to eat at the diner on the way. And (b), it was neither a date nor was it secret. There are no secrets in Shallow Pond."

"Speaking of secrets," Shawna said, "did you guys hear that the sophomore chick with the nose ring is pregnant?"

"Don't change the subject," Jenelle said to Shawna, then to me: "Why the hell wouldn't you answer your phone last night?"

"Annie's sick," I said. It was the first thing that came to mind. It wasn't a lie, but it didn't have anything to do with why I hadn't answered my phone. It wasn't like I was providing round-the-clock care or anything. As far as I knew, Annie had done nothing but sleep all night. I hadn't seen her that morning, which might have meant she was still asleep. I hoped she was all right.

"Like, hospital sick?" Jenelle asked.

"No," I said. I didn't add that, as this was Annie, getting her to go to a hospital or even a decent doctor was pretty much impossible. "I don't think it's that serious."

"So, then, maybe you could have spared a minute or two to talk to someone who may or may not still be your friend."

"I was tired," I lied. "Annie does a lot around the house every day."

"It's like you don't even care about us anymore," Jenelle said. "I mean, you could have at least told us that you and Zach were hanging out."

"We aren't hanging out," I said. "I already told you. He gave me a ride home, that's it."

We drove the rest of the way to school in silence. Jenelle had a reason to be upset. I mean, I should have taken her calls. It wasn't like I had anything to hide from her. There was nothing to hide. Zach and I were friends. That was it, end of story.

"Hey," I said as the three of us walked into school together. "I'm sorry if it seems like I've been ignoring you."

"Friends come before boys," Jenelle said.

"No, that's not it," I said. "It's just that things have been kind of weird at home."

"Weird how?" Jenelle asked.

"My sisters," I said with a wave of my hand that I hoped would clear everything up, but Jenelle planted herself in my way with her hand on her hip, waiting for me to elaborate. I sighed. "Gracie is dating Cameron Schaeffer."

"Oh my God!" Shawna yelled. It was so loud that I think everybody on the school grounds turned to stare in our direction.

"Yeah, it's messed up," I agreed.

"So when you said that Annie was sick, you meant more of an upset kind of thing?"

I thought about this. I'd just assumed Annie was physically sick again, but it did seem strange. She'd been doing so well. Now I wondered if maybe she wasn't actually sick, just upset about the Gracie-Cameron thing. I couldn't believe I'd been such an idiot; of course that was what was going on.

"Maybe," I said. "I don't know."

Just a few days prior, Annie had been feeling great. In fact, she'd been practically bouncing off the walls with energy. Baking biscuits, even humming to herself, but that was all before she found out that there was something going on between

Gracie and Cameron. As I thought about it, I realized something else. Annie had started feeling better almost as soon as she'd learned that Cameron was back in town. And she hadn't just been feeling better—she'd been super happy, almost like someone who was in love or something.

I didn't want to believe it, but I didn't see any alternative. Annie was still in love with Cameron. Just seeing him again must have brought back all those old feelings, must have made her feel young and alive again. Well, until she found out the bastard was dating her younger sister.

"Are you okay?" Shawna asked.

"I'm fine, why?" Then I realized I was standing in front of my locker; I must have walked there on autopilot.

"Because you're just staring off into space."

"I was just thinking about something," I said.

"Bunting, you really need to get your head out of the clouds," Jenelle said. "This is starting to get annoying." But she was smiling as she said it, and I felt like things were back to good again between us.

"So are we cool?" I asked. "Can I hitch a ride with you this afternoon?"

"Yeah, we're cool, but I can't help you out in the rides department. I've got to go straight over to the hospital after school. Candy striper orientation."

"Crap," I said. I'd completely forgotten about the women's support hotline thing. It started that afternoon. It didn't really matter, but I'd been hoping to go straight home after school and check on Annie.

The call center was located inside the municipal building, and we had our training in a tiny cramped office. There were only four of us: me, Meg Kelly from my class, and two younger girls who were smart enough to get their volunteer time in before their senior year.

There were three training sessions before we could start volunteering, and the time spent in training didn't count toward our volunteer time. I think if I'd realized that, I might have signed up for a different volunteer job. Surely there wasn't that much training involved in cleaning out animal cages.

There was a crazy, spazzy sort of woman with artificially bright red hair who ran things: "Just-call-me-Danielle." She thanked us about a million and one times for choosing to volunteer. We had to go over a very boring training manual.

"Now," said Just-call-me-Danielle, "it's time for our special guest speaker. Put your hands together for Officer Hantz."

The four of us, reluctantly, began to applaud along with Danielle, and the police officer stood there looking a bit sheepish at the warm welcome.

"Well, I can't promise I'll be entertaining," Officer Hantz said, "but what I do have to say is very important. I'm here today to talk about sex offenders. I work for the regional police and specialize in dealing with convicted sex offenders making a re-entry into society. Sex offenders sound like scary monsters you would find lurking in the alleyways of a big city, but the truth is they usually seem like ordinary folks, and they can be found just as easily in small towns. They can be a boy from school, a neighbor, even a relative."

"There are perverts in Shallow Pond?" asked one of the younger girls.

"I don't like to use the word 'perverts,'" said Officer Hantz. "While some sex offenders are individuals with unhealthy sexual appetites, others are just individuals who got lost in the heat of the moment or let their feelings for another turn to obsession."

I felt my mind wandering. I couldn't help but think about Annie. I should have called the house before I went to the training, just to see how she was doing. Was she obsessed with Cameron? It seemed pretty clear that she was. What was so special about Cameron? Was it just because she'd never dated anyone else? Maybe if she met someone else, she would realize that Cameron wasn't so great after all. The likelihood of Annie meeting anyone in Shallow Pond, especially since she seldom left the house, was pretty slim. Annie was not going to find anyone unless she got out of this town, and she was never going to get out of this town.

The police officer droned on and on about different types of sex offenders and the different ways they victimized people. It was interesting, and I should have been paying attention, but I couldn't focus. I was thinking about love and obsession, about what Annie said in the kitchen the other day. Love seemed like an ugly, dangerous thing. I wondered why more people didn't avoid it at all costs.

"Now, to get back to your question about Shallow Pond and sex offenders," Officer Hantz said, "it's pretty simple to check. Pennsylvania has a Megan's Law registry website. All you need to do is enter your zip code and you can see if there are any registered sex offenders in your town. I urge all women to do it as a safety measure. It's good to know who these individuals are and where they live, to keep yourself safe." He wrote the website address on the board at the front of the room, and I copied it down in my notebook: www.pameganslaw.state.pa.us.

It was dark out by the time we left the municipal building, and after all that talk about sex offenders, I didn't feel like walking home by myself. I called the house, and Gracie picked up on the second ring. She acted like driving over to pick me up was a big inconvenience, but she showed up.

"When I was in school," Gracie said, "I just volunteered at the animal shelter. I got to cuddle cute kittens all day. It was super easy. I don't know why you didn't do that."

"This sounded interesting," I said.

"You're weird," she said.

"Speaking of weird," I said, "are you still dating Cameron?"

"What the hell is that supposed to mean?" she asked. "And, yes."

I shrugged. With her job at the grocery store, Gracie almost always had the latest scoop on gossip, but maybe it didn't work that way if the gossip concerned you. I'm sure the rumor mill had already started buzzing about Gracie and Cameron. Could she really be that clueless?

"How's Annie?" I asked.

"The same." I didn't know what she meant by that, but I couldn't believe I was related to such an insensitive bitch.

"You have to stop seeing Cameron," I said. "She's really hurt by this."

"Oh, give me a break. She needs to grow up."

I didn't point out that Annie was like a thousand times more mature than Gracie. "She still loves him," I said.

"Well, he doesn't love her. So she needs to get over him already."

"Why do you have to date him, of all the guys out there?"

"First of all, there aren't a whole lot of guys out there, and second, because I like him."

But why? I wanted to ask. *Why Cameron Schaeffer? What makes this guy so special?* I kept my mouth shut. I could see I wasn't going to get anywhere with this line of reasoning.

TEN

Zach was waiting for me at my locker when I got to school. I was surprised to see him there.

"What are you doing here?" I asked.

"I think the traditional greeting is something more like hello or good morning or something, but I'm not from around here."

"Right, good morning," I said. "But what are you doing here?"

"I thought maybe you were mad at me or something," he said.

"I'm not mad."

"You barely talked to me in English yesterday."

"I was busy trying to get an education."

"You're not going to get one in that class. That woman can't even remember your name."

He had a point. The truth was, I'd wanted to prove that everything I'd told Jenelle and Shawna was true—that I didn't really know Zach, that we were just friends. I hadn't so much been trying to ignore him as I was trying to avoid looking like I was flirting with him.

"Look," I said. "I'm not mad at you, but you've got to back off a bit. You come on a bit strong, is all."

"Okay," he said. "I understand." He nodded as he considered what I said, then took a physical step back. I was going to say that wasn't what I meant, but he seemed like he was about to say something. Then he shook his head.

"What?" I asked.

"Nothing. Never mind."

"I guess I'll see you later, then?"

"Sure."

I watched him walk away. Maybe his benefactor was European. Those sleek, perfect clothes of his didn't look like anything that came from this continent. He most certainly didn't look like he belonged in this little town.

"Drool much?"

I jumped. It was Jenelle. Shawna was a few steps behind her, and she looked to be hobbling. I glanced down at her feet. She had on a pair of bright blue open-toed flats. The open toe did seem a bit much for February in Shallow Pond.

"New shoes," Shawna explained as she caught her breath. "I have to break them in."

"For your information," I told Jenelle, "I was just talking to Zach about English class." It was mostly true.

"Admit it already," Jenelle said. "You're completely and totally in love with him."

"I'm not," I said.

"You should ask him to the Valentine's Day dance," Shawna said.

"I don't go to dances," I reminded her. "And it wouldn't make any sense anyway, since we're just friends."

The Valentine's Day dance wasn't really a big deal, just your average school-cafeteria sort of affair, a fundraiser for the Key Club or one of the school groups. It was the sort of dance that the guys put on their best pocket T-shirt for. No matter what Zach wore, he would be overdressed. Before I could stop myself, I was imagining what it would be like to go to the dance with Zach. He would be dressed to the nines; it wouldn't be enough for me to just throw on a denim skirt. Gracie had a cute red dress, and maybe if I asked nicely she would let me borrow it. We never shared clothes, which was silly since we were the exact same size. What shoes would I wear? Wearing heels might make dancing uncomfortable, but they would look nice. I felt like Shawna.

What was I doing? Why was I worried about what shoes would go with a dress I wasn't going to borrow to wear to a dance I wasn't attending? I needed to get control of things. I was being ridiculous.

"I've got to get to homeroom," I told Jenelle and Shawna, who gave me strange looks. It was early—we had almost ten minutes until the bell rang. "I didn't finish my math homework. I want to try and get it done."

But I'd done my math homework. I wanted to be alone, to try to rein in my racing thoughts. And before I'd even made it to homeroom, my mind went spinning off on a new tangent. Did Zach even know about the Valentine's Day dance? Being new, it was possible he didn't. Then I remembered the way he'd been waiting for me at my locker. The way it had looked like he was going to say something before he changed his mind. What if he'd been waiting there because he wanted to ask me to the dance? What if the way I'd told him to back off made him chicken out? I tried to mentally replay the conversation in my head. Had Zach said anything about the dance? About Valentine's Day? I didn't think he had. That didn't mean anything, though.

The thing was, I didn't even know why I was so concerned. It wasn't like I would go to the dance with Zach even if he did ask me, right? I mean, that might be going too far.

Try as I might to put Zach out of my head, he seemed to be always there. When I closed my eyes, I saw him with a sly grin on his face. I heard his voice, cool and gentle but with a thrilling undercurrent of sexiness. I thought of our afternoon at the diner. There'd been something that afternoon, hadn't there? A sort of connection between us. He'd shared his life story with me—that counted for something. Then there was the way he looked this morning. I couldn't stop picturing the way he'd stood there by my locker waiting for me, and I couldn't stop mentally cringing at my cold dismissal of him. What was wrong with me?

I was being ridiculous. So we'd spent a few minutes together at the diner. That didn't mean anything. Even if Zach liked me, even if he was planning on asking me to the Valentine's Day dance, I couldn't suddenly lose my head over him. He was just some boy. He really wasn't that great. Good-looking, yes, but almost too good-looking. He was sort of a jerk, wasn't he? He didn't really act like a jerk, but there was something about the way he walked around, all cool and nonchalant like he knew he was better than everyone else. He was sort of like a nice jerk, which didn't really make sense, I knew, but it didn't even matter whether or not he was a jerk, because the fact of the matter was I neither needed nor wanted a boyfriend.

I tried to focus on such thoughts, but instead my mind kept straying to Zach, and I went through the day feeling slightly lightheaded and giddy. I felt as if over-carbonated soda was flowing through my veins, with those little bubbles popping constantly.

I'd never before looked forward to a class as much as I looked forward to that afternoon's English class. I wondered if Zach would pass me a note. Maybe it would be cut into the shape of a heart for Valentine's Day. Probably, though, he would just whisper something devastatingly romantic and I would have to lean in close to hear him. I tried to banish the foolish thoughts from my mind, but they kept returning.

I was on my way to English class when I heard the announcement: Zach was called to the main office. I should have been relieved, but I was disappointed. I sat through class completely unable to focus, watching the clock and expecting Zach to walk through the door at any moment, but he never did. When the bell finally rang I burst out of my seat, propelled by nervous energy. I knew which way he normally headed after class and I headed down that way, even though it was the opposite direction from where I had to go. My heart was racing and I had this weird all-over achy feeling.

I caught a glimpse of his hair, the sleeve of his shirt, and I called out his name, too loud in the crowded hallway.

At a more normal volume, I asked, "What happened? Why weren't you in class?"

"Some problems with my transcripts," Zach said. He made no attempt to stay and talk with me. Instead, he headed away from me, in the direction of his next class. The hallway crowd was already thinning out, a sure sign the bell would ring at any moment. I turned around and sprinted down the hall to avoid being late.

It was a relief to have the hotline training that afternoon. I wanted something to take my mind off Zach Faraday. Unfortunately, the boring training program was not enough to keep my mind occupied. I thought of how cool and distant he'd been in the hallway. Was he upset about the problem with his transcripts? Was he annoyed with me for being kind of unpleasant to him at my locker, after he'd bought me pie a couple of days before? Perhaps I'd read too much into everything.

The thing was, it didn't matter what Zach thought of me. I didn't want to be anything more than his friend. My head felt like it was spinning. I wished I could press some button to put everything on pause while I regained control of my scattered thoughts. This was why I'd tried to keep my distance from Zach. From the start, I'd felt that weird pull he seemed to have over me, and now what I'd feared had come true. I'd been sucked into the Zach vortex. I needed to remember that being his friend was all that I wanted and needed.

Was it even possible for me to be just friends with Zach? It seemed like the more contact I had with him, the more dizzy I became over him.

Thinking of Annie and how crazy she'd been, and still was, over Cameron Schaeffer was a cold dose of reality. If I wanted to get out of this town, then I needed to purge any vaguely romantic thought involving Zach from my head. Seeing myself following in Annie's footsteps was enough to bring me to my senses. I felt better, and at least for the last portion of the training I was actually able to focus on what Danielle was saying. It wasn't exactly riveting, but I forced myself to at least make an attempt to be interested.

It was dark out when we got out. I called the house, but no one picked up. Annie should have been home. Where was she? I tried her again, but still she didn't pick up. I couldn't help picturing her still lying in bed, wasting away before my very eyes. I tried Gracie's cell and it went straight to her voicemail. Maybe Annie was so sick that Gracie had to drive her to the hospital. It seemed like a distinct possibility, but Gracie would have at least called me to let me know what was going on, unless in her panic to get Annie to the hospital she'd forgotten about calling me.

Meg Kelly waved goodbye to me and headed for her car. I could call Jenelle, but she was volunteering at the hospital again and I didn't know what time she finished. I thought briefly of Zach, but I didn't know his phone number, and besides, I could not call him. My mind toyed with this idea, imagining myself calling Zach and asking him for a ride, even though I didn't actually know his number. Perhaps he would be out cruising around. Perhaps he would just happen to drive past the municipal building. Well, he'd shown up just when I needed him before. Maybe on top of all the rest of his perfection he could read my mind as well.

I glanced out toward the road, but I didn't hear or see any sign of Zach in his Mustang. Out of the corner of my eye, I did see Meg backing out of her parking spot. I ran toward her and knocked on her window. She jumped. Well, spending a couple of hours learning about sexual predators can make a girl a little nervous. She relaxed and rolled down her window when she saw it was me.

"What's up?" she said.

"Do you think I could get a ride?" I asked. "I can't get a hold of my sister."

"Sure. Hop in."

I didn't really know Meg too well. She was pretty and more in the popular crowd than I was, not that she was some stuck-up snot or anything. In fact, in training she had been really nice to me and easy to get along with.

"So, are you going to the Valentine's dance?" she asked after she'd pulled onto the road.

"Oh," I said, startled. I wondered if perhaps Meg had some mind-reading abilities. "I'm not sure. It depends." *It depends on whether or not Zach asks me*, I was thinking, even though a part of my brain was also screaming *NO! NO! ABSOLUTELY NOT!*

"Yeah, I know what you mean," Meg said. "It's such a crappy stupid dance. Nobody even gets dressed up for it."

"Yeah," I said. I felt so lame. It wasn't like I was really a part of the social scene at all. But I knew I should at least try to act normal so Meg didn't think I was a complete loser. "Are you going to the dance?" I asked.

"Yeah. It's funny. I wasn't going to go, but then that new guy, you know the cute one?" My heart pounded in my chest. There was only one new guy in Shallow Pond, and I knew I didn't want to hear what Meg was about to say, but I had no choice. "Zach? He asked me to the dance today in gym class. I mean, he barely knows me, right? But I guess he doesn't really know anyone yet."

The words *he ate pie with me* almost burst out of my lips but I held them back, not sure I could say them without getting weirdly emotional.

"So, are you...?" I couldn't even finish my question.

"Oh, yeah," she said. "I said I would go with him. I mean, he's pretty good-looking, right?"

"Oh, I hadn't really noticed." I said. Lame, lame, lame. I felt like such a loser, but really, I didn't care what Meg Kelly thought of me.

Meg Kelly? Seriously. That's who Zach asked to the Valentine's Day dance. What was that about? What did he see in her? Well, besides the fact that she was gorgeous and smart and popular. I couldn't believe I was such an idiot. Of course he would prefer a girl like that over someone like me. Besides, I was the one who'd told him we were just friends. I wondered again if he'd been thinking of asking me. Was that the reason he was waiting at my locker? If I'd been a little nicer to him, maybe he would have asked me instead of Meg. And if he had asked me? Would I have said yes?

I hated myself for caring so much about this. I hated myself for even thinking that Zach could have been planning to ask me to the dance. I hated myself for wishing that I was going to the dance with Zach.

———————

Annie was in the kitchen when I got home. Dinner was some sort of casserole, which she'd obviously been trying to keep warm in the oven. I was glad to see she was up and about, but she didn't look good. There were dark circles under her eyes and her skin looked too pale.

"I didn't know what time you were getting in," she said. It wasn't really an accusation, but I heard it that way. The urge to snap back at her was strong, but I shrugged it off.

"I had the training for my volunteer thing after school," I said.

"You should have called," she said. She glanced outside. "Did you walk home?"

"I got a ride with a girl from my class, and I did call. No one picked up."

"Oh," Annie said. "I was taking the trash out before."

"Where's Gracie?" I asked.

"She called to say she wasn't going to make it home for dinner."

I didn't point out that this wasn't really an answer to my question. I was pretty sure I knew exactly what this meant. Gracie was too busy with Cameron to make it home for dinner.

Annie and I sat down to a meal of over-cooked casserole and began to eat in silence. I stole glances at her while I ate. She really didn't look good. It was like I was looking at myself a few years down the road—this is what would happen to me if I became all lovesick and obsessed with Zach. I needed to drop this thing right now. He wasn't worth it.

"He's not that special," I said.

"What?" Annie asked.

"Cameron. He's not worth all this trouble. You should just forget about him."

"I don't really want to talk about this," she said.

We returned to our silent eating. I tried to think about college, about moving out of Shallow Pond. I tried to think of anything but Zach Faraday, but he kept creeping back into my thoughts.

ELEVEN

I didn't tell Jenelle or Shawna about Zach asking Meg to the dance, but by Friday morning they'd heard about it. Jenelle stood by my locker fuming. She looked like she was ready to bite somebody's head off.

"I can't believe the nerve of that guy," Jenelle said. "How could he ask some stupid airhead like that to the Valentine's dance?"

"She's not an airhead," I said. "She's actually kind of nice."

"It's okay," Shawna said. "You don't have to put on a brave face for our benefit. We're your friends."

But the thing was, I wasn't putting on a brave face. I'd told Zach I just wanted to be friends with him, and he'd listened to and honored that request. I couldn't really blame him, and I kind of liked the idea of being friends with him. I mean, sure, he was good-looking and perfect boyfriend material, but I didn't need a boyfriend. I didn't want a boyfriend.

"Guys, really," I said. "It's okay. I told Zach I just wanted to be friends with him."

"You're hopeless," Jenelle said. "Completely hopeless, you know that?"

"Are you still going to the dance?" Shawna asked.

"Do I ever go to dances?" I asked.

"Bunting, we really need to get you out of your shell, pronto," Jenelle said.

"I like it in here," I said. This only made the two of them shake their heads. I could sense they would probably spend the day engaged in some text message chat, trying to come up with some scheme that would get me to the Valentine's dance and into Zach Faraday's arms.

I didn't wait for Jenelle and Shawna after school. I nearly ran out the doors and walked home as quickly as I could. They'd been on my case all during lunch. Their new plan was to have me go to the dance with some sophomore guy they described as marginally attractive, the thinking being that it would drive Zach into a jealous rage. I declined their offers to meet this guy, but I had a feeling they weren't really going to take no for an answer.

Two blocks away from school, I stopped looking over my shoulder every couple of steps and slowed down my pace. I was glad that it was Friday afternoon, glad that for a couple of days, at least, I could avoid the high school social scene.

Annie was on the couch when I got home. When I opened the door, she actually let out a little yelp. Apparently she'd dozed off and I had startled her.

"Are you okay?" I asked.

"Fine," she said. "It's just this weather, the cold. It makes me sleepy."

"Maybe you should go see someone, a doctor."

"I'm perfectly healthy," she said. She didn't look healthy. Did perfectly healthy people fall asleep in the middle of the day? She'd been going to sleep earlier and earlier. She must have been averaging twelve hours of sleep a day, maybe more.

She stretched and got up from the couch, and with stiff, awkward steps headed upstairs, saying she had some laundry to put away, but I couldn't help wondering if she was planning on crawling into bed to finish her nap. I went into the kitchen to hunt around for a snack.

I saw him standing at the back door. I wasn't sure how long he'd been there. I supposed he must have just gotten there. He waved when he saw me. I didn't want to let him in, but I didn't see any choice.

"Cameron," I said as I opened the door. "What are you doing here?"

"I was supposed to pick up Gracie," he said. He stepped into the kitchen without actually being invited.

"She's still at work," I said.

"Yeah, I guess I'm early," he said. "I just needed to get out of the house. My mother was driving me crazy."

Did he expect me to commiserate with him about how annoying mothers were or something? Could he really be that big of a jerk? He did know that my own mother had died shortly after I was born and I'd never had the chance to know her, didn't he? He smiled at me, but bright as that smile was, it wasn't going to be enough to win me over. Perhaps Cameron was one of those guys who'd been using that smile his whole life to get what he wanted.

"Are those the kind with the cinnamon on top?" he asked as I took out a box of graham crackers. "I haven't had one of those in years."

I offered him some, and the two of us sat there munching them in a slightly awkward silence. I didn't know where to look. I began reading the back of the graham cracker box, but it was short of captivating, and I could feel Cameron staring at me.

"You look just like your sister," he said. "She used to have a shirt that same color." I had on a dark purple T-shirt. It was one of my favorites.

"Which one?" I asked. It was a valid question, considering.

"Annie," he said. It was a perfect opportunity to give him hell for dating Gracie, but I really didn't feel up to it.

"Do you have any milk?" he asked.

"Would you like me to fix you dinner too?" I asked, unable to hold in my annoyance. He began to apologize, but what I'd said gave me an idea. "I mean, you should stay for dinner. Annie was going to make something. She's really a great cook."

"Oh, I think Gracie and I were going to go out and grab something."

I went into the fridge, pulled out the milk, and poured Cameron a tall glass. All he had to do was see how awesome Annie was and he would forget all about Gracie. Annie was smart and talented, and she was a good cook; I wasn't making that up. Gracie, on the other hand, was Gracie. She was silly and flighty. She couldn't hold a candle to Annie. Cameron had gotten confused—it was only natural. Gracie was younger, and looked more the way Annie had looked back when Cameron used to know her. It just made sense that he would fall for Gracie. It was like what he'd said about me, that I looked like Annie. Of course, once he had a chance to spend time with Annie, he'd see that she was the one he was really in love with.

I handed him the glass of milk. He grabbed it, and his hand closed over mine around the glass. He held it there a moment or two. His eyes stared into mine like he was searching for something in them. Then he adjusted his grip on the glass and let my hand go.

Nothing had happened. Nothing, really, but I'd felt something, some weird connection between me and Cameron Schaeffer. I wasn't sure what to make of it.

"I remember this time when you were little," Cameron said. "We took you to get ice cream. You got a vanilla cone with rainbow sprinkles. You and I got into a debate about whether or not rainbow sprinkles have different flavors."

"They're just sugar," I said.

"Ha, that's what you said then, too, but I'm sure they're different fruit flavors."

"They aren't."

"Do you remember that?"

I shook my head. I remembered Annie taking me to get ice cream, but I didn't really remember Cameron there.

Maybe we'd met him at the ice cream stand. Sometimes Annie had run into her school friends there.

"We should get out the photo album," I said. A plan began to take shape in my head. "Hang on. Annie will know where it is."

"She's here?"

Annie was always here, but I didn't want to tell Cameron that. "Upstairs. I'll be right back."

Annie didn't understand my urgency about looking at the photo album, possibly because I'd deliberately left out the fact that Cameron was there. I didn't tell her until we were walking downstairs, and by then it was too late for her to turn around. Cameron was already in the living room, staring at the picture of my mother on the wall.

"Cameron," Annie said. Her voice sounded different than normal, lighter and airier. I thought of it as her southern belle voice, but without the accent.

"I didn't mean to interrupt you," Cameron said. "I was just—"

I knew he was about to say something about coming over to pick up Gracie, so I quickly said, "Cameron was talking about old times, when you two were my age, and I said we should get out the photo album. We never look at it." I was talking so fast my words were running together. I sounded like Gracie after she drank a big cup of coffee.

"I'm not even sure where it is," Annie said.

"It's right here," I said as I pulled it off the bookshelf. I shoved the album into her hands as I steered the two of them toward the couch. Annie laughed at me. She could tell that I was behaving strangely, but she also didn't try to fight it. She wanted to spend time reminiscing about the good old days with Cameron.

I arranged it so that Cameron and Annie had to sit next to each other. I sat on Annie's other side. I felt like I was being something between an annoying little sister and cupid.

The photo album was a big fat one that went way back, back before I was even born. I didn't make Annie skip ahead to the stuff where she and Cameron were a couple, though. I figured the more time they spent side by side together on the couch, the more chance there was that those old flames would be rekindled.

So, together, we looked at shots of a toddler Annie holding an Easter basket nearly as big as she was, of her and my father posing in front of a lake somewhere. There was a picture of her in some nursery school pageant, another of her skinny-dipping in a kiddie pool in the backyard, which she flipped quickly past. Eventually a baby Gracie began appearing in pictures beside her older sister, sometimes with, but mostly without, my father in the shot.

It was a dark shadowy picture with a Christmas tree in the background that made me grab hold of the couch arm as if the floor had dropped out from under me and I was holding on for dear life. That's what it felt like, anyway. The picture was too fuzzy to really make out, but I could have sworn I was staring at Zach Faraday.

"What?" Annie said.

"Who is that?" I asked. She looked at me like I was crazy.

"It's Dad," she said.

I took another look at the picture and realized she was right. It wasn't a very good picture, but something about the shadows in the photo made it into a sort of optical illusion, like those pictures where if you look at it one way it's a young woman, and if you look at it another way it's an old lady.

"Who did you think it was?" Annie asked.

"It looked like this boy I go to school with," I said. I shook my head. "He wouldn't even have been born yet." I tilted my head and looked at the picture, but I saw only my father. Whatever it was that had made me see Zach was gone. I wondered if I'd only seen Zach because subconsciously I was still obsessing over him.

A couple of more pages and we came to my baby pictures.

"Look at you," Cameron said. "You were a chubby little baby."

He reached right around Annie to gently squeeze my shoulder. It filled me with a happy warmth—not the fact that Cameron was squeezing my shoulder, but the fact that for however briefly, his arm was around Annie. Perhaps things were already starting to happen.

There was a picture of my father holding me in his arms. His face looked grim and cheerless. It was the face that naturally sprang to mind when I thought of my father, but it made me realize what an unpleasant time my infancy must have been for him. On the one hand, he had a new daughter, but on the other hand, he'd lost his wife. It must have been difficult for him to try to pretend to love me. I was staring at that picture of my unhappy father, my chubby infant self, when it hit me.

"Why aren't there any pictures of Mom?" I asked.

"Babie, she died right after you were born," Annie said.

"No, I know that, but I mean, what about before that? There aren't any pictures of her with you and Gracie."

"That's because she's the one who took all the pictures," Annie said. "I think she didn't really like having her own picture taken. She used to shy away from cameras."

There were pictures of her, though, from when she was younger. The picture on our wall, others I'd seen of her from when she and Dad were dating. One where she looked so much like Annie I'd actually been confused when I saw it as a kid, assuming it was a picture of Annie.

I wondered if she'd put on weight after having kids and didn't want to have her picture taken. Maybe something about being a mother had made her have the same dark circles beneath her eyes that Annie presently sported. I tried to imagine what she would have looked like, this woman on the other side of the camera lens capturing the smiles and giggles of her two daughters on film. It didn't seem fair that they'd been able to have her there, if only for a short while, when they were growing up, when all I'd had was a sad and bitter father.

The three of us were huddled together, laughing at a picture of me at two years old not at all happy about being dressed up in a robot Halloween costume made from a cardboard box and part of an old vacuum cleaner, when Gracie stepped into the room. We must have been laughing so hard we never heard her come in the back door.

"What's going on?" she asked.

"We were just looking at some old pictures," Cameron said. He seemed suddenly aware of the fact that he'd been sitting so close to Annie, and he stood up.

"Remember the year you were a cowgirl for Halloween?" Annie asked. She pointed toward the photo in the album, but Gracie didn't seem interested.

"Cameron and I are headed out," she said. "I just want to change my shoes."

Gracie slipped out of the sneakers she wore for work, into a dressy pair of flats. I watched Cameron watching her. I waited for him to look back over at Annie, but he didn't. When I glanced at Annie, I could see that some of the light had gone out of her face. She'd been so happy, so animated when we'd been laughing at the pictures, but now her face looked pinched and tired again.

Gracie grabbed hold of Cameron's arm and steered him toward the back door.

"Don't wait up for us," Gracie said.

"You two have fun," Annie said. I hated to hear her say those words. I wanted to shake her, to slap her. I wanted her to say what she really felt.

"Thanks," Cameron said as he turned back and looked at us still sitting there on the couch. There was the briefest flash of that smile. I didn't know if he was thanking Annie for telling them to have fun, or for sitting with him and looking at the photo album. Maybe he was thanking me for the milk and graham crackers. I watched him leaving with Gracie and wondered if he really couldn't tell he was with the wrong sister. Was he really that blind?

TWELVE

Jenelle's car horn blared outside, far too early on Monday morning. I was still in the bathroom trying to do something with my uncooperative hair.

"Babie, Jenelle's here!" Gracie shouted from the other side of the bathroom door, in case I'd missed the beeping.

I grabbed an elastic off the counter and ran out of the bathroom, throwing my hair into a ponytail on the way. I slipped on my grubby sneakers without bothering to tie them and grabbed my backpack, hoping that everything I needed was inside it. I didn't have time to check. Jenelle sat behind the wheel making hurry-up gestures as I ran down the front steps. I considered flipping her the bird, but I figured that probably wouldn't go over too well. She would probably leave without me, and I wasn't much in the mood for walking.

"Took you long enough," Jenelle said when I slid into the back seat.

"You're early," I said.

"Not even close," Jenelle said.

"Did you have a rough weekend?" Shawna asked. I realized she was referring to the fact that I had that just-rolled-out-of-bed look, even though I'd showered and put on clean clothes.

"My God, what happened to you?" Jenelle asked, finally getting a good look at me in the mirror.

"Just drive," I told her.

"You should have gone to the dance," Shawna said. "We had such a good time. Didn't we have a good time?"

"It was magical," Jenelle agreed.

"Magical?" I asked. "You don't think maybe you're exaggerating just a tiny bit?"

"You had to be there," Jenelle said. She paused, then said, "No really, you *had* to be there."

"You should have seen Zach," Shawna said. "He had on this shiny blue shirt and these black pants. Not jeans, pants. He looked like someone in a magazine or something." I didn't point out that he always looked like someone in a magazine. That would have proved I noticed what he looked like.

"He actually made Meg look kind of underdressed in her jean skirt," Shawna said. "I kind of felt bad for her."

I noticed Jenelle taking a supposedly surreptitious swing at Shawna to get her to stop talking about Zach.

"It's okay," I said. "I really don't care. I told you I'm not interested in him."

I wasn't just saying that. An entire weekend without seeing Zach had pretty much washed him from my mind. Maybe it had something to do with the fact that Gracie had spent nearly the whole weekend with Cameron, and Annie had spent nearly the whole weekend bundled up on the sofa reading some paperback book or flipping through television channels, drifting in and out of sleep the whole time like she was in some sort of drugged fog. All I knew was I had better things to do than spend my days pining for some stupid boy.

"He's not the right guy for you," Jenelle said. "He's too full of himself. There's something about him I don't like."

"He's a nice guy," I said.

"So, wait, you do like him?" Shawna asked.

"I mean nice as a friend," I said. "Can we please change the subject?"

"Well, on a cheerier note," Jenelle said, "I'm pretty much guaranteed to fail that chemistry test today."

"Crap," I said. I'd forgotten all about the test. I'd left school in such a hurry Friday afternoon I didn't even bring my notebook home with me. "At least you won't be the only one failing it."

"Tell me you didn't study," Jenelle said.

"I forgot."

"So, wait, what exactly *were* you doing all weekend?"

"Contemplating the day when I'll finally get the hell out of this worthless town," I said.

"Hey, guys," Shawna said, "I know it's Monday and all, but do we have to talk about pessimistic stuff?"

But the thing was, I wasn't being pessimistic at all. I liked Shawna and Jenelle, but it was becoming more and more apparent how different we were. Our lives were taking us in completely different directions. I rested my head against the seat, feeling strangely alone even though I was in a car with my two best friends. It was like I was an outsider, even though I'd lived in this town my whole life. Maybe I'd never really fit in. Maybe I'd only been pretending like I belonged.

I saw my chemistry teacher, Mrs. Kirk, on my way to first period. She'd always struck me as a reasonable sort of person, so I figured it couldn't hurt to try to see if I could make up the test I hadn't studied for. I was fully prepared to play the sick sister card, but I never got the chance.

"I was wondering if I could get an extension on taking today's test, make it up tomorrow. It's just that I forgot to bring my book home with me because—"

"Gracie," she said with an exasperated sigh and a shake of her head, "you really need to start to learn some responsibility. You can't always expect someone else to pick up the slack. Why should I give you an extra day to study? How is that fair to the other students?"

"But I'm not—" The bell rang before I could finish correcting her, and Mrs. Kirk waved dismissively at me as she hurried to her classroom.

I hurried off to my own class through the suddenly empty hallway.

"Annie, you're late," Mr. McDevitt said. I heard some of the kids snickering. I didn't even bother to correct him.

Behind me on the lunch line, I overheard two boys saying something about witches. I remembered what Zach had said, about stories he'd heard about my family. The one about us being a coven of witches seemed particularly fitting. Could this be what those boys were talking about? It was just some stupid rumor, but it bothered me. I spun around, ready to tell the boys to mind their own business, when I heard one of the names of the people they were talking about—not Annie, Gracie, or Barbara, but the name of that actress who was rumored to be a drug addict.

"Yeah," one of the boys said, "the ending was totally lame."

I realized they were talking about a movie. I felt my face flush in embarrassment, but was thankful I hadn't made a complete idiot of myself. As it was, people were starting to stare at me because I was holding up the lunch line.

———————

I caught my breath when I stepped into English that afternoon. It was an involuntary reaction. Zach was already in his seat, and I realized something that had sort of slipped my mind when I'd resolved to have no feelings other than those of friendship for the boy. He was incredibly good-looking. It was one thing to make a resolution at a safe distance, but having to stick fast to that resolution while in close proximity would be more of a challenge.

"Hey," he said when I sat down.

"Hey," I said. I wanted to sound casual, but my throat had gone dry and the word sort of squeaked out. It felt like someone had turned up the dial on the thermostat. I blushed; I could feel myself beginning to sweat.

"Are you okay?" he asked. Was it really that noticeable?

"I'm fine," I said. My voice sounded sharp and angry. I turned toward him, thinking I'd say something a little less harsh, but when I looked at him I caught a glimpse of a smug smirk on his face, which he quickly dropped when he realized I was looking at him. Stuck-up jerk.

"I think I saw your sister the other day," Zach whispered a few minutes later.

"What?" My question came out a little loud. I looked up in time to see Mrs. Grimes give me a warning look.

"Does she work at the grocery store?"

"Mr. K's," I whispered back.

"Yeah. I can see why people confuse you two. You do look a lot alike."

"What's your point?" Again my voice was a bit too loud. I was something short of pleased to hear Zach telling me how much I looked like my sister. I didn't need him to tell me that. I'd been hearing it my whole life.

"Gracie," Mrs. Grimes said, "can we please postpone our personal conversations until after the class is over?"

"I'm not Gracie," I said. I could have left it at that. I should have left it at that, but something had been building in me all day, and now it burst forth. I rose from my seat. "My name is Barbara. Not Gracie, not Annie. Barbara! I'm sick and tired of people thinking they can just call us whatever name they want. I'm sick and tired ... " I paused long enough to give Zach a long, hard stare, though I was really thinking of Cameron Schaeffer when I said, "of people assuming we're interchangeable with one another!"

I'd always been the kind of person who went through school on cruise control. So shouting in front of my entire class? Not the sort of thing I usually did. I could feel everyone staring at me. My face grew hot. Mrs. Grimes stood there looking stunned, not sure what to say. I knew I couldn't stay there. I ran out of the room, and only when I was halfway down the hall did I realize I'd left all of my books back in class.

I stopped and rested against a wall in the empty hallway. I took several deep breaths and tried to relax, staring up at the random speckled pattern in the white ceiling tiles as if mesmerized. I figured I could wait here in the hallway until class was over, then go back in and claim my stuff, apologize to Mrs. Grimes. If I was lucky she might be understanding and not require me to serve two weeks in after-school detention or write a ten-page essay on the inappropriateness of my outburst.

"Hey, are you okay?"

I jumped at the voice. It was Zach. He stood there holding my books. I wondered how long he'd been there.

"I'm fine," I said.

"You keep saying that," he said, "but I'm having a hard time believing you."

"I shouldn't have jumped down her throat like that," I said.

"I told her you'd been under a lot of stress lately, a family thing. She bought it."

I wonder if Zach knew how close to the truth he was.

"Thanks," I said. It would have been easier to not like Zach if he wasn't such a nice guy.

"So, what is the matter?" he asked.

"It's just been kind of a crappy day," I said. I could feel my resolve beginning to melt in his presence. I couldn't remember ever feeling so helpless around a guy. I didn't like the feeling. I wanted to feel in control. "I have to go."

"Now? What about your next class?"

"There's just something I need to do. Off campus."

"You need a lift?"

"It's something I have to do alone."

He nodded, but it was a slow, hesitant nod, like he didn't really believe me. I guess it did sound like a made-up excuse, but I wasn't lying. There really was something I needed to do. It was an idea that had only occurred to me a few seconds before, but now I knew I had to do it. In fact, I couldn't believe that I hadn't thought of this sooner.

———————

The bored cashier at Rite Aid looked kind of familiar, and my suspicions were confirmed when she said, "You're Gracie's little sister, aren't you?"

"Yeah," I said.

"Of course you are, you look just like her." I hoped I never had to hear those words ever again. "She's dating that new guy in town, isn't she?"

"He's not new," I said. I guess she didn't know that Cameron used to date Annie. Maybe Gracie was deliberately trying to keep the weirdness of her relationship under wraps. The cashier was staring at me blankly. "He used to live here," I explained. "He went to school with my oldest sister."

"Oh," said the cashier. She finally looked down at my purchase. "Midnight?" she asked as she read the package. "So you're like one of those goth-type chicks?"

"How much do I owe you?"

She finally got around to scanning my package. "It comes to $8.37," she said. I paid her, and she handed me my change. "Hey, you can tell your sister that if she ever gets tired of that guy to let me know, 'kay? He's pretty cute."

"Sure," I said. I didn't have the heart to tell her that based on what I knew of Cameron's dating history, she wasn't his type. Who knows? Perhaps he'd be interested in trying something different. Better her than me, I figured.

———————

Annie was dozing in front of the television when I got home. Gracie was still at work. I grabbed the scissors from the kitchen drawer and headed up to the bathroom with my Rite Aid bag. I soaked my hair in the bathroom sink, combed it out, and began cutting. I gave myself bangs, then I trimmed the rest of my hair until it fell just below my ears. It looked sort of cute, but I wasn't done yet.

I tore open the package of Midnight hair dye and read through the directions. I took a deep breath. Was I sure about this? What if I came out looking like a freak? I decided that even that would be an improvement. Maybe it would mean people would recognize me as being a truly unique person.

It might even make Zach finally stop chasing me around. I hesitated. I remembered Zach in the hallway, bringing my books to me like the chivalrous young man he was. I felt my heart rate increase at the thought of him. Did I really want to drive him away? Yes, I had to. It was for the best.

I opened the hair dye and began to apply it to my newly shortened locks. It needed to set for twenty-five minutes. The phone began to ring almost as soon as I'd coated the last of my hair with the dye. A few seconds later, Annie called my name from downstairs. I knew it would be Jenelle on the phone; she'd sent me approximately half a million texts demanding to know where the hell I was. I hadn't replied to any of them. I debated not answering Annie, but didn't see the point.

"I'm in the bathroom," I yelled. "I can't come to the phone."

After the twenty-five minutes, I washed out the dye and combed out my hair. I stared at the vaguely familiar-looking girl in the mirror. My skin looked so pale against the dark hair. It looked weird. It didn't look that good. I looked like someone who'd cut her own hair in her bathroom and then dyed it with cheap dye.

I smiled at myself in the mirror. I liked it.

Thirteen

There was a soft tapping on the bathroom door, almost too faint to be heard.

"Babie?" Annie asked. "Are you feeling all right?"

I'd been in the bathroom a long time. I glanced around and saw the floor covered in clippings of strawberry-blond hair. I looked back at my new reflection in the mirror and saw how it would look to Annie's eyes—like I had snapped. What would she think? Probably she would want to search my room for drugs. I couldn't go out there. I couldn't face her. Not yet.

"I think I've come down with a stomach bug," I said. I used my best intestinal-distress voice.

"Can I get you anything?"

"No, I, um, I'm just going to clean up in here, and then I think I'm going to bed."

"Well, I hope you feel better soon."

I swept up the hair from the floor with my hands and dumped it into the trash can. I stared down at it, lying there.

It used to be a part of me, and I had this weird feeling that I was looking at my old self there in the trash can. That was Babie Bunting, younger sister of Annie and Gracie Bunting, and she was history. This new me was Barbara, a free spirit, independent. Clearly, the new me did not belong in Shallow Pond. I was a citizen of the world, ready to spread my wings and fly. Well, just as soon as I was ready to announce this independence to the rest of the world. In the meantime, I had evidence to bury.

I buried the clippings under the hair-dye package. I buried all of it beneath the plastic Rite Aid bag, then crumpled up a few tissues and threw those on top for good measure. I ran out of the bathroom and into my room, and shut the door behind me. I hardly ever kept the door of my room closed, but figured I could chalk it up to my illness. I needed my rest, couldn't be disturbed, that sort of thing. I knew Annie. She would still poke open my door later to check on me. So I would have to pull the covers up over my head when I went to bed. I knew I couldn't hide forever, but I decided I had to get used to things before I could find the courage to let my sister see the new me.

I went to bed early without dinner, and woke up in the middle of the night warm from sleeping burrowed under the covers, with a stomach that was growling in protest at its neglect. I tried to be as silent as possible as I scoured my room for something edible and found a package of M&Ms in a purse in my closet. I couldn't remember how long they'd been there, but figured they were probably safe to eat. I devoured them and went back to bed.

As a result of my late-night dinner of M&Ms, I woke up feeling like I really had come down with a stomach bug. My head was pounding and I felt nauseous. It wasn't so much courage that forced me to leave my bedroom, but the need for real food.

There was a note on the kitchen table from Annie. She'd already called the school to let them know I would be out sick. Then she'd gone to a doctor's appointment. I nearly had a heart attack. My sister had gone to the doctor? Perhaps we were all making some radical changes in our lives. Well, maybe not all of us; according to Annie's note, Gracie hadn't come in until late and was likely still asleep. Annie told me to get plenty of rest and feel better soon, and that she would see me later.

I did feel better after a full breakfast and a hot shower. In fact, I felt perfectly fine, and a little bit guilty for not going to school. I glanced at my phone. There were now roughly a billion text messages from Jenelle. She wanted to know how I was feeling. She wanted me to know that she was feeling extremely bored. She told me Zach had asked where I was. I was sitting on my bed scrolling through Jenelle's messages when Gracie finally stumbled down the hallway.

"Good afternoon," I said. I'd forgotten momentarily about my hair.

"Oh my God," she said. She stood there staring at me. Her eyes looked ready to pop right out of her skull. "Please tell me that's a wig."

"It's not a wig."

She marched into my room, grabbed hold of a hunk of my hair, and gave it a tug on the off-chance that I was lying.

"Ow," I said, shoving her away.

"What the hell is wrong with you?" she asked.

"I'm not the one who goes around pulling people's hair."

"You look horrible."

"I like it."

"You can't possibly think that looks good. What did Annie say?"

"She hasn't seen it yet. She's at the doctor's."

"What?" she asked. I shrugged. It was one of those mysteries of the universe, apparently. "Why aren't you at school?" she added.

"I'm sick," I said.

"Sick in the head."

"Stomach bug," I said. "But I'm feeling better."

She shook her head and walked away. I wondered if my hair really looked as bad as Gracie said it did. Perhaps she just needed time to get used to it.

The doorbell rang a few minutes later, and I heard Gracie answer it. I heard her using her flirting voice and assumed she must be talking to Cameron. I had no desire to see him, but I heard a familiar voice say my name. Barbara, not Babie. I jumped off the bed and ran down the stairs two at a time.

Zach stood at the front door while Gracie all but batted her eyelashes at him. It was hard to believe I was related to her. It was hard to believe that anyone could have ever mistaken me for her.

"Barbara!" Zach said. He was clearly surprised by my hair,

but at least he hadn't said something along the lines of Gracie's "Oh my God."

"So, I just want to know where you've been hiding this good-looking guy," Gracie said. She gave Zach a playful pat on the arm, like they were old friends and not like he was someone she'd met a minute ago.

"Safe from your grabbing hands," I said. I slipped past her and grabbed Zach's arm to lead him down the front steps. "I'll be back later," I called over my shoulder.

We didn't say anything until we were seated in his car, and then we both tried to talk at once.

"Ladies first," he said.

"Why aren't you in school?" I asked.

"I decided to leave early. I wanted to check on you."

"You're not responsible for me."

"I never said I was."

"Let's just go somewhere," I said. I glanced back up toward the house. I couldn't see Gracie, but I'm sure she was watching us from a window. Annie would probably be back any minute.

"Where do you want to go?" Zach asked.

"I don't care," I said.

The car roared to life, and he drove a little too fast up the street. I thought at first he was headed back toward school, but then he turned, and we pulled into Memorial Park and parked facing the pond.

"So," he said, "you did something different with your hair, right?" He was grinning like a fool. I punched him playfully on the arm. It felt like the sort of thing a girlfriend might do to her boyfriend. I blushed, but I think he was too busy staring at my hair to notice. Zach had this thing about him, and once again sitting there beside him I felt like I had known him my entire life, not just a couple of months.

"You think it looks awful," I said. "It's okay, you can say it."

"No, I don't think so. It's just a big change. I'm still getting used to it. It makes you look kind of artsy."

I wondered if that was a compliment. I decided to take it as a compliment.

"Should we get out?" he asked. "You picked a good day for skipping school. It's pretty warm outside."

It was one of those freakishly warm winter days that's sort of like a teaser of the spring weather that will eventually arrive. I didn't even mind that I hadn't grabbed a jacket, and only had on a sweatshirt over my T-shirt. There was still plenty of snow on the ground, but there was also a path cleared that led up to the frozen pond, and we walked toward it.

"So tell me," Zach said, "is this radical transformation all for Mrs. Grimes's benefit?"

I laughed. "I just wanted a change."

"Change is switching to mousse instead of gel. This is more like a complete overhaul."

"You don't like it," I said again. "My sister thinks it looks ugly."

"This would be Gracie? The one who opened the door?"

"Yeah," I said.

"For a moment or two I thought she was you. Then she opened her mouth."

"Our voices are that different?" I asked.

"Not the voice, so much, but the way she was speaking —all bubbly and happy."

"So, what—you think I can't be bubbly and happy?"

"Oh, you're probably fully capable of it, but I've never actually seen it."

I couldn't tell if he was kidding around or if he was serious. Maybe he was a little bit of both. I hadn't been exactly easygoing with him since the day we met, so probably he thought I was a difficult person, someone who wasn't all that fun to be around. But if that was the case, why had he shown up at my house?

We walked over some frozen snow to get to a weathered park bench that faced the pond. I sat down first. Zach sat beside me, but it seemed like he was being careful not to sit too close to me.

"You don't like your sisters?" he asked.

"I didn't say that," I said. "I like Annie. Gracie is ... well, she's nothing like me, like you said. It's not that we don't get along—it's just that we're so different. We don't always see eye to eye on things."

"Still, it must be nice to have siblings. They're like older versions of you."

"Have you even been listening to what I was saying?" I asked as an angry sigh passed through my clenched teeth.

"What I mean is, they've gone through all sorts of stuff before you, and they can help you out, give you advice, that sort of thing."

"Both of my sisters have spent their entire lives in Shallow Pond. I hardly think they've got any advice worth giving."

"So no one in Shallow Pond knows anything?"

"Pretty much," I said. "The thing is, once I get out of here, I don't plan on coming back."

"Not even to see your sisters?"

"Maybe," I said. "But there's no reason they can't come visit me."

"We're alike, you know," Zach said.

"You plan on getting out of this town as soon as you can too?"

"I mean we're both independent. We don't need anyone else's help."

Zach was definitely independent. He lived on his own, but me? Was I independent? I didn't really feel like it. If I was really independent, I would just pack my bags and leave, pull together enough money for a bus ticket and just dive right into the rest of my life. But I couldn't just run away, and that was because I wasn't independent. Not really.

"I'm tired of being all alone," Zach said. "I'm tired of having to face everything on my own. Why am I telling you this?" He stood up suddenly and jammed his fists in his pockets. He began to kick stubbornly at the frozen snow. He muttered a few times beneath his breath like a crazy person. That, and the violent kicking, made me a little bit scared. I wanted to ask him what was wrong, but I couldn't find the courage to speak.

"Look, I know you don't like me," he said.

"I didn't say that."

He held up his hand to silence me. "You didn't have to say it. I can tell. And it makes sense—what would ever possess you to be with a loser like myself?"

"You're *not* a loser."

I wasn't sure if he heard me or not, because he turned away and looked out over the frozen pond.

"I try to imagine them, my parents, what they would have been like when they were my age," he said. He didn't look at me. He stared out across the past as if he could see his unknown parents somewhere out there. "Maybe they were my age when they had me, too young to take care of a kid, and they didn't know what else to do with me. Maybe I was just something that would have gotten in the way of their life. Instead of going away to college or what-ever, they would have had to spend their time taking care of me and working crappy jobs just to pay the bills."

"So instead they just dumped you on the steps of a con-vent?" I asked. I couldn't imagine someone acting so heartless and cruel. What kind of life could their child ever have? That was completely unfair.

"What would you do?" he asked.

"If I were you?" I asked.

"What would you do if you got pregnant? Would you give up on all your dreams and just stay here in Shallow Pond to raise a kid?"

"I wouldn't get pregnant in the first place," I said, but before the words had even left my mouth, Zach's question jogged loose something in my head. I knew someone who had given up on all her dreams and stayed in Shallow Pond to raise a child. Allegedly that child was her younger sister, but I recalled the photo album.

There were no pictures of Mom even when Gracie was a baby...like Mom was already dead at that point. Could it be? Could the girl who I'd always thought was my oldest sister actually be my mother?

I forgot about Zach, the bench I was sitting on, the pond, the entire external world. Annie wasn't old enough to be my mother. Only how did I know how old Annie really was? She looked older than she said she was. She looked old enough to be my mother. My heart was racing. I thought of the way Annie had always treated me—not the way one would treat a younger sister, but the way one would treat a daughter. It all fit—the reason she'd never left Shallow Pond, never gone away to school.

If Annie was my mother, then that meant Cameron was my father. It gave me a chill. I'd thought Cameron was a jerk before, but now I saw that he was downright vile. How dare he date Gracie? No wonder Annie was so upset. He hadn't even made an attempt to keep in touch with me all the time he'd been gone. Or had he? Memories spun around my head. I recalled Cameron's story about getting ice cream with him and Annie. I'd assumed they were in school then, but that couldn't be possible if they were my parents. Unless maybe I was getting it wrong in my memory. I closed my eyes, tried to picture it. I pictured spending time with Annie and Cameron when I was a kid. They certainly did seem old in my memory, older than just teenagers, in which case it would all make sense. It was all true. I knew it.

"What's wrong?" Zach asked. He must have seen the look of panic on my face.

"I have to go," I said.

"We just got here," he said.

My head was spinning. I paid no attention to him. I began running up the path we'd come down.

"Barbara, wait!" Zach called after me. "Let me give you a ride." I picked up my pace. I didn't want to talk to him. I needed to get home, but I didn't want to go with him. I ran toward the street.

Fourteen

I stood at the front door sweating and panting. I shoved my hands into my pockets, but I realized as soon as I did so that I didn't have my key. My key was in my jacket, and I hadn't brought that with me. It was still in the house somewhere. I rapped on the door. I waited. Nothing. I pounded on the door. Gracie couldn't have gone anywhere—Annie had the car. Unless Cameron had come and picked Gracie up. I became convinced of this when I squinted inside and saw only the empty living room. I slid down to sit on the top step.

My cell phone, like my key, was inside the house somewhere. What now? At least it wasn't that cold out. My head hurt. I shut my eyes, but saw only confusing images. Annie at various ages in her life... the ages I had always presumed her to be versus the age that she probably was. It was dizzying.

Then I heard something. The car—only it wasn't coming back from the doctor's office like I first assumed, but down the driveway. I saw Gracie behind the wheel, and Annie in the passenger seat. My reeling mind didn't even know how to begin to process this additional confusion. I did have enough sense to stand up and flag down Gracie.

"Hey," I yelled. "Where are you going?"

Gracie rolled down Annie's window and shouted to me, "There you are. We've been trying to find you. Get in the back."

"Where are you going?" I repeated.

"I didn't know where you were," Gracie said. "I tried your cell phone." Annie was being remarkably quiet during this whole exchange.

"I left it in my room."

"Yeah, I realized that. Also, you have like a billion text messages on there. You might want to read them sometime."

"You were reading them?" My voice came out sounding angrier than I had intended.

"Relax, I just saw the little box blinking. Get in the car please."

I pulled open the back door. I recalled too late about my chopped and dyed hair, but Annie seemed to barely even notice when I got in. Had they put her on some sort of drugs at the doctor's office?

"How are you feeling?" Annie asked.

"I'm fine," I said, remembering I was supposed to be home sick from school, "Better," I added. "How are you feeling?"

"I keep telling Gracie I'm fine, but she won't listen."

"You collapsed in the middle of the living room floor," Gracie said, her voice cracking as she zipped through the stop sign at the end of our street.

"What? You collapsed?" I asked.

"It's my own fault," Annie said. "That's what you get for not eating breakfast."

"This has nothing to do with skipping breakfast, and you know it," Gracie said. She continued to drive too fast as she raced through town toward the highway. I watched Shallow Pond fly by outside the window as I tried to make sense of what was going on.

"I thought you went to the doctor this morning," I said.

"Yes, and he said I was perfectly healthy," Annie told me. She sounded normal, but she really didn't look well. Could it be something as stupid as not eating breakfast? I'd felt pretty lousy when I woke up that morning and it was probably because I hadn't eaten anything the night before.

"You need to go to a real doctor," Gracie said. "They have machines and tests they can do and stuff at the hospital."

"I feel better," Annie said. "Just turn the car around."

Gracie didn't listen to her, and I was glad. Annie had been sick for a while and if she'd collapsed, then maybe there really was something seriously wrong. It could be something stupid—maybe she just needed to take some pills or something. I hoped it was something like that, something simple, treatable. The fact that Gracie had managed to get her into the car meant that Annie realized she needed help.

As we neared the highway entrance, Gracie turned on the right blinker and headed toward the southbound entrance ramp.

"No, we're going north," Annie said.

"What? Are you delusional on top of everything else? The hospital is south of us."

"We're not going there," Annie said in that clipped, firm tone that made it sound like she was so angry she could barely open her clenched teeth.

"Jenelle volunteers there," I said. "Maybe she could make a phone call for us. Make sure we get a nice doctor."

Gracie pulled onto the ramp, but Annie grabbed hold of the steering wheel, jerking it hard to the right. I cried out as I was tossed around in the back seat. Gracie got control of the car and steered us carefully onto the shoulder of the road, bringing the car to a stop. Both of my sisters were breathing heavily in the front seat. It looked like Gracie's heavy breathing was due to shock. Annie, on the other hand, looked completely exhausted.

"What the hell is wrong with you?" Gracie demanded. "You could have killed us all."

"Listen to me. We'll go to the hospital, but we're going up to University Hospital."

"What? That's more than an hour away! What do we need to drive all the way up there for?"

"Dad had a friend who worked there," Annie said.

"And Babie's got a friend who works at Shipley, which is only twenty minutes away."

"Volunteers," I corrected, somehow hoping to smooth over the tension in the front seat. Jenelle had only just started volunteering; she might not even know anyone at the hospital yet.

"We go to University Hospital and meet with Dr. Feld,

or you turn the car around and we go home. Those are your two options."

"You're being ridiculous," Gracie said. Annie didn't respond. She just glared at Gracie until Gracie finally sighed, popped the car into reverse, and slowly drove backward down the shoulder of the entrance ramp so that we could get onto the northbound ramp.

"Do you even know this Dr. Feld?" she complained when we were finally on the highway headed toward University Hospital.

"He was a good friend of Dad's. They were close."

"Couldn't have been that close," Gracie said. "I don't remember ever meeting him."

"They used to work together," Annie said.

The whole time I'd known my father, he was a misanthropic hermit, but Annie always told me that he'd been a smart man. A genius, she'd told me, but this was probably hyperbole. He'd been some sort of medical researcher. That was before I was born, and maybe before Gracie was born if my new theory was correct.

"You don't even know this guy," Gracie complained. "I don't understand what the big deal is." I felt like telling her to just shut up and drive, but she did have a point. It was an awfully long way to drive just so that we could see some doctor who had once worked with my father twenty years ago or more.

"Do you know if Dr. Feld even works there anymore?" I asked.

"Yeah, good point," Gracie said. "He probably won't even be there."

"He still works there," Annie said.

She turned around to look at me, reaching our her arm to pat me on the hand like I was a little kid. She had dark circles beneath her eyes and her face looked so thin and pale. I hoped this Dr. Feld, whoever he was, was a genius like my father had supposedly been.

"You cut your hair," Annie said. She smiled as if it took her all her energy to do so. "It looks cute."

"Cute?" Gracie said. "I'm going to ask them to examine your head as well when we're there. She looks like hell."

Annie didn't respond. She rested her head on the back of her seat. Within a few seconds I could hear her snoring softly. I caught Gracie's eye in the rearview mirror and we exchanged concerned looks with each other. For a brief moment I found myself wishing it was Gracie who was the sick one. I quickly chased those thoughts from my mind. Annie would be fine, I told myself. It was probably nothing.

FIFTEEN

As bad as Annie looked, there were worse-looking people in the crowded emergency room. This was only mildly reassuring. The woman behind the counter offered us a clipboard loaded up with forms to fill out, but Annie ignored it.

"We're here to see Dr. Feld," she said.

"Do you have an appointment?" the woman asked.

"Just tell him that Annie Bunting is here to see him."

"Have a seat," the woman told us. She sighed in an extra-loud way, to let us know this request was quite a burden for her.

We sat down in the waiting room chairs. Gracie had picked up the clipboard and was starting to fill things out. I realized this would give me the perfect opportunity to double-check Annie's birthday, but before Gracie could get more than Annie's name on the clipboard, Annie took it away and stuck it on an empty chair.

"Don't worry about it," Annie said. "We don't need it."

The woman came out from behind the desk and stood

before us. She looked disgusted. Apparently protocol was very important to her.

"Dr. Feld asked me to show you into an examination room. He'll be with you in a few minutes."

The other folks sitting in the waiting room gave us annoyed looks as we followed the cranky woman back to one of the rooms. I felt sort of like royalty, getting to jump the line so easily. Sometimes it helped to know the right people. Maybe it had been a good idea to go out of the way to go to this hospital.

"You know, the two of you don't have to wait here with me," Annie said.

"What if you collapse again?" Gracie asked.

"Do I look like I'm going to collapse?" Annie said.

She sat on the paper-covered exam table. She might not have looked like she was about to collapse, but she didn't exactly look healthy.

"I don't understand why you didn't go see someone when you first got sick," Gracie said. "You're so stubborn. You're just like Dad."

"I'm nothing like him!" Annie's voice came out sharp and angry. Other than when she'd grabbed the steering wheel, it was the most energy I'd seen her use all day. I tried to remember if our father had also refused to go see someone when he got sick. I couldn't recall him ever being sick. Well, except for when he died. Was that what Gracie meant? If he'd gone to the hospital, would they have been able to help him? Would he still be around if he'd gotten treatment?

I didn't have a chance to ask because the door opened and Dr. Feld stepped in.

Dr. Feld was a large, red-faced man who looked a bit like Santa Claus without the beard and the suit. He broke into a smile when he walked into the room, and I half-expected him to start ho-ho-ho-ing.

"Look at you three," he said, with a laugh and a shake of his head. "This is an unexpected surprise. Look at how grown-up you all are. Amazing."

I hardly thought it was amazing, but I guessed he hadn't seen us since we were babies. I supposed to him it was like we went from being infants to grown-ups in the blink of an eye.

"How's your father doing?" Dr. Feld asked. I sucked in a big mouthful of air and I heard Gracie gasp. "It's been a while since I've heard from him."

Annie looked over at us, a sort of pleading look on her face. I assumed she wanted one of us to deliver the much-belated news of our father's passing.

"He died," I explained.

"Oh, God," Dr. Feld said. "I had no idea. My condolences."

"It's okay," Gracie said. "It was like six years ago."

"No, it couldn't be that long," Dr. Feld said.

"I'm afraid Gracie is correct," Annie said in a stiff, unnatural voice. The doctor shook his head stubbornly, but his face changed a bit; he became more of a sad Santa as he processed that it had been more than six years since he'd last heard from his friend.

"So I'm guessing this isn't a social visit?" he asked.

"It's probably nothing," Annie said.

"She hasn't been feeling well for a while," Gracie said. "Then earlier today, she collapsed."

"It was because I hadn't had anything to eat," Annie said.

"And have you been eating normally lately?" Dr. Feld asked. "I only ask because you do look a bit on the thin side. Well, of course, everyone looks thin to me." He laughed at this comment, but none of us bothered to join him. "And how old are you now, Annie?"

I noticed the way Annie glanced over at me and Gracie before she answered, "Twenty-six." Why would she need to look at us to answer such a simple question, unless she was lying? Dr. Feld nodded at her answer as if there was something magical about the number twenty-six—unless perhaps he knew that she was lying, knew why she was lying.

"Well, we always feared something like this might happen," he said.

Something like what? Had I missed something? Annie cleared her throat quietly and then looked over at me and Gracie again.

"Yes, of course," Dr. Feld said.

"What?" I asked. There seemed to be a whole silent conversation going on that I wasn't hearing.

"Ladies, I'm going to ask you to step out while I examine your sister." It was subtle, but I heard the extra emphasis he placed on the word "sister." I wanted to just shout that I already knew everything and we could have everything out in the open instead of these weird silent conversations, but now wasn't the right time. I walked to the door, and Gracie followed me. She looked back at Annie, who waved us out of the room.

"That was weird," I said when we were out in the hallway.

"I don't like that guy," Gracie said. "What's with all the smiling and laughing and crap? I swear I've never seen that man before in my life."

"Dad probably sent him Christmas cards or something."

"And if they were such good friends, how could he not know Dad was dead?"

I shrugged. Dr. Feld didn't seem like such a bad guy. I wondered if he'd been Annie's doctor when she was pregnant. They did seem to know each other, and that weird secret, silent conversation they'd had would then make sense. Plus, if you were going to have a secret baby that you raised as your younger sister, you would want someone you could trust—a family friend—involved with all the paperwork, to make sure you could keep your secret safe.

"You know now that we aren't in there she's just going to tell him she's fine, and he's going to send her on her way without doing anything for her," Gracie said.

"He did ask her if she was eating," I pointed out.

"Speaking of which," Gracie said, "I'm starving. Let's go see if we can find any grub around here."

We did some exploring and found a smaller waiting room, with some cushioned chairs and a few different vending machines. We scoured our pockets for money and came up with enough to buy ourselves a feast of chips, a shared candy bar, and a couple of sodas.

"What do you think is wrong with her?" I asked.

"I don't know," Gracie said. "Maybe it's nothing—a lingering flu or something. Maybe he'll give her some antibiotics and they'll knock it right out."

"She seemed like she was getting better, and then the whole Cameron thing seemed to make her sick all over again." I'd deliberately avoided saying that this was all Gracie's fault, but she was still offended.

"Don't you dare," she said. "Who I date is my business, so mind your own. It was a long time ago that Annie was with Cameron. She had years to rekindle that romance, and she never even tried. So I don't feel bad about dating him." She turned sideways in her seat and refused to look at me, like a spoiled little girl. But wasn't I the baby of the family? Wasn't I the one who was supposed to act like a little kid? Unless, of course, I wasn't.

"Do you ever think it's weird that you can't remember Mom at all?" I asked. "I can remember stuff when I was three years old."

"Like what?" she asked.

I was sure I could remember something from being a little kid, but when I tried to think, all I saw were some vague hazy scenes in my head. I could remember some party...it must have been a birthday party, with a present wrapped in pink polka-dot paper. I remembered sitting in a little plastic wading pool in the backyard. As these different scenes surfaced in my memory, I realized that these were moments that were captured in the photographs in our family album. Maybe I wasn't really remembering them at all...maybe it was just the picture etched in my brain; not a real memory, just a sort of copy of a memory.

"See?" Gracie said. "You don't really remember anything from when you were that age."

Like a spark, a memory—complete, and with only the slightest bit of haziness—arose fully formed in my head.

"Wait!" I yelled, even though Gracie was right next to me. "I can remember a campfire. We caught fish and cooked them on the fire, and then we roasted marshmallows. Dad must have taken us on a family camping trip or something. It was by this lake." I knew the memory had to be a real one because I hadn't seen any pictures of it in the album.

"Dad never took us on a camping trip," Gracie said. "It must have been something you saw in a movie. We never went anywhere with Dad."

"I can remember the taste of the fish," I said. "I remember how gooey the marshmallows were."

"Actually, I think you did go on some sort of camping trip when you were little, but you went with Annie and Cameron's family. It wasn't Dad who took you." As I pictured the scene in my head, I realized I couldn't actually recall Dad being there, but for some reason I thought he had been. Well, of course I did. My dad, my real dad, *was* there. Cameron. It all made sense.

"I think you were probably like four or five at the time," Gracie added. "It was a long time ago, but still, you were older than three, and you can't even remember it that well."

"How come you didn't go with us?" I asked. I knew

the real reason Gracie hadn't gone—she wasn't part of that family. But I wondered if she knew this.

"I don't know," she said. "Probably I had something else that weekend." Right. Like at age eight or whatever her social calendar was completely full. Yet I didn't think she was lying. She probably was too young to remember anything clearly—she had no idea that Annie was really my mother, that Cameron was my father, that she was really my aunt. But it all fit. It all made sense, and it made the fact that she was dating Cameron even more wrong, somehow.

"About Cameron," I started.

"We're not talking about that," Gracie said.

"No, wait. Listen, I know that you think I'm picking on you, but you don't understand."

"No, you don't understand, Babie. This isn't some stupid high school romance, okay? What Cameron and I have, this is real."

"Yeah, but Annie—"

"Forget about Annie. This doesn't have anything to do with Annie."

"What doesn't have anything to do with me?"

We both looked up to see Annie standing there in the entrance to the little waiting room. She still looked pale and ill, and she was holding on to the door frame as if she didn't have the strength to stand without some sort of support.

"Nothing," Gracie said. She looked over at me with narrowed eyes. It wasn't like I was going to say anything in front of Annie; well, not right now anyway.

"You ready to go?" Annie asked. She had a smile on her

face, but it looked like she was trying too hard to look happy and relaxed.

"Did the doctor say what was wrong?" I asked.

"I have a prescription," Annie said.

"Isn't he going to do any kind of tests or anything?" Gracie asked. "He seems like a quack."

"He's not a quack," Annie said.

"You probably told him you were fine," Gracie said. "Did you tell him how sick you've been?"

"He understands," Annie said. "The medicine he prescribed should help. Hey, why don't we stop somewhere for dinner on the way home. When was the last time we all went out together? It'll be fun."

Fun? Something told me this would be about as much fun as ripping out my own toenails one by one.

SIXTEEN

Gracie gave me a ride to school the next morning. It was such an uncharacteristically charitable act that I was on my guard. I sat silent on the ride there, expecting her to ask me to do something in return for her, but she didn't say a word. That same nervous tension that had hung over us since we'd left the hospital was still there, and when she pulled up to the curb in front of school, I was so eager to get out that I swung the door open before she'd come to a complete stop.

"Relax, you've got plenty of time," Gracie said.

"Well, thanks. Bye," I called over my shoulder as I hurried into school.

Jenelle and Shawna spotted me as soon as I started down the hallway. With everything that had happened, I had kind of forgotten about my hair again. It was old news now. Except, of course, it wasn't. Jenelle's mouth hung open as I walked up to her.

"Oh my God," she said.

"Good morning to you too," I said.

"You look just like that actress," Shawna said. "What's her name? In that movie?"

"She looks like she's completely lost her mind," Jenelle said.

I headed past them and to my locker, but they followed at my heels. Shawna couldn't come up with the name of the actress, and Jenelle made a few more choice remarks about my hair. I ignored both of them while I hung up my coat and grabbed my books.

"Is this what you were doing yesterday?" Jenelle asked.

"No," I said.

"Where were you then?"

"Annie was sick," I said. "We had to take her to the hospital."

"Oh my God," Shawna said. "Is she all right?"

"Yeah," I said. "No. I don't really know." I closed my locker and turned around. Zach was walking down the hallway. He didn't even look in my direction. Was he mad at me for running off yesterday? I stared at him, and there was a fluttery sort of achy feeling in my chest.

"You're mental, aren't you?" Jenelle said.

"What?"

"I asked you what was wrong with your sister."

"Right," I said. "I don't really know. She won't talk about it. The doctor gave her some medicine."

"No offense," Jenelle said, "but your family is pretty weird."

"Yeah," I agreed. My family was weirder than Jenelle

knew, but I wasn't about to tell her what I'd figured out. "I've got to go."

"Go where?" Jenelle asked, but I didn't answer her. I needed to talk to Zach. I was pretty sure I would explode if I didn't talk to him.

His locker was all the way at the end of the hallway. I stood a few yards away, watching him grabbing books from his locker, and for a moment I felt short of breath. God but he was gorgeous. He closed the locker door and I was about to call his name, but I caught myself just in time. He wasn't alone. Meg stood beside him. She must have been standing on the other side of the locker door, and I saw that they were talking about something. They walked together up the hallway, and I shrunk back against the wall trying to make myself invisible, though neither one of them even glanced in my direction. They were too caught up in each other.

I felt flushed and slightly sick. They were a couple. Of course they were. How could I be so stupid? I knew they'd gone to the dance together, but for some reason I'd assumed that hadn't meant anything. Why? Just because Zach the snake Faraday had shown up at my front door yesterday? What was wrong with me? Why was I so obsessed with this guy?

I forced myself to stop thinking about Zach and instead spent my day thinking about Annie and Cameron. I tried to piece together my fragmented childhood memories, looking for clues. My father—well, the man who I'd always assumed was my father—had barely spoken to me my entire life, and I realized now that it wasn't because he'd blamed me for his wife's death. It was because I made him uncomfortable. He was ashamed of me, of my illegitimate birth. Maybe he was angry that I had completely ruined his daughter's life, kept her from going to college and becoming more than yet another girl drowning a slow, sad death in Shallow Pond. I was angry that this secret had been kept from me my whole life. Did they really think this would make my life easier? My whole life had been a lie.

Annie was still asleep when I'd left for school in the morning, and she would probably be asleep when I got home. It wasn't fair to bug her about this right now, not when she was sick. I needed to know, though. Of course, there was someone else who would know the story, and lucky for me, he was back in town after years of trying to escape his past. I needed to talk to my father. I needed to talk to Cameron Schaeffer.

When I stepped into English class, Zach was already in his seat. As usual, I felt a little weak when I saw him. Why oh why did he have this effect on me?

"Hey," he said when I sat down. "What happened to you yesterday? Why did you run off?"

"I just remembered something I needed to talk to my sister about," I said. He nodded slowly, like he didn't really believe me. Well, it did sound like a lame excuse, but it was also pretty much true. "It's complicated," I explained.

"Right, sure," he said. "Well, hope you got everything worked out."

"Actually, I didn't get a chance to talk to her. We had to take her to the hospital." His eyes grew wide, and at first I thought it was because he was surprised by this news, but

I think he thought I was making that up too. "She's fine. I mean, she got some medicine, and she's home now."

"Whatever," Zach said. "You don't need to explain it to me." He didn't believe me.

"Mr. Faraday, Ms. Bunting," Mrs. Grimes said. "Kindly pay attention, please." I blushed in embarrassment, but I was also secretly pleased. I liked hearing our names together like that. She hadn't called me Barbara, but on the other hand she hadn't called me Gracie or Annie either. Maybe my new hair had done the trick.

I was silent through the rest of the class, but I wasn't paying attention. That wasn't going to happen with Zach sitting right next to me. How serious were he and Meg? Did he think I was a complete bitch for running off on him yesterday? Did he hate me for lying to him, even though I hadn't really lied to him?

When the bell rang I hurried silently out of class without looking in Zach's direction, but he caught up with me in the hallway and stopped me by grabbing my sleeve.

"Hey, how about a rain check?" he asked.

"Rain check?"

"Well, we didn't get to talk much yesterday. Maybe we could hang out again."

"Sure," I said. I was confused. By "hang out," did Zach mean as friends? Is that what he saw me as? One of his buddies?

"Great. How about after school? It's colder today, so we might have to find an indoor place. Maybe the diner?"

"Uh, I can't today," I said.

"It doesn't have to be the diner. We can go wherever you want. We could go bowling, go to the mall—you can pick."

"No, it's just that today's not good for me," I said. "I have something I have to do after school."

He nodded. He looked hurt. He thought I was blowing him off. I mean, I was sort of blowing him off, but it was because I needed to talk to Cameron.

"It's something important that I have to do," I said.

"No, that's fine," Zach said. "I'll catch up with you another time."

He walked away, and that ache that had been gnawing away at me all day suddenly flared up.

"Zach!" I called after him, but he didn't hear me.

———————

After school, I hadn't even made it out of the senior hallway when Jenelle and Shawna caught up with me. I'd been hoping to disappear before they noticed, because I knew I couldn't tell them that I needed to go over to Cameron Schaeffer's house or why I needed to go there.

"What, you're not even going to wait for us?" Jenelle asked.

"I feel like walking," I said.

"You can walk up the hill."

"What?"

"We're going sledding with the boys," Jenelle said. "Why don't you invite Hot Stuff?"

"He and Meg are together." I instantly regretted saying the words out loud. It was proof that I was interested in Zach.

"I never liked that girl," Shawna said.

"She's fine," I said.

"It's your fault for not making your move when I told you to," Jenelle said. "You've got to show some interest in a guy for him to notice you. Let's go. The boys are waiting."

"I can't," I said. "There's something I have to do."

"Your homework can wait, Bunting."

"No, it's not that. It's…" I struggled to find an excuse. "I can't really talk about it."

"You should come," Shawna said. "It will be a lot of fun." She was wearing a ridiculously short skirt. I hoped she planned on getting changed before she went out to play in the snow.

"Another time, guys," I said.

"I can't believe you're totally ditching us again," Jenelle said. "What is with you lately?"

"It's just something I've got to do," I said.

I tried to look apologetic as I left them behind, but Jenelle still sneered at me.

———————

Yesterday's freakishly warm weather hadn't lasted. It was cold out, but I didn't even notice it as I walked. My mind was on Cameron, everything I knew about him and everything I didn't. All this time I'd thought he was nothing but the stupid guy my sister had fallen for, the guy who'd broken her heart. Other than the fact that he had ruined Annie's life, I'd never really thought of him as an important person in my life. Well, and why should I? What had Cameron ever done for me? It had been years since he'd seen me. He'd never called. He'd never sent so much as a Christmas card.

At least, I didn't think he had, but I wondered if he had tried to get in touch. Had Annie kept him from contacting me? Had she removed his cards from the mail? Was it all part of the lie that was my life?

I wondered what Cameron thought of me. Was he ashamed of me? Did he wish he'd had the chance to get to know me better? Had he been so scared at the responsibility of being a father that he'd run away? I wondered what had brought him back after all these years. Perhaps he'd come back to see me. I even entertained the notion that the reason he was dating Gracie was that he thought it was the only way he'd be able to see me.

I reached the Schaeffers' house in record time, having kept up a good pace as all the confusing thoughts swirled around my head. I actually felt a bit warm from the exertion, despite the cold. I was also having second thoughts.

I didn't know Cameron at all. Wouldn't it be weird if I just showed up at his front door and said I wanted to talk to him? What had seemed like such a good idea when I was at school was now looking completely idiotic. How did one even start a conversation like this? Maybe I could write him a letter. I decided that was what I would do. I would go straight home and write up everything I had to say, then mail it to him.

"Babie?"

I gasped. I hadn't realized that he was in the driveway. He was loading a bunch of stuff into the trunk of the car parked there.

"That's a pretty different look you've got going there," he observed.

"Oh," I said. I patted my shortened and dyed locks.

"If you're looking for Gracie, I think she's working this afternoon."

"No, I was..." Just about to leave? My heart raced in my chest. Inside my gloves I felt my hands sweating. "Are you going somewhere?" I asked.

He'd packed a bunch of stuff in the trunk and now slammed it closed. Was he getting set to leave town again? Was my father leaving my life again before I even had the chance to get to know him?

"To the pond," he said.

"The pond?"

"Ice fishing. Gotta go while the ice is still thick."

"Oh."

I thought of that camping trip, all those years ago. Had Cameron caught those fish we'd cooked on the fire?

"Remember that time we went camping?" I asked. He broke out in a grin and laughed. When he smiled like that, he was a good-looking guy. I searched his face for traces of me in it, but I couldn't tell. I looked so much like Annie that whatever I'd gotten from Cameron was probably buried.

"I can't believe you remember that," Cameron said. "You were just a little bit of a thing then."

"I remember we had fun."

"Yeah, those were good times." He brushed his hands off on the front of his jacket and his eyes got a faraway look to them, like he was remembering that camping trip.

"Well, I guess I should let you go," I said. I'd lost all nerve whatsoever. "Be careful!" I turned to head back up the street.

"Wait!" Cameron called. I stopped in my tracks but didn't turn around. "It's kind of boring to go fishing alone. Are you doing anything? Why don't you come with me?"

I felt my face break out in a huge grin, but I composed myself before I turned around.

"Okay," I said.

"Cool, hop in."

As I sat down in the passenger seat and Cameron started up the car, I couldn't believe how perfect this was. We were going on a father-daughter fishing trip. Out on the ice, it would be the perfect time to talk about everything with him. I couldn't help but feel that he knew that, that he had invited me along for just that reason. Maybe he was ready to finally get to know me.

SEVENTEEN

Cameron parked the car in a gravel lot on the far side of the pond. It was a pretty spot. Tall evergreens hid the rest of the town from view and it felt like we were out in the middle of the wilderness. The smooth surface of the frozen pond and the steely gray expanse of sky only added to the wild beauty of the place. Cameron opened the trunk and began to remove the gear: a tackle box, something that looked like a giant screw with a crank on the end of it, a couple of folding chairs, a thermos, and a fishing rod. He handed me the rod and the tackle box and juggled the other things in his arms.

I followed him down a well-worn path to the pond, and shuffled onto the ice beside him as he looked for a good fishing spot. The pond was deserted. I wasn't surprised that no one else was crazy enough to come out here in the freezing cold. The fact that it was a weekday afternoon, and most folks were at work, was another good reason no one else was around. It made me wonder about Cameron. Obviously he didn't have a job, but he must have had one at one point, right? What was it that he did for a living? I knew next to nothing about this mystery man. I glanced over at him and caught him staring at me.

"What?" I asked. He shook his head and laughed. "What?" I repeated, a little bit more of an edge to my voice.

"It's just, you look so different with your hair like that," he said. I had a weird dizzy moment as I recalled one of my reasons for dyeing my hair: I'd wanted to make sure I didn't become Cameron's next love interest. Of course, all that was before I realized that Cameron was my father.

"Gracie hates it," I said. I almost immediately regretted bringing up Gracie, but Cameron didn't flinch.

"It takes some getting used to, but it suits you."

I wondered what that was supposed to mean. Did my dark hair suit me because it made me look dark and mysterious? Did he think of me as the black sheep of the family?

Cameron settled on a spot. He unfolded the two chairs, then set to work drilling a hole in the ice with the giant screw thing. I sat down in one of the chairs and watched him.

"I used to go ice fishing with my father all the time," Cameron said. To me, this sounded like an admission. I nearly fell out of my chair. He used to go ice fishing with his father, just like I was now going ice fishing with my father. I stared at him, but he didn't look up at me. "You ever gone before?"

"No," I said. I was about to tell him that my dad didn't do that sort of thing, but then I realized that wasn't true. Not the part about him not doing that sort of thing, but the part about him being my dad. How did I refer to my dad without sounding weird?

"The late Mr. Bunting was not much of an outdoorsman," I finally said.

"And yet he chose to settle down in the middle of nowhere, Shallow Pond," Cameron said. He'd created a small, perfectly round hole in the ice and now stood back to admire his handiwork and catch his breath. He picked up the fishing rod and knelt down to rummage through the tackle box. "Was your mother from Shallow Pond?"

I wondered if he meant it as a trick question. Was he testing me to see if I'd already figured things out?

"I don't know," I answered. I tried to watch his eyes, but he was absorbed in adding a lure to his fishing line. "I don't really know much about my mother. It's all sort of a mystery."

Cameron nodded without giving any sign that what I'd said was not very accurate. He must have thought I didn't know, and wanted to keep playing along with the lie that everyone had been telling my whole life. He sat down in the other chair.

"It must be difficult for you," he said. "Your mother dying when you were only a baby, and your dad dying when you were a kid."

"It is," I said, even as I thought, *but it would be a whole lot less difficult if I knew the real truth about who my parents were.*

"I felt lost when my father died," Cameron said, "and I was an adult. It was like this big giant chunk had been ripped out of me. I can't imagine how you handled it as a kid. I still miss him. Every day I miss him."

I didn't miss my father. I had never known him well enough to miss him. It wasn't that I was happy when he died. It was more like a numb feeling. It was probably the way a person would feel if a distant relative died.

"I went through some really dark times after my father died," Cameron said. "I guess I'm still trying to recover from it."

"I never felt like I knew my father," I said. "We weren't close." I looked hard at Cameron, but he remained stoic. "He was kind of aloof, I guess," I continued. "But I always thought that was because he hated me."

My father's dislike of Cameron now made sense. What father would have anything but hate in his heart for a guy who'd gotten his teenage daughter pregnant?

Cameron attached a lure to the end of his fishing line. He struggled for a few minutes with his gloves on, then took them off to get the job done.

"I only packed the one rod," he said.

"It's okay," I said.

"It's going to be pretty boring just sitting there."

"Isn't ice fishing pretty boring in general?"

"Yeah, I guess it is. I like it though. It's quiet out here. It gives me a chance to think about things."

He was right about the quiet. We couldn't hear a thing out in the middle of the pond. Every once in a while the wind would blow hard enough to rustle the trees, but that was pretty much it. Otherwise, an eerie silence hung over everything. The world could have ended and we were the last two people left alive; that's how quiet it was.

"Can I ask a question?" I asked. I wondered if he would

be annoyed at me for disturbing the quiet, but he smiled, so I figured I was safe.

"You can."

"Why did you come back to Shallow Pond?"

"Circumstances beyond my control," Cameron said. I didn't know what that meant. He shook his head after a moment and added, "That's a load of crap. It wasn't really beyond my control."

"What wasn't beyond your control?"

"It's a big mess. I don't really feel like getting into it."

I nodded. Cameron hadn't really answered the question, and I was still completely clueless about him and his life. I tried to pretend I was satisfied with his non-answer, but I wasn't, and after a minute or so I tried again.

"The thing is, when I make it out of this piece-of-crap town, I don't see myself ever coming back unless maybe my life depended on it," I said.

"I take it you are immune to Shallow Pond's bucolic charm."

"This place is hell."

"Yeah, I hated this town when I was a teenager too," Cameron said. "I couldn't wait to leave."

"And you did," I pointed out. "So, seriously, why move back here?"

"Now that I'm older, I realize this place isn't so bad. There's something to be said for small towns."

"So you moved back here because you suddenly decided you liked small towns? It didn't have anything to do with someone who might live in this particular small town?"

Cameron turned to look at me. There was a flash of emotion in his eyes that quickly subsided. Had I pissed him off? Had I surprised him? Did he suddenly realize that I'd figured out who he was in my life?

"I moved back here because I lost my job," he said. "I was flat broke and I needed a place to live."

"Oh," I said. "I'm sorry."

"Apology unnecessary. It was all my fault."

What do you say to a comment like that? I waited for him to say more, but he didn't. He turned back to his fishing, staring at the hole in the ice as if hoping to telepathically bring the fish to the surface.

"What did you do?" I asked.

"I don't really feel like getting into it," he repeated.

"I mean, what did you do for a living, before you got fired?"

"Oh. I was a teacher."

I'm not sure why, but this surprised me. I hadn't really had any idea about what Cameron did, but I kind of pictured him working at some boring office job somewhere. He didn't really seem like the teacher type. He was too young. Also, he didn't really act like a teacher. Maybe it was because I was used to Shallow Pond's teachers. Probably only the most pathetic teachers in the world could be enticed into working at a school in this crappy town.

"Maybe you could get a job at the high school," I suggested.

"Not likely," Cameron said.

We sat silent. I could feel the cold seeping up through

the soles of my shoes. Either it was getting colder, or sitting there with nothing to distract me made me notice it more. I hunched over a bit against the cold, then shoved my gloved hands into my pockets to keep them warm.

"Hey, I'm sorry," Cameron said. "Are you cold? There's hot chocolate in the thermos if you want some."

I took him up on his offer. I unscrewed the cup from the thermos and poured out some hot chocolate into it. It was still scalding hot. I burned my tongue on the first sip. It was also super sweet.

"How is it?" Cameron asked.

"Hot," I said, "and extremely sweet."

"Sounds like someone I know," Cameron said.

"What?"

His face, already pink from the cold, turned an intense red. I realized he must have been referring to Gracie.

"Sorry," he said. "My father always used to make a thermos of hot chocolate when we came out here. I wasn't sure how many packets of hot chocolate mix to add."

"It's okay."

"Could I have a little?"

I poured some more into the cup for him and passed it over. His gloved hands fumbled to take the cup from me, and he smiled. This is what it would have been like, I figured, to have a real dad. We would have shared fun moments like this, laughed together while doing stupid father-daughter things like ice fishing. It wasn't like I had some sort of nightmare childhood, but I felt like I'd been cheated out of some of the usual rites of passage. My father should have been there to help me ride a bike or to practice with me when I signed up for the softball league in middle school. I'd never watched a professional sports game on television. Maybe I would find it insufferably boring, but I should have at least had the opportunity to spend a Sunday afternoon watching a Steelers game with my dad. It wasn't fair, and I was about to say this out loud—about to let Cameron know that I wasn't okay with the fact that he hadn't been there my whole life, and I didn't think that he could make up for it this late in the game.

"I think I got one," Cameron said.

"What?"

"A fish! Here, grab this!"

He meant the cup of hot chocolate. He passed it to me while clutching the rod with his other hand, spilling some of the hot chocolate over the sides of the cup. Startled, I took it, and watched him as he attempted to reel his catch in. I sipped from the cup as he grappled with the line. He wasn't quick enough. I saw the line go slack.

"What happened?" I asked.

"He got away."

"I can't believe a little fish outsmarted you."

"It happens. It's okay. There'll be others."

"I wouldn't be so sure about that. It is a Shallow Pond, you know."

"Okay, smartypants," he said. "It's your turn."

"What?"

"You're catching the next one."

"I don't know how to."

"What, afraid that a little fish will outsmart you?" He

laughed at this, so I thought he was joking, but then I realized he was handing the fishing rod to me. He was serious.

"I don't know what to do," I protested.

"I'll help you. Just shout if you feel anything tug at the line."

I put the cup of hot chocolate down on the ice and accepted the fishing rod. I held it in a clumsy grip until Cameron directed me where to put my hands. It wasn't riding a bike or practicing softball, but it was a start. Cameron smiled at me and I thought I saw pride in that smile.

"You're a natural," he said.

I smiled back at him. Even though it was cold and getting colder, I wished we could stay out here longer. Already the afternoon light was starting to fade, and it wouldn't be long before we would have to go back.

"Hey," I said, "do you think maybe we could do this again sometime?"

He seemed startled by the question, even though it wasn't really a startling sort of question.

"Yeah, sure," he said. "Maybe your sisters would want to come."

My sisters? Was he thinking we could make it some sort of family outing? A seriously messed-up family outing. It would be mother, father, daughter, and aunt, except aunt would also be father's current girlfriend. Could Cameron really not see how completely awkward that would be? I wondered if it would completely screw up this moment if I pointed out the awkwardness, but then I felt a tug on the line.

"Fish!" I said. I was so freaked out I attempted to hand

the rod back to Cameron, but he waved at me to keep hold of it. He got up and stood behind me. He guided my hands to steady the rod and slowly reel in our catch. He leaned over me, and together, though it was mostly his doing, we reeled in a fish.

"Pickerel," Cameron announced as he carefully removed it from the line.

"Is that good?" I asked.

"Always in season," he said. "What do you think? You interested in taking him home, cooking him up for dinner?"

"Annie usually does the cooking," I said. "And you probably know better how to cook a fish." I had a vision of Cameron coming home with me and cooking up dinner for us. I'll admit, in this fantasy I saw Gracie having to work late so that she didn't spoil our pretty little domestic scene.

"He's kind of on the small side," Cameron said. He gently tossed the fish back down into the water.

"After all that you're not going to keep him?"

"I'm not really in the mood for fish."

I shook my head. Cameron Schaeffer was a complete enigma.

"It's starting to get dark," Cameron said. "I should probably get you home."

I nodded. As we gathered everything up, I wondered if this had been a one-time thing, a fluke. Would Cameron go back to being the guy I only knew at a distance as the occasional boyfriend of my sisters? It made me sad to think it.

Cameron had managed to grab both chairs and the corkscrew drill in his left hand, and I grabbed everything else. He threw his free right arm around me and hugged me to him to keep me warm as we shuffle-stepped our way back toward shore and the parking area. He didn't say anything, but I couldn't have heard his message any clearer if he was shouting it from the top of a mountain. He was my father. He was here for me. He would take care of me and protect me.

I should have left well enough alone. Why wasn't I content to bask in the happiness of knowing that after all these years I'd found my real father? As Cameron drove me home through the twilit streets of Shallow Pond, though, I kept thinking about how weird things were with Cameron dating Gracie instead of being back together with Annie. If only he was with Annie. If only he had never left Annie. Then we could be like a normal family.

"Can I ask you a question?" I asked.

"Another one," he said, briefly looking away from the road to give me one of those smiles. "I see a bright future for you as a journalist."

"Why did you break up with Annie?"

"What?"

"She loved you. She still loves you." I regretted saying it as soon as the words were out of my mouth, but it needed to be said. "Why did you break up with her?"

"Babie, I never broke up with Annie," he said. I excused his use of the nickname, but I shook my head at his blatant lie. He stopped the car at a stop sign. There was no one behind us, so instead of pulling forward when the road was clear, he turned and looked at me. His eyes were deadly serious and a little bit sad. "I never broke up with Annie. I loved Annie. She broke up with me."

"No she didn't," I said, ready to defend my sister.

"When I went away to college," he said, "it was like someone had taken a knife and stabbed me in my heart."

Cameron resumed driving. I shook my head again. He had to be wrong. He had to be lying. Annie was completely and totally in love with him. She never would have broken up with him. Plus, the timing didn't make sense. They couldn't have broken up when Cameron went away to school. I could remember going on that camping trip, getting ice cream with them. Annie couldn't have had me until right after high school. I could feel hot tears beginning to form, and I blinked them away.

We'd pulled up in front of my house.

"Hey," Cameron said softly. "Are you all right?" I nodded. I was afraid if I tried to speak I would burst out crying. He reached over and gently lifted my chin so that I was looking into his eyes. "It's okay. You were probably just confused. It happens. If it helps any, the reason she broke up with me is that she'd met someone else, another guy. Maybe that's the guy she's been in love with."

I knew this couldn't be right, but I nodded. Silent tears streamed down my face. I pulled away from him and quickly got out of his car, shutting the door behind me. I should have said goodbye. I should have thanked him, but I couldn't speak. Halfway up the front steps I turned and saw Cameron watching me. I tried to smile at him, and he smiled back.

EIGHTEEN

I stepped into the house, and Gracie all but leaped on top of me before I could even make it through the doorway.

"Who was that?" she demanded, her voice a little more shrill and high-pitched than usual.

I glanced over my shoulder to see Cameron's taillights headed down the street.

"Was that Cameron?" Gracie asked. "What were you doing with Cameron? Where is he going?"

I didn't know which question to answer first. I didn't want to answer any of them, but I had a feeling she wouldn't let me off the hook that easily.

"Ice fishing," I said. I shut the door and started to take off my coat.

"Ice fishing? Since when do you go ice fishing?"

Since I've come to the conclusion that there's something about our family that doesn't quite add up and I'm hoping to find some answers, I thought but didn't say. I didn't see any point in explaining my theory to Gracie, especially since she would completely dismiss it and since it probably wasn't even true anyway. Couldn't be true, I now told myself. Cameron Schaeffer was not my father. I felt like I was missing something. I needed some time to sit down and think things over, to figure out what it was that I wasn't seeing.

Standing there just inside the front door, my coat half on, I closed my eyes and took a deep breath. I sucked in a lungful of burnt-smelling air.

"What's that smell?" I asked.

"French toast!" Gracie shrieked, running into the kitchen. I heard her cursing. I finished taking off my coat and my shoes and followed her in to see the damage. The kitchen was thick with smoke. I opened the back door and wafted cold fresh air into the room while Gracie scraped the ruined slices into the trash.

"Was this supposed to be dinner?" I asked.

"Annie's still not feeling that well," Gracie said. "She's taking a nap. Crap, what are we going to do now?"

"We can make more," I said.

"That was the last of the bread," Gracie said. She looked about ready to cry. I actually felt a little bit bad for her, but only a little bit.

I shut the back door and started to scavenge around in the fridge for something dinner-worthy. I'd just located a package of hamburger buns when the smoke alarm sounded an ear-piercing wail. I thought we'd done a good job of clearing the smoke out of the room but perhaps it was just that I had gotten used to it, or maybe it had all risen to the second floor. So much for Annie's nap.

I wafted more cold air into the kitchen and the smoke alarm went silent. Annie was downstairs in seconds, and even though she looked like someone who'd just been rudely awakened from a nap, she also looked a bit more like her normal self. Maybe the medicine was actually helping her.

"What's going on?" she asked.

"Burnt French toast," I explained. Gracie glared at me, but what did she want me to say?

Annie shook her head and said, "Babie, grab all the vegetables you can find in the refrigerator. Gracie, grab the step stool and get the big pot off the top of the cabinets. We should have enough ingredients to make Mom's vegetable soup."

We didn't have all the ingredients listed on the recipe card in Mom's neat handwriting, but Annie did her best to improvise. Together we chopped and added vegetables to the pot. Annie added broth and water. Gracie set it on the stove to simmer, and before long the burnt smell was replaced by the aroma of soup. Annie was like some sort of magician. I'd always looked up to her, but now I felt something else—awe, I guess it was. I also felt scared.

What if she was really sick, seriously sick? How would we manage if she got worse and had to be admitted to the hospital? I didn't want to think about it, but it was unavoidable. People in my family had a knack for dying young. What if Annie died? I imagined Gracie and me trying to make it on our own. It would be awful. I pictured us sitting at a messy kitchen table eating a dinner of stale hamburger buns.

No, I couldn't think like that. Annie would get better. The medicine already seemed to be having a positive effect.

She would be fine, and everything would go back to normal, or what passed for normal in the Bunting household. That is, until that day when I finally left this town. Then I would be on my own, all on my own. For the first time, I had a little bit of doubt. How would I make it out there in the world on my own, without Annie? Annie was a grown-up. She was smart, resourceful, and always completely in control, and that's the way she'd been for as long as I could remember. Compared to her, I was nothing but a helpless child.

"Hello, space cadet," Gracie said in an annoying voice; that is, her usual voice. I looked up. "Are you paying any attention? I asked you to get out the bowls and set the table."

"A 'please' would be nice," I said.

"Puh-leeze would you get the damn bowls out already."

"Stop it, you two." Annie raised her hand to her temple as if her head was in pain. Probably it was, but for a moment there I had the suspicion that she was faking in order to make us feel bad for arguing. Either way, I resolved to try to get along with Gracie at least through the rest of dinner. As it turned out, I didn't have to try that hard.

Gracie started telling some story about some woman at the store, a customer who dropped a can of beans; when the customer leaned over to pick them up, her pants fell down. The problem was, Gracie kept laughing as she was telling the story and she couldn't get out more than a few words at a time. Even though Annie and I could barely understand what she was saying, we started laughing at her laughing. Then Annie told a story about the time when I was little and I dropped my favorite stuffed animal into the freezer case at the store when no one was looking. I started bawling, and it wasn't until a few aisles later that anyone realized I was missing my toy. We had to retrace our steps, looking everywhere for the stuffed animal to no avail while I screamed. They finally asked the store to make an announcement about the missing toy, and a woman found it on top of a bag of frozen peas. It made us laugh until tears rolled down our faces. It felt good. It felt like old times.

I was in my room after dinner when the phone rang. A few seconds later Gracie called my name, then appeared at my door with the phone in her hand.

"It's for you," she said.

"Who is it?" I asked.

"What do I look like? Your personal answering service? It's one of your friends."

It would be Jenelle or maybe Shawna, I thought. Maybe, and my stomach did a little flip-flop thing at the thought, it was Zach. I was surprised when I heard Meg on the other end. Then realization crept over me.

"We had a training session tonight, didn't we?" I asked.

"Yeah," Meg said. "I was surprised you weren't there."

"I completely forgot."

"Actually, you didn't really miss much. I was just calling to let you know we got our schedules for when we work with our mentors on the phone lines. Danielle's going to be a mentor for both of us."

I got out my notebook and jotted down the dates and times that Meg read off to me. I'd been thinking some pretty dark thoughts about her, but she really wasn't that bad. In fact, she was pretty nice. She didn't have to go out of her way and call me with the schedule information. Was it any wonder that Zach was interested in someone like her? Compared to Meg I probably came across like some sort of ice-princess bitch.

"So, see you at school, I guess," Meg said.

"Hang on," I said. I hesitated. I wasn't sure how to ask what I wanted to ask. I wasn't sure if I *should* ask what I wanted to ask. "Are you and Zach Faraday, are you, like, a couple?" I came across sounding completely stupid.

"Oh, no," Meg said. "No. I mean, he's completely gorgeous, but we're not really a couple or anything. Not that I would be opposed to that, but I think he's got a girlfriend, or maybe an ex-girlfriend who he's not over or something."

"Oh," I said. "I didn't know he had a girlfriend."

"Maybe from where he used to live? He just seems like there's someone else he's really into, you know?"

"Sure," I said. Even though I didn't, not really. "Okay, thanks for the schedule."

"No problem," Meg said.

I hung up and sat there in a daze. Who was this girl that Zach was really into? Could it possibly be me? Why did I feel myself getting so excited by the thought?

"Hey there."

I jumped. It was only Annie. She was standing in my doorway.

"How are you doing?" she asked. "I feel like I haven't talked to you in forever."

"I'm fine," I said.

She nodded, then stepped into my room. She came over and stood beside me, brushing her hand over my hair.

"It's quite the look," she said. "It's growing on me. It looks a lot better than that perm I got when I was fourteen."

I laughed, because I'd seen the pictures. It was, in a word, heinous.

"Who was on the phone?" she asked.

"A girl I know from school. We're in training together for volunteering at the women's support hotline." For a moment Annie's face looked a bit strained and pale, like she was in pain. Perhaps she was still sick and trying to hide it for my benefit.

"How's it going? The training?"

"Fine." I decided not to tell her that I'd accidentally missed a session. It would only make her worry about me.

With her standing beside me, her hand on the top of my head, she felt more like a mother than ever. I felt a wave of sadness thinking that I had been wrong after all, but I wondered if I'd only been partly wrong. What if Annie was my mother and this mysterious *other* guy was my father? Except what about the time we'd spent together with Cameron when I was younger? That didn't make sense. Unless...

"How old are you?" I asked.

The sudden question surprised Annie. She lifted her hand and looked at me like I'd suddenly sprouted an extra head.

"I'm twenty-six. You know that," she said.

She was still claiming to be only eight-and-a-half years older than me. But what if she was lying? What if she was five years older than she said she was? At thirteen, someone could technically have a kid. Stuff like that happened, didn't it? It was a lot less socially acceptable than having an out-of-wedlock child in your late teens, which would be all the more reason to keep the real story of my parentage a secret. I thought of the pictures I had seen of Annie in that awful perm. It would have been right around that time. Maybe that had been her way of trying to look older, of dealing with what must have been a huge change in her life that she couldn't have been anywhere near ready to deal with. It made me respect her that much more.

I turned and threw my arms around her waist and hugged her tightly. She laughed, then hugged me back.

"What was that for?" she asked when I let go. I shrugged. "Okay, well, I think I'm going to head off to bed." It was only nine o'clock, but at least she'd been up and about for a few hours. "Don't stay up too late," she said as she left the room.

I couldn't even think about sleep. There was too much going on in my head. What if Annie and Cameron had been just kids when I was born? It was only a few years, but it made a huge difference. Having a kid at seventeen or eighteen was not exactly ideal, but it happened pretty often. Having a kid at thirteen or fourteen? That was crazy. It wasn't the sort of thing that should ever happen. In a small town like Shallow Pond, it wouldn't be the sort of thing you could ever escape from. It would be all the more reason to want to get the hell out of this town as soon as possible. That made Annie's refusal to leave that much more mysterious, but I realized she'd done it all for me. She'd sacrificed everything so that I could have a reasonably normal childhood, or as normal as one's childhood could get when one's mother was only fourteen years older than her.

But who was this other guy, the one she'd broken up with Cameron to be with? As far as I could recall, she'd never had another boyfriend. Why would she make up something like that? It didn't make any sense. Cameron could have been her ticket out of this wretched town. Unless... what if what she'd said to Cameron was that there was someone else—not another guy, but someone else—and by someone else she meant me? What if she'd broken things off with Cameron because she felt she had to spend her time taking care of me, and because she knew the best chance I had at normalcy was if she stayed in town with me?

My head was spinning, and I wanted to march right into Annie's bedroom and attack her with questions, but that wouldn't be fair. She was exhausted. She needed her rest. And I needed answers. I squirmed restlessly in my chair, unable to get comfortable, unable to relax.

I flipped idly through my notes from the hotline training. According to the schedule I'd jotted down, my first day of being on the phones was next week. That was too soon. I felt nowhere near ready. The notes I'd taken were sparse and not especially helpful.

I came across the website I'd written down when the cop spoke to us. Turning on the computer, I typed the address in the address bar. I couldn't remember what the site was supposed to be, but I realized as soon as the page began to load. It was the state's Megan Law site. If you wanted to find out whether there were any registered sex offenders in your town, you typed in your zip code. So I typed Shallow Pond's zip code. In the few seconds it took to load the results page, I thought about the possible suspects among Shallow Pond's small population. The guy who collected the shopping carts in the parking lot at Mr. K's had always made me uneasy. There was that older guy who always seemed to be at the library. He could be a sex offender.

I had an image in my head of what a sex offender looked like, so when I saw the picture of Shallow Pond's lone sex offender, I was surprised. I let out a little yelp, and then, because I didn't know what else to do, I quickly flipped off the computer.

NINETEEN

I debated turning the computer back on and retrying my search. Maybe there'd been some error, but I knew what I'd seen. His picture had been there, some sort of mug shot. How could that be a mistake?

Why was he there? This time I did turn the computer back on. I returned to the site and typed in our zip code. I shut my eyes as the results page loaded, willing some completely different person to appear, or better yet, a friendly little message that said *Hooray, there are no sex offenders in Shallow Pond!*

No such luck. I found myself looking at a horrible picture of Cameron Schaeffer. His name, age, and physical details appeared beside the photo. What was *not* there was any information about his crime. Was he a rapist? A child molester? Falsely convicted?

With a chill, I realized that I'd spent the afternoon alone with him. I'd been together with him in his car. We'd been out there on the ice all alone for hours. Anything could have happened. Yet nothing had. Maybe that counted for something. If Cameron Schaeffer was such a horrible criminal, then surely he would have at least attempted something. Perhaps the fact that he didn't proved he was reformed, or maybe not such a bad guy after all.

"Babie!" I heard Gracie call. She was headed down the hall toward my room. I quickly snapped the computer off. Cameron's mug shot had already burned itself into my mind.

"You never gave the phone back." Gracie walked right into my room without knocking. The phone was on the desk beside my now-dark computer screen. She grabbed it.

"Wait, Gracie," I said. I needed to tell her. She needed to know. I couldn't keep something like this from her.

"What?" she said. The friendly, laughing sister from dinner was gone. She was back to being her usual annoying self.

"There's something I want to talk with you about," I said. I was stalling. I didn't know how exactly to tell her that her boyfriend was a sex offender. It felt like the sort of thing I should break to her gently.

"Can this wait? I've got a phone call to make."

"Yeah, sure," I said. I was too relieved to be let off the hook.

———

I didn't sleep well. I kept having nightmares. Someone was chasing me. Every time this mysterious person was about to catch me I would wake up, my heart racing. I peered around my darkened bedroom, half-expecting Cameron

Schaeffer to be lurking in the corner or crouched behind my door. I even turned on the light a couple of times in the middle of the night, just to be sure.

I sleep-walked through school the next day, and Jenelle told me about fifty times that I looked like crap. I felt like crap, too. Maybe I wasn't just tired; maybe I was sick. Maybe whatever Annie had was contagious. When school finally got out, I wanted to go straight home and crawl into bed, but I couldn't. Instead, I walked all the way out to Mr. K's.

I found Gracie working one of the registers. She didn't look pleased to see me. I stood at the end of her checkout lane while she rang up an order.

"What are you doing here?" she asked.

"I need to talk to you."

"In case you didn't notice, I'm kind of busy."

"This is important. Can you take a break?"

"Just took one half an hour ago."

"It's about Cameron."

I saw the customer look up from her wad of coupons with a flash of interest. She obviously wanted to hear the latest gossip.

"Stay away from him," Gracie said. Her voice was like ice.

"Actually, you're the sister who goes around stealing other people's boyfriends," I said. I hadn't gone there with the intention of being mean, but Gracie always brought out the worst in me.

Gracie blushed, then turned to me, her eyes slitted in anger. I think if she hadn't been at work she might have gotten physically violent. Instead, she read off the total to the now-flustered customer, who fumbled to get her money out of her wallet. Gracie shut off her light and told the guy who had already loaded about half a million cans of cat food onto the conveyor belt that she was closed.

She led me over to the corner where the lottery machines were, looking around to make sure that no one was listening to us.

"I don't appreciate you coming here and bugging me at work," she said. "This better be important."

"It is," I said. "It's very important. I think you're in danger."

"In danger? In danger of losing my job because of my irritating little sister, maybe."

"No," I said. I thought about that idea of breaking the news to her gently. That wasn't going to work. "It's Cameron. He's a registered sex offender."

"What?" I expected her to be incredulous, but I didn't expect her to start laughing like I'd told a hilarious joke.

"I'm serious," I said. "I had to look something up for school, and he's on the Megan's Law site."

"Cameron is not a sex offender."

"But he's—"

"Look, I think I would know if I was dating some sort of criminal, okay? I'm sure this is all Daddy's fault." I tried to think of a way my dead father could be involved in this. "He hated Cameron, you know that, right?" Gracie said.

"Yeah," I said. I recalled what Cameron had said about the two of them not getting along.

"Well, he probably filed some sort of complaint against

Cameron when he was dating Annie. It's the sort of thing Dad would have done."

"But Cameron had to have been convicted of a crime to be on there," I pointed out. Gracie shook her head.

"Drop it," she said. "And don't go shooting your mouth off about this to anyone, okay?"

It was on a public website for anyone to see, but perhaps Shallow Pond's rumor mongers were not that tech savvy. I nodded and watched Gracie storm off back to her register, shaking her head as she went.

I wondered if she could be right. If Dad had filed some sort of fabricated charge against Cameron, maybe he had gotten in trouble for something he'd never done. It made sense and I found myself buying the idea, because some part of me still believed that Cameron Schaeffer was more than just some guy that Annie had dated—that he was indeed my father, messed up as the whole thing was.

"You look lost. Let me guess—you forgot your shopping list." I recognized the voice and felt myself blush. Zach stood beside me, a pair of shopping bags in his arms.

"I was just here to see my sister," I said.

"Well, in that case, I was going to make a pit stop for pie on the way home. Want to join me?"

"Yeah," I said.

A few minutes later we were sitting once again in a booth at the diner, a plate of pie before Zach and a chocolate milkshake in front of me. It felt so natural sitting there with him. It really was like I had known him my entire life. I felt like I could say anything to him.

So I blurted out, "You're so much like my sister."

"She wears more makeup than I do," he said. "Also, I don't think my giggle is quite so high-pitched."

"Not Gracie," I said. "My other sister, Annie."

"I haven't met her yet. So, is she particularly manly or am I very feminine?"

"What I mean is, the way you're kind of like a grown-up even though you're still a kid—how you do your own grocery shopping and live on your own and everything. Annie pretty much raised me single-handedly even though she was still a kid when I was born." I didn't tell him about my conviction that Annie was my real mother. Maybe I wasn't ready to share everything.

"How is she doing? She's the one that was sick, right?"

"Yeah, she's better. I mean, she's still sick, but she seems to be doing better."

He nodded and shoveled one last giant piece of pie into his mouth. I watched as some of the filling missed his mouth and slid slowly down his chin. He wiped it off with his napkin, his mouth bulging with pie.

"That old-flame situation still going on?" he asked.

"I guess," I said. Cameron's mug shot popped into my head. "It's strange. All these years I always thought that he was the one who dumped her, but yesterday he told me she was the one that broke up with him."

"You two spend a lot of time chatting?"

"I went ice fishing with him," I said. I knew it sounded weird, but it all made sense when you knew I'd been convinced that Cameron was my father. Of course, Zach lacked the benefit of that knowledge.

"Huh," Zach said. He nodded as he considered this. He pushed his empty plate out in front of him. "So that's what you had to do yesterday after school."

"Yeah." Why did Annie still act interested in Cameron if she was the one who'd broken up with him? Maybe I'd misunderstood Annie's reaction; maybe she wasn't interested in Cameron. "I just don't get why my sister would break up with Cameron."

"What's that supposed to mean?"

"Cameron said she had someone else, but I can't remember her having any other boyfriends."

"Maybe she just decided the guy was a jerk," Zach said. He sounded sort of pissed off when he said this. Did he know something about Cameron that I didn't know? Maybe he'd looked at the Megan's Law site. Oh my God. What Zach said finally sank in: *Maybe she just decided the guy was a jerk.* Not just any old jerk—a rapist jerk. What if it wasn't my father but Annie who'd filed the complaint against Cameron? Maybe the way she'd acted when she found out about Cameron's return was nervousness—the kind of nervousness that's actually fear. I couldn't believe I'd been so blind, but it all made sense.

"I need to go home," I told Zach.

"Well, okay. I'll drive you."

"Right now!" I said. I shouted a bit in my excitement.

"Was it something I said?" he asked.

"Yes!" I realized this came out sounding all wrong. "No, I mean, what you said made me realize something."

"Right, okay, well, let me just pay for this."

I was only half done with my milkshake, but I knew I couldn't drink another sip. I practically sprinted out of the diner while Zach paid, only to pace around until he got outside. During the short car ride to my house I could barely sit still.

"Listen," Zach said in a serious tone. "I know you don't really like me, and I get that you are trying to be nice to me because you feel bad for me or whatever, but it's okay. You can be straight with me."

"What?" I said. Really, my head was spinning so much I could barely understand what he was saying.

"I guess you must think I am completely annoying."

No, I didn't think anything of the sort. "That's not true," I said, but we'd pulled up in front of my house and I had to talk to Annie. "I have to go. And no, you're not annoying."

I got out of his car and looked back at him with what I thought was a sweet smile as I shut the door. Then I sprinted up the stairs.

Annie was on the couch when I walked in. The television was on, and I couldn't tell for sure, but it didn't look like I'd woken her up.

"What's wrong?" she asked.

"He raped you, didn't he?" I said. The words burst out of my mouth, where I'd been holding them in for the past few minutes.

"What?" Annie asked. Her already-pale skin looked like it had grown even paler. She looked like someone whose dark secret had just been exposed. It was true.

"He raped you, and that's why you never left home."

"Why..." Annie began, but seemed to reconsider and said instead, "Where did you get this idea?"

"It was something Zach said."

"Zach?"

"A friend of mine from school," I said. Annie looked confused. Confused and scared. "I mean, Zach didn't say anything about rape," I went on. "I figured that out from the Megan's Law site. Well, and yesterday Cameron told me you were the one who broke up with him."

"You were talking with Cameron?"

"Yes, I was talking with Cameron. And if you want to know why I was talking with Cameron, it's because no one in this family ever tells me anything! So, yes, I went ice fishing with some rapist all because my stupid family can't tell me anything."

"Cameron's a rapist?"

"You don't need to deny it," I said. "He's a registered sex offender. His picture is on the Megan's Law site."

"There has to be some mistake," Annie said. "Cameron is not that sort of person."

"But he raped you!"

"Cameron? Babie, you don't know what you're talking about."

I'd been so sure. That look on Annie's face—she'd looked so scared—but now she just shook her head at me like I was the crazy one.

"Well, then what's he doing on the Megan's Law site?" I asked.

"I don't know. It must be some sort of mistake."

"Why did you break up with him, then?"

"It was a long time ago," Annie said with a sigh. "I really don't feel like getting into this now."

"He said you said there was someone else. Is that true?"

"Yeah," Annie said, and she got a sort of far-off look in her eyes. In a faint whisper she said, "There was someone else."

TWENTY

"So, I don't even know if I should bother asking you this," Jenelle said as she stood beside my locker, "but Shawna and I are going to go look at prom dresses this afternoon, and if you want to—"

"It's February," I pointed out.

"Do you have any idea how long it takes to find the perfect dress? Plus, if you wait too long, there's nothing but crappy ones left."

"I can't," I said. "I have something I've got to do."

"Oh my God, Bunting, it's like you completely hate us all of a sudden."

"I don't hate you," I said. I closed my locker and tried to get my lips to curl into what I hoped was a warm and friendly smile. Beyond her, I could see Zach and Meg walking down the hallway together. They looked awfully close to one another. Were they holding hands? I squinted, but there were too many other kids in the hallway blocking my view.

"Who is he?" Jenelle asked.

"What?" I said, snapping back to reality.

"This guy you're sneaking around with?"

"I don't know what you're talking about."

"Oh come on, what are all these mysterious things you're always having to do? Danielle Roberts swears she saw you riding in a car with Cameron Schaeffer the other day, but I told her it must have been Gracie she saw. Unless perhaps he's going for the complete set."

"Don't be disgusting," I said. "And I'm not sneaking around with anyone. I have to go do something for my volunteer thing."

"Honest?" Jenelle asked. The fact that she had to ask bothered me. Had we really reached the point where she no longer believed the things I said?

"I swear," I said. I immediately felt bad. While I did have to do something for the volunteer job, I also had an ulterior motive.

―――――――

I had to wait for a little while in the police station's uncomfortable vinyl-covered chairs. Officer Hantz was out on patrol. I suppose it was a bit of a relief to find out how little activity there was in the Shallow Pond branch of the Regional Police on a typical weekday afternoon, but it wasn't like I'd ever feared for my safety in this town. I think I would have traded a little of my security for a little less boredom.

He walked right past me when he came in, until the receptionist in whispering tones let him know I was there to see him. He turned around to look at me with a slightly puzzled smile, and in a burst of words I explained that I was one of the volunteers at the hotline.

"You're here for the background check? I'm sorry they didn't explain it better. You didn't need to see me directly. Anyone here could have helped you with that."

"So, you can't do it?" I asked. I tried to make my voice sound deflated and pathetic. I probably didn't need to worry about trying so hard.

"No, of course I can. Just give me a minute. I'll be right with you."

He disappeared for a few minutes, and when he returned he led me to a desk and offered me a seat. I handed him the birth certificate and the form I'd filled out.

"You're a Bunting," he said as he looked over the form. "I thought you all had red hair." *Strawberry-blond*, I mentally corrected.

"The miracles of Lady Clairol," I said with a smile.

He smiled back at me. He looked at the birth certificate again, and then his smile froze. He squinted at the print on the certificate as if he was trying to make out some detail.

"This can't be right," he said.

I'd only glanced at the birth certificate, which Annie had dug out for me the night before. I didn't want to look at it. No matter what the exact circumstances of my birth were, and I honestly didn't have a clue, I knew that it wasn't a happy occasion.

"What's wrong?" I asked. Perhaps it listed the age of the mother on the birth certificate. If Annie had given birth to me at some horribly young age, it would look all wrong to a police officer.

"The doctor that signed the form," he said. He held the birth certificate up for me to see and pointed toward a scribbled signature. Was he criticizing the doctor's penmanship? I shook my head, not seeing whatever it was that he saw. "Dr. Hantz," he said. "My father."

"It's a small world." I mentally breathed a sigh of relief. There wasn't anything wrong, just an interesting coincidence. My relief was short-lived.

"He died two days before you were born. In a car accident."

Did no one in this town have a living father?

"I'm sorry," I said, because it's what you say when someone tells you his father died, even if it was seventeen years ago.

But how could his signature be on my birth certificate if he was already dead? My mind began to churn through possible explanations. Someone forged his signature. No, why would they do that? The date on my birth certificate was wrong. Maybe whoever had typed it up had been off by a week, or their fingers slipped or something. It could happen, right? But weren't these things triple-checked?

It became suddenly clear. Someone had doctored the date on my birth certificate. There would be little benefit in changing the month or the day—so what they had to have changed was the year. How old was I really? Only sixteen? Fifteen? I had been robbed, cheated, and for what? To preserve some messed-up sense of normalcy? Like anyone had ever considered the Buntings normal.

"You know," Officer Hantz said, "this doesn't even really look like his signature. Maybe one of the nurses signed it. He delivered a lot of babies there. It was probably just out of habit or something."

"I guess," I said, but I was too stunned to pay much attention.

Officer Hantz went ahead with processing my paperwork while I zoned out, thinking about the irregularities of my birth certificate and what it meant. All those times I'd felt like I was completely behind my other classmates, all those times I had felt immature—it all made sense. I wasn't young for my age, I was just young—well, younger than I ever thought I was, anyway.

I was so distracted, I almost forgot the real reason I'd come down to the police station.

"Remember you told us about that website we should look up?" I said. "The Megan's Law site?"

"Sure," Hantz said.

"Well, I was wondering, is there some way to find out why someone might be on the Megan's Law site? I mean, it doesn't really give any specific information."

"Is there something you were concerned about?" he asked.

"No. Not really. But, I mean, if someone was on there it would be because they have a record, right? You could tell me what they did and when they did it?"

"I can't freely dispense that information," he said. The seriousness of his tone frightened me a little. "Did something happen?" I took in his look of concern, and realized that he thought I was there because I wanted to report an incident.

"No," I said. My suddenly high and squeaky voice must have made my words sound like a lie.

"It's not something you have to be embarrassed about. If something happened, it's not your fault." He looked at me with that serious and concerned face of his and I made some attempt to laugh the whole thing off, which only made me sound like a complete lunatic. I realized he must know who I was talking about. There was only one sex offender in Shallow Pond.

———

The anger broiled inside me as I walked home. I had visions of storming in the front door, marching right up to Annie, and demanding she tell me the truth for once in her life, but Annie wasn't in the living room when I got home. She was in the kitchen. So was Gracie. Annie was heating up the leftovers we were eating for dinner while Gracie set the table. I hadn't really counted on Gracie being there, or the fact that both of them greeted me in warm, friendly tones as if they were genuinely happy to see me. I played the obedient girl and sat down. I'd waited this long; what was another hour or so? I could corner Annie later and force her to be straight with me. It was a good plan ... but I'd kept all of my questions locked inside of me for too long.

"You're my mother, aren't you?" I said.

I stared at Annie as I spoke. She dropped her fork on her plate. Gracie looked up in surprise.

"What?" Gracie said. "Are you completely insane?"

"I don't know where you got that notion," Annie said. She sighed, then forced a smile. I could see she was trying to shrug the whole thing off, but she was trying too hard.

"She's only twenty-six," Gracie added. "How could she possibly be your mother?"

"And how old am I?" I asked.

"Weirdo, what are you talking about?" Gracie said.

"Somebody doctored the date on my birth certificate."

Annie had given up on dinner. She pushed her chair a few inches back from the table and folded her hands neatly in her lap. She looked scared and a little sad, and I knew that I'd figured it out. She'd been keeping secrets from me for years. Gracie, though, was still clueless.

"What the hell are you talking about?" Gracie asked.

"The doctor who signed my birth certificate died two days before I was born."

"But then, if the date was changed, that would mean you're older, not younger," Gracie said.

She was right, of course. How had I missed that when my airheaded sister had picked up on it?

"Maybe the whole birth certificate is a fake." I spat the words out in anger, feeling for some reason like a cornered animal. I glared at Gracie. "How come you can't remember Mom, if she didn't die until *I* was born? How come there aren't any pictures of her with you when you were a baby? Mom's not my mother!"

I shot to my feet, and my chair toppled over. My anger had turned to sadness. All I wanted to do was cry, but I didn't want to do it there. I needed to get out of there. I needed to be alone.

I had my hand on the front doorknob when Annie finally spoke.

"She's not your mother," Annie said. Her voice was so quiet and faint I could barely be sure I heard her.

"What?" Gracie said.

"She's not your mother," Annie repeated. "She's not the mother of any of us."

TWENTY-ONE

Gracie didn't say anything. She got up from the table, went into the living room, and returned carrying the photo from the mantel. She held it up beside her face.

"We look just like her," Gracie said.

"Exactly," Annie said.

I was confused. This wasn't making any sense. I thought I had everything figured out, but now nothing seemed to fit.

"She died before any of us breathed our first breaths," Annie said. "We're her clones."

Gracie started laughing, like this was all some big joke. It was too early for April Fools', though. And Annie looked deadly serious.

"Clones," I said in a whisper. I felt like I was trapped in a nightmare, but I didn't think I was going to be able to wake up and shake this off like a normal sort of nightmare.

"She's obviously just messing with us," Gracie said. "You're just messing with us, right?"

Annie shook her head. The overhead light sparkled on the tear tracks running down her face.

No, no, no, no, no. This was not the answer I'd wanted. I wanted to rewind the conversation. Annie would make her big grand admission, but it would be something trivial and mundane. She would confess to secretly being my mother. She'd gotten pregnant in her teens and given birth to me, but the decision had been to raise me as her sister. A birth certificate had been fabricated to preserve the illusion. I would have given anything in the world to be just your garden-variety illegitimate child. It was so simple and neat. I wouldn't even be mad at Annie for keeping the secret all these years. After all, it wouldn't really matter.

"It's not possible," Gracie stated.

"He was a brilliant scientist," Annie said. It took me a moment to realize that she was talking about our father. "One of the best in the world."

"Nobody goes around cloning people," Gracie said.

"It's not legal," Annie said, "but it is possible."

"What else don't I know about?" Gracie asked. "Did he have conversations with space aliens? Did he build a time machine?"

I wish he had built a time machine, because right now all I wanted to do was go back in time and undo everything. I wanted things to go back to the way they were before I started asking all my questions. I wanted to just be a teenage girl from a slightly eccentric family living in some middle-of-nowhere Pennsylvania town. I wanted to go back to being me.

"But we're different from each other," I said. My voice

was choked with tears. "We look alike, but it's not like we *act* alike." I felt sure I'd proven Annie wrong. Clones were all the same person, but we weren't all the same. We weren't anything alike. How could Gracie and I possibly be the same person?

"We've got the same DNA," Annie explained.

"That just makes us sisters," I said.

"The same *exact* DNA," Annie said.

"Does this have something to do with the medicine you're on?" Gracie asked. "You're hallucinating, right?"

"I'm not hallucinating," Annie said. Her voice was flat and weak.

"No, you are," Gracie insisted. "Because if what you're saying is even remotely true, then we're freaks. We're nothing but some crazy science experiment, and I don't know about you, but I am not cool with that. Not one bit." She punctuated her sentence by slamming the framed picture she was still holding on the edge of the table. I heard a tinkling noise as the glass over the picture shattered. A spiderweb of cracks now distorted the familiar face that looked out of the frame, the face that I'd always thought belonged to our mother, but it was the face that actually belonged to each of us. Our face.

"I didn't plan on telling you like this," Annie said. She still sat there in her chair with her hands neatly folded.

"How long have you known?" I asked. She didn't answer right away. I stared at her as a few lonely tears slid down her face.

"Awhile," she said after several seconds. I didn't know what that meant. Had she known her whole life? Why was it that she knew and we were in the dark? I wished I was still in the dark. It would have been easier than knowing. Knowing made everything different.

I leaned my head against the door, resting my cheek on one of the cool glass panels. My whole life flashed through my mind, and it was all a lie. Everything that I thought I knew had been wrong. My whole life I'd been pretending to be a real person, a unique person, but I wasn't. I was a clone of some woman I'd never met. I was a freak. We were all freaks.

The door rattled suddenly, and I jumped. I spun around and saw Cameron Schaeffer standing on the other side.

He smiled at me through the glass. I stared at him as if he was a ghost. It seemed like a million years ago that I'd spent the afternoon with him, convinced he was my father. My father? I didn't even *have* a father. No wonder the man who I'd always assumed was my father was so distant from me. He was probably repulsed by our very presence, the monsters that he'd created—living, breathing monsters.

Cameron's brow furrowed when I didn't open the door right away. I thought of the Megan's Law site, the mug shot that was there. He was a sex offender. I knew this should make me feel something, but it didn't. It didn't seem to matter anymore. Nothing mattered.

I opened the door, and Cameron stepped into the kitchen. His eyes swept the room, taking in the mostly uneaten dinner, the smashed picture frame, Annie so sad and serene in her chair, and Gracie looking about ready to jump out of her skin. Unless he was a complete idiot, he must have realized that something was seriously amiss.

"Hello, Cameron," Annie said in a voice that tried too hard to be casual and friendly.

"I think maybe I've caught you at a bad time," he said.

"You could say that again," Gracie said.

"I'm sorry," Cameron said. "I should have called. It's rude to just show up unannounced. I should probably go."

"No!" Gracie screamed. "I mean, I was just about to go out too. Just let me go grab my jacket."

"If you were in the middle of—" He looked around, as if the appropriate word might be sitting on a shelf somewhere. "Dinner, or whatever, I can wait for you in the car."

"We're done," Gracie said. She turned and looked at Annie with narrowed eyes, then ran out of the room to grab her coat.

"So, Babie, how're things going?" Cameron asked as he stood there awkwardly waiting for Gracie. I stared at him in confusion. How were things? I didn't even know where to begin with that question. Thankfully, Gracie swept back into the room and grabbed Cameron by the arm to steer him past me and out the door. She didn't look back at us or even say goodbye.

I didn't watch them as they walked out of the house, but Annie did. The look on her face said it all. She looked wistful and heartsick. It was the look of lost dreams and unrequited love, and I thought for the first time in my entire life that I finally understood Annie.

Everything I'd thought I knew about her had been wrong, but now, with the information I'd been lacking for so many years, I could finally piece together the mystery that was Annie. All these years, I'd blamed the fact that Annie had never left Shallow Pond on Cameron and her foolish love for him, but now I could see the true explanation. It wasn't love that had kept her from living her life, but shock—and a knowledge that she didn't know how to deal with. How do you go forward with your life when you find out you aren't even a real person? What is the point of anything if your whole life has been some sort of cruel lie? She didn't go to college, and she broke up with Cameron, because college and Cameron were things that belonged to the real world, a world that she no longer belonged to. My sister had dealt with the knowledge that her whole existence was some cruel science experiment by becoming a recluse, a response that seemed pretty rational to me.

I turned to look out the window, but Gracie and Cameron had already disappeared from view. I looked back to Annie. She was staring out into the darkness with that wistful look on her face.

"There never was anyone else, was there?" I asked. That had only been a lie to appease Cameron, because telling him the truth was out of the question.

"No. There was someone else."

I didn't believe her. For some reason, it was easier for me to believe that we were the clones of some woman we'd been told was our mother than for me to believe that Annie had ever had another boyfriend.

"Does it ever get easier?" I asked. She looked at me and smiled that warm smile of hers.

"It does," she said. "I know it's a lot to take in at once. I'm sorry."

"It's not your fault."

"I didn't mean to tell you so suddenly like that, but it's best that you know."

I nodded, though I didn't entirely agree. Why was it best to know?

"I think I'm going to head up to bed," Annie said. "Do you mind cleaning up the dishes?"

She was going to bed? Now? She dropped a bomb like that on me, and then she was just abandoning me?

I told her I didn't mind. I began to clean up the dishes with slow, methodical movements like some sort of robot, even though I wasn't a robot. I was a clone. Well, at least there was that. I mean, being a robot? That would really suck, right?

TWENTY-TWO

I awoke suddenly. I felt my heart racing. It was dark, so I rolled over to look at my alarm clock. It was only a few minutes after five. Too early, way too early. I knew I should try to get some more sleep, but my racing heart thought otherwise. There was something I was forgetting. A nightmare, I told myself—that was the nagging feeling that was keeping me awake at this hour. But the nagging feeling refused to go away. After I'd tossed and turned for another minute or so, it came back to me. *Last night. Annie's announcement.* I wanted for it to have all been a nightmare, but I knew it wasn't.

I sat up and hugged my knees to my chest in the dark. I'd slept in this room my whole life, and it had always seemed like such a warm, welcoming space. Now, in the darkness of early morning, there was something menacing about it. I felt like I didn't belong. Maybe I didn't. After all, *she* (my mother, for lack of a better word) had not grown up in Shallow Pond. I belonged to a different time and a different place. I was an interloper here. I could never be anything but.

All I'd wanted for as long as I could remember was to get the hell out of Shallow Pond. I'd always thought this was because it was some crappy small town where dreams went to die, but what if that wasn't the reason at all? What if the only reason I longed so desperately to get out was because my body instinctively knew it wasn't supposed to be there?

Suddenly, everything I'd ever thought, everything I'd ever said, everything I'd ever done was suspect. Why had I done any of the things I had done? What if everything was due to forces beyond my control or understanding? I felt scared, like I couldn't even trust my own mind; like it wasn't my mind to trust.

———————

Forty-five minutes before the first bell rang, I stepped out our front door. I couldn't remember ever being ready for school this early. The weekend had passed by like a confusing dream—I didn't sleep through it, exactly, but I'd barely left my bedroom for two days. At least now the groggy fog had lifted.

An icy wind blew, and the cold felt good on my skin. It made me feel alive. I should have called Jenelle, but I didn't feel like talking to her. I didn't feel like talking to anyone. I walked toward school, taking my time despite the cold. I told myself I needed time to think, but what I was trying to do was *not* think, keep my mind empty of anything important. I studied the bark on the side of a tree, the grit that speckled the snowbanks at the side of the road, a crow who cawed at me from atop a chimney. I immersed myself in the physical world to shut out all thought.

The school was still pretty empty when I walked in. It felt strange. I went to the library and found the shelf with the old yearbooks. I found the one from a couple of years earlier, Gracie's senior year, and the one from Annie's senior year. I'd seen them before, of course, but that was before I knew what I was looking at. Annie and Gracie looked alike, but so did plenty of sisters. Did they look identical? It was hard to say. They had different hair styles, and the angle the pictures were taken at was slightly different. But if you looked at the two photos side by side, without knowing anything else, it would seem like you were looking at two pictures of the same girl.

I flipped through the rest of the book. Annie had been on the debate team and worked on the school newspaper. I'm sure she'd told me that at some point, but I'd forgotten until I saw her picture on the activities pages. Gracie had played field hockey and worked on the yearbook and the prom committee. She'd been popular in school—her photo appeared again and again in the candid shots.

If we were all the same, then why wasn't I in the popular crowd? How come Gracie hadn't been on the debate team? It didn't make sense.

When I glanced up at the clock, there were only three minutes until the homeroom bell rang. I'd lost track of time. Shoving the books back on the shelf, I ran to my locker. I should have known that Jenelle and Shawna would be waiting there for me, but it didn't really hit me until I saw Jenelle standing there, her hand on her hip, her expression murderous.

"What the hell?" she said.

"Not now," I said. "I've got to get my things."

"You don't answer any of my messages this weekend. You walk to school without even bothering to call me. This isn't cool."

"I'm sorry, okay? But I've got some stuff going on right now," I said.

"Stuff that's more important than your friends? That's bull, Bunting."

"It's like you barely talk to us anymore," Shawna said. She had a big pouffy bow tied in her hair. Was it some new style? It looked ridiculous, especially since part of it kept flopping in her face.

"I can't explain," I said. "You wouldn't understand."

"No, what we don't understand is why you're treating us like you don't even know us," Jenelle said. "What's up with that?"

I grabbed my books from my locker and slammed the door.

"Not now," I said. I started to walk away down the hall.

"If that's what you think of us," Jenelle said, "if you're not our friend anymore, then keep walking."

I paused. I took a deep breath. Would it really be that much trouble to walk back to Jenelle and pretend like everything was fine? I probably could have done it, but I was sick of pretending. My whole life had been nothing but pretend. The only alternative was to tell the two of them everything, and that was definitely not going to happen. I resumed walking at almost the same moment that the bell rang.

"Hey," Zach said, falling into step beside me.

"I'm not really in the mood to talk right now," I said.

"So, not a morning person I take it."

"No, I just … there's this thing, a family thing, I don't really feel like talking about it."

"Maybe I should be thankful I'm an orphan," he said. He was smiling as he said it, but it sounded more like a self-pitying sort of thing to say than the funny remark he was trying to pretend it was.

I came to a stop in the busy hallway, and a few people bumped into me as they hurried to get to their homerooms.

"I don't want to be here," I said.

"Yeah, I get it already. Shallow Pond is small and pathetic and nothing ever happens here. You know, you really should give this place a chance. It's not that bad."

"No," I said. I sighed through my clenched teeth. "I don't want to be here, at school, today. Drive me somewhere."

"We can't just walk out of here."

"We can, and we have to. Come on."

I grabbed his sleeve and started walking toward the parking lot door. He walked with me, but still didn't seem entirely sure about it. I didn't care. I couldn't be there one more minute. I needed to be somewhere, anywhere else.

"What's this all about?" Zach asked when we were safely in his car. His keys were in the ignition, but he hadn't started the car yet. "I don't like this. We should go back. They'll give us a late pass."

"Just drive."

"I shouldn't really skip school like this."

"You're like Mr. Perfect, aren't you? You can't have a hair out of place and you can't possibly do anything that isn't exactly by the book."

"That's not true," he said. "It's just I kind of got in trouble the last time I skipped." I wondered if he meant the day he'd shown up at my house. "Strings had to be pulled for me to be enrolled here," he continued. "I'm not really supposed to be living on my own without a guardian, and I'm somewhat lacking in documentation. I don't even have a birth certificate."

"Join the club," I said. The bitter laugh that escaped my lips surprised me.

"I'm just saying that it probably makes more sense to fly below the radar."

"Then go back to school," I said. I put my hand on the door handle. I didn't need him. I could walk. I was about to open the door when the car roared to life.

"You're impossible," he said. He peeled out of the parking lot too fast, but it felt good. It felt reckless. It felt like we were alive. I liked that feeling.

Zach didn't say anything until he pulled into the parking lot by Memorial Park. I wished he'd kept driving. If I'd been the one behind the wheel, I would have gotten on the highway and kept going all the way to California.

"What is it about you, Barbara Bunting?" he asked. I shrugged, because how do you answer a question like that?

"You've got this pull over me. So, what's going on? Why aren't we at school?"

"I just didn't want to be there," I said. I opened the door and stepped out. The cold tore through my clothes. My coat was back in my locker. I should have gotten back in the car, but I didn't want to. I folded my arms across my chest and tried not to shiver.

Zach got out of the car holding a scratchy wool blanket in his hand. He shook his head at me, then draped one end of the blanket over my shoulders before pulling the other end over his own shoulders. I had no choice but to huddle next to him for warmth. The blanket had a musty smell, but Zach smelled clean and soapy. Everything about Zach was perfect. He was good-looking and sweet. He wasn't from Shallow Pond; he was the exotic stranger with the mysterious past. Best of all, we were alike, orphaned, the dark shadow of questionable parentage hanging over our childhoods. We belonged together. It seemed so natural. I was surprised it had taken me so long to see it clearly.

I turned to him, the scratchy blanket twisting around me. I stared into his blue eyes, eyes so deep they sucked me right in. When he exhaled, a small white cloud condensed in the space between us and I could smell minty toothpaste. It was warm beneath the blanket, with Zach inches from me.

"Why can't I resist you?" Zach asked me, and this time I knew he didn't expect me to answer. Instead, he leaned toward me. His lips brushed mine; they were soft and warm. They filled me from head to toe with intense heat. It was over in a moment. He pulled back and looked at me as if seeing me for the first time, as if trying to answer his own rhetorical question.

But I needed him. I needed to lose myself in him. I reached up and brushed my fingers along the rough skin of his cheek, then gently guided his face back to my own. Our lips met again, but this time they stayed locked together as if by some magnetic force. Zach tasted the way I imagined a bubbling forest stream to taste. I raised both hands to his face and held on. The blanket slid from my shoulders and then to the ground as Zach's hands found my hips and pulled me toward him. With our bodies pressed together, I didn't feel the cold. Zach's hand, just above the waistband of my jeans, was warm against my bare flesh. I could feel the pounding of his chest against my own.

The world fell away. Nothing else mattered. There was only us, and I could have stayed there forever and ever. If only it was possible to stay there forever and ever. He leaned against the car and pulled me to him. Our lips explored each other as his hands, strong but gentle, explored my body. I slid my own hands from Zach's face to his chest and then down to his waist. I'd never needed anything as badly as I needed Zach Faraday.

Zach pulled away from me. I reached for him, but he turned his head away. With his hands on my waist, he held me at bay.

"No," he said. "Why are we here?"

"What are you talking about?" I couldn't understand what he meant. I only knew that I needed him desperately.

"I mean, what's going on, Barbara? Why are we ditching school? What's wrong?"

"I don't want to talk about that now," I said. I pushed his hand from where it held my waist, then reached up and guided his face back to my own. Our lips tore into each other, desperate to taste each other, but then he pulled away again and shook his head. When he stepped away from me, I suddenly felt the cold. He lifted the blanket from the ground and handed it to me, but he didn't drape it over my shoulders, and he didn't take up the other end for himself. He paced across the unpaved parking lot.

"I can't do this," he said. I thought of Meg and hated her. He shook his head, as if he could read my thoughts. "You need to talk to me."

"There's nothing to talk about," I said.

"The hell there isn't. You dragged me out of school and then won't even say anything to me. What's going on?"

"Nothing."

"Was it Cameron? Did he do something to you?"

"No!"

"I don't like him. I don't like the way he looks at you."

"It's not Cameron," I said. My voice was soft and quiet. I looked at Zach, and his eyes looked damp. Was he crying? Was it the cold?

"Get in the car," he said. He opened the passenger door, then went around and got in on his side. I sank into the seat, the blanket still wrapped around me, and pulled the door closed after me. I was too stunned to speak. Zach was about to start the car, but then he stopped, sat back against his seat, and sighed. "I wish I'd never met you. I think about you all the time. I can't get you out of my head."

"Zach," I began, because I knew I needed to say something, but he cut me off.

"No, let me finish. You're . . . I can't explain it. I don't understand it. You've got this power over me, and I like you even though you clearly aren't interested in me. I know that I should just forget you, but I can't."

"I *am* interested in you," I said. I thought of how we had been kissing just a couple of minutes before. How could he say that I wasn't interested in him?

"You don't act like it," he said. "You won't even tell me what's bugging you."

"It's a family thing," I said. "I can't really talk about it. You wouldn't understand."

"Are you forgetting who you're talking to? I was found in a basket outside a convent. I was raised by nuns."

"Trust me, you're normal compared to me," I said. It was more than I'd meant to say. For a second or two, I considered telling him everything, but I thought of how it had been to feel his lips on mine, his hand against my skin. I needed Zach Faraday, and if I went ahead and told him everything, he would never even look at me again. He would be repulsed by my very presence. I couldn't handle that. I might have been sort of a freak, but I wasn't ready to let the rest of the world know that.

"You and your sisters are aliens, here from another planet to observe life in a small American town?" he asked.

"Something like that," I said.

He smiled at me, but when I didn't say anything more, he looked away. "Why do you shut me out?" he asked.

"It's not something I can talk about," I said.

"Why not?"

"You wouldn't understand."

"How do you know unless you tell me?"

I shrugged. He pounded his fist on the dashboard and I flinched. He shook his head and turned the key in the ignition.

"We're going back to school," he said.

I didn't say anything. I turned and looked out the window. I watched as Shallow Pond flew past. I hated this place more than ever, but I would have traded places with just about anyone in town whose last name wasn't Bunting. It wasn't fair. I wished I had some nice, normal life, but I was some sort of monster. How could I explain any of that to Zach? Zach thought *his* life was messed up? He didn't have a clue.

I looked at him sitting there beside me, perfect in every way, and my heart ached with hunger for him. I wondered if this was what Annie had felt when she broke up with Cameron. It would be easier to reject someone than to have them run from you when they found out you were nothing but a complete freak. The fact that I could understand and relate to my sister scared me. Annie was no longer a mystery. Her peculiarities all made sense now; she was looking a whole lot more like a sensible and logical person.

I realized that no matter how hard I tried, I might have no choice but to become my sister—and then I reminded myself that she wasn't my sister. We were much closer than that. We were just different versions of the same person. Was my fate already decided? It seemed I might have no choice but to spend the rest of my miserable life in this town.

TWENTY-THREE

When I got home from school, Annie was waiting for me. She clicked off the television as soon as I stepped in the door.

"I got a phone call from the school today," she said. Crap. "They said you were late this morning, which I thought was kind of strange since you left pretty early."

"You're not my mother," I said. "You can't yell at me."

"I'm not yelling," she pointed out.

"Look, it's not a big deal," I said. I hung my coat up and started up the stairs. We weren't going to have this conversation.

I figured Annie would give up and turn the television back on, but I'd underestimated her. I threw my backpack on my bed, and when I turned around, she was standing there in my doorway.

"I know this hasn't been easy for you," she said. "Maybe I shouldn't have told you, but I didn't think I could keep it from you forever. You're too smart for that." She smiled at me, like complimenting me on my intelligence would somehow wipe away all my problems.

"I don't really feel like talking about this right now," I said.

She nodded, but she kept standing there as if I might change my mind. I glared at her and she finally walked away. I threw myself down on the bed beside the backpack. I curled myself around it as if it was some piece of flotsam keeping me afloat in an endless ocean. I wanted to cry or scream or do something, but instead I just lay there staring at the wall in front of me.

"Who is Zach?"

I jumped. Annie had crept silently back into my room. I rolled over and saw her standing there, just inside the doorway. Why couldn't she just leave me alone?

"When the school called to say you signed in late, they said you were with another student, a boy, Zach Faraday. I didn't recognize the name."

"He's not from here," I said.

"Is he ... ?" She let the half question hang there in the air. I sat up and shook my head.

"Don't do this," I said. "Don't try and act all motherly. It's annoying."

"Is he your boyfriend?" she asked.

"Genetic mutants don't have boyfriends."

"We're not genetic mutants."

"Yeah we are." I stared at my sister; well, not my sister, my clone. She looked old, with the dark circles beneath her eyes and her skin pulled tight across her face. This was what I would look like in a few years.

"It's not like that. It doesn't really matter where you come from."

"If that's true, then why the big secret? Why the phony birth certificate?"

"There are laws," Annie said. She waved her hand in the air as if this was only some trivial thing. "It makes things easier."

Easier? Or did it just keep us from getting locked up in some lab somewhere, where government scientists would poke, prod, and study us like the science experiments gone awry that we were? What would happen if the truth ever got out? Did we risk more than complete and total ostracism by everyone we knew? Was our very security at stake?

"There's a lot of people who wouldn't be cool with what we are," I said. "Does anyone else know?"

"A few of Dad's old colleagues."

"Dr. Feld?" I asked. I thought of his weird reaction to seeing us. Annie nodded in confirmation. "But you've never told anyone?"

"No," she said.

I lay back down on the bed and stared up at the ceiling. I thought of Cameron Schaeffer. With the memory of Zach's lips on mine so fresh in my mind, I wondered how Annie had done it, how she'd shut Cameron out of her life. Only she never really did shut him out, did she? She tried to pretend she did, but she'd never stopped loving him. It had eaten her up inside, turned her into a hollow shell of herself.

"If you hadn't broken up with Cameron, you would have had to tell him."

"That doesn't have anything to do with this," she said. Her calm motherly voice had given way to the clipped, angry tone. I'd had to go and pull that scab off the Cameron Schaeffer wound. I was such an idiot.

"But it's true." I was nothing if not persistent. "We can never have a normal life. We'll always have this big dark family secret hanging over our heads."

Annie's face softened. She came in and sat beside me on the bed. "Lots of people have secrets," she said. "This is about Zach, isn't it?"

She let her hand rest on my shoulder, and I jerked it away. Why did she have to drag Zach into this?

Of course, I couldn't help but think about him. Did he have secrets? He'd told me his whole life story; it was hard to imagine he could have any secrets, but perhaps there were secrets even he didn't know about. After all, he didn't know where he came from. We were so alike that it was like we were fated to be together. Maybe that's what Zach meant when he said he was drawn to me. I knew what he meant—after all, there was something about him that was irresistible to me. We belonged together.

"Why did you fall in love with Cameron?" I asked.

"Why? Love doesn't really work like that. It's one of those things that happens whether you want it to or not."

"Because two people have a lot in common?"

"Maybe, or simply because. Sometimes it doesn't make

much sense at all. This Zach, he must be something special, I take it."

I started to blush and tried to will the telltale heat away, but it only seemed to grow hotter.

"He's a nice guy," I said, "but it's not like that. He's not my boyfriend."

"Well, why not?"

Because I'm a complete genetic freak and I can never ever tell him that was the first answer that came to mind, but I didn't voice this out loud.

"I don't need a boyfriend," I said.

"Need," she repeated in a quiet voice. She looked off into space. I worried that I'd upset her somehow, but there was a smile on her face. She returned to earth and said, "When it comes right down to it, nobody needs a boyfriend. We'd probably all be better off without them. Better off, but not necessarily happier."

I puzzled over this comment. Annie was the last person I expected to be singing the praises of romantic love. How could she, after everything, still equate love with happiness? I thought of that mysterious "someone else." I hadn't really believed he'd ever existed, but now I wasn't so sure. Could that be who she was thinking about whenever she got that dreamy expression on her face, this mysterious other guy that she refused to talk about? Who was he, and what had happened to him? If she was so in love with him, where was he?

"What happened to the guy you dumped Cameron for? Did he die?"

"Yeah," she said. Her response arrived too quickly, and

I saw the way she went rigid, the color draining from her face as soon as the words left my lips. Who *was* this mystery man, and why wouldn't she talk about him?

"How did he die? How come you never talk about him?" I knew I sounded like a demanding child, but she was being such a pain about this.

"The thing with love," Annie said, "is that if you aren't careful, it can consume you. It doesn't take much for love to turn into obsession."

Obsession? Was she talking about Cameron? The mystery man? I wanted answers, but I wasn't going to get them, at least not just yet. Gracie had gotten home and was shouting up to us, referring to us as lazy slugs for not checking the mail.

"I should get down there," Annie said. She patted my leg as she stood up. "I didn't realize how late it was. I've got to get dinner started."

I could tell by the speed (practically running) at which she left my room that she was eager to escape. My questions were not going to be answered. Maybe they would never be answered. After her big revelation, this did seem a bit strange. If she could tell us that we were clones, you would think that telling us something, anything, about some boyfriend she used to have would be nothing.

———

Twenty minutes later, I finally got up off my bed and trudged downstairs to see what we were doing for dinner.

"You got mail," Gracie said. She pointed at my place, where I saw a white business-sized envelope.

I went over and picked it up to look at the return address, and saw a college's name and seal. It was a mark of how completely things had changed for me. As little as a week earlier, the sight of such an envelope would have caused my heart to start racing and a furious tumult of excitement and nervousness to overtake me. Now I felt numb as I stared at it.

"Aren't you going to open it?" Gracie asked. But I couldn't see the point of that. It was pretty obvious that I wouldn't be going off to college, that I would never leave Shallow Pond. The evidence was staring me in the face; Gracie and her supermarket job, Annie and her reclusive ways. If they were both still living in this crappy town long after their eighteenth birthdays, then I knew there wasn't any possibility that I would ever escape. The sooner I gave up hope, the less painful it would be.

"What is it?" Annie asked.

"From a college I applied to," I said. Annie turned away from the stove, and Gracie was pretty much ready to explode with anticipation. Great, I had an audience. I sighed, then slipped my fingernail beneath the flap and began to gently pry the envelope open. I pulled out the letter and began to read.

It was a long letter, two pages. I knew that was a good sign. I read it through once, then went back and double-checked it to be sure.

"What does it say?" Gracie asked. In her excitement her voice had grown so high-pitched she was practically squealing.

"I got in," I said.

"That's great," Annie said. "Congratulations!"

"They're giving me a full scholarship," I continued.

"Oh my God!" Gracie screamed. "That's awesome!"

In the second or so it took me to glance back at the letter one more time, Annie and Gracie attacked me as if they were boa constrictors, squeezing me so tight with their hugs that I nearly couldn't breathe.

"We're so proud of you," Annie said. Her voice was choked with tears.

I wouldn't have minded being able to cry, or at least being able to feel some sort of emotion. Anything would have been better than the weird blankness I felt. My dream had come true. Not only did I get accepted into college, but they were offering me a scholarship. There was nothing standing in my way. The road was clear. But I knew deep down that it didn't matter. Somehow or other, this was not going to happen.

"I would think you would be at least a tiny bit excited," Gracie said when she finally released me from her grasp. I shrugged.

"It doesn't change anything," I said. It took her a moment, but then Gracie's face fell when she realized what I was talking about.

"We're not going to talk about that," Gracie said. "Besides, I'm not really sure I believe any of it. Annie, you can't believe anything Dad told you. He was completely crazy."

"It's true," Annie said, "and it doesn't change anything. Babie is going to college, but first we're going to eat some dinner."

I went to bed early. I crawled into my bed, pulled the covers over my head, and tried to escape from everything. I sank into a world of disturbing nightmares. Creepy men in white lab coats chased me down narrow twisting hallways. I escaped only to find myself in a room filled with cages housing scientific experiments gone wrong. A normal-looking girl with octopus tentacles writhed against the bars of her cage. A half-bird, half-human creature made pitiful squawking noises in its cage. There were people with multiple heads and people with too many limbs. Then suddenly I found myself trapped in a cage. I clutched at the bars, shook them in a futile effort to free myself. The men in white lab coats appeared and began to reach through the bars of my cage. They poked and prodded at me. One grabbed my arm. I told myself it was all a bad dream and forced myself to wake up.

My heart raced. I was damp with sweat as I struggled to remember where I was. I wasn't in the lab anymore. I was in my bedroom. I was safe. The dream still clung to me, and something else. I let out a yelp when I realized one of the men in white coats was still clutching my arm.

"Relax. It's just me," Annie said, her voice soft and comforting in the dark room. Fully awake now, I stared into the darkness and saw Annie sitting on the edge of my bed in her white nightgown, her hand on my arm. "You were having a nightmare."

I sat up and rubbed my eyes. Pieces of the nightmare

flashed through my memory. A glimpse of tentacles, the long hallway, a boy with too many heads. I shuddered.

"Are you all right?" she asked.

"Yeah," I said, but I didn't want her to go. It was nice to have her there in the darkness. I wasn't ready to be alone again. "Do you ever get used to it?"

"Does where you come from really matter that much?" she asked.

For some reason, her question made me think of Zach and his mysterious origins. "I think it does matter," I said.

"Sometimes, if you're lucky enough," Annie said, "you find that one person who completes you, the person so perfect that it seems like they were made for you. Love, the truest of loves, is a magical thing. There's nothing more beautiful or more wonderful, but there's a dark side too. The world can be a cruel place. Sometimes the person we love is torn away from us, leaving behind an emptiness that can never be filled."

Was she talking about Cameron? Her mystery man? Her vagueness made things confusing.

"Is that why you never went to college? Is that why you stayed here?"

"He loved her," she said. "It was like a storybook romance. They were perfect for each other. Theirs was the truest sort of love out there. Then she died suddenly, and way, way too young. He was beside himself with grief. He was left with a big emptiness he had no way of filling. What he did, he did out of desperation; out of love and grief as well."

She was talking about our father. It took me a few seconds to realize it.

"It wasn't a rational thing at all," she went on, "but he needed her, and it was the only way he knew to bring her back to him."

"Lots of people have their hearts broken without going off and cloning their dead lover," I said.

"Yeah," Annie said. "People deal with a lost love in all sorts of different ways. I guess what I'm saying is that if you're looking for an explanation of what you're doing here, maybe it helps to think that you're here because of love. It's why most people are here. Maybe our creation took a slightly different route, but it's still the age-old story. Two people fell in love, and now we're here."

When she put it that way, it didn't sound at all like the crazy world of my nightmares. It made us sound almost normal.

TWENTY-FOUR

We had a half day, because of a teacher inservice, and there were still a couple of hours before I was due at the call center. So, instead of heading home, I walked to the cemetery. I could remember visiting it when we were kids, placing flowers on our "mother's" grave on Mother's Day, but it had been years since I'd been there.

When my father died, he was cremated. His ashes sat in an urn in his old room. There had been no procession to the cemetery. That had all happened six years before, and it had been at least that long since we'd been to the cemetery. Probably even longer than that. I didn't know what drew me to the place now.

A short stone wall topped by an iron fence surrounded the small graveyard. The big iron gate was standing open when I got there. Large towering elm trees lined the perimeter, with a few more in the center. Their leaves had long since been shed, and their bare branches looked dark and menacing against the pale gray sky. It was cold out, but it felt even colder as I stepped through the gates. It was a bleak and creepy place. I wondered if this was why we'd stopped coming here.

I had a vague idea of where her grave was, but I couldn't remember for sure. I wandered in what I thought was the general direction, stumbling over the frozen, uneven ground. Each marker I passed represented a dead Shallow Pond resident, and I wondered about these people who had lived and died in this sad town. Had they been born and raised here? Had fate brought them here? Had fate kept them here against their wishes? I imagined three more headstones that would someday join the others here. The three strange Bunting sisters who would be buried along with their secret. It felt weird to think about, but I was spared these morbid thoughts when the familiar name caught my attention.

Susie Bunting. I stared at the engraved name on the smooth marble surface. Below her name it read, *Beloved wife and mother.* I stared at the epitaph without really seeing it. There was something weird about this tombstone, and it took me a few minutes to realize what it was. There were no dates. I glanced around. All the other markers I saw had birth and death dates. Many only had a name followed by the dates, which were the sole bits of information about these other Shallow Pond residents. But how old was Susie Bunting when she died? *Too young* was all I knew, since there was no indication on her tombstone of how young she'd been.

Staring at the tombstone, I noticed something else. The surface of the stone where the epitaph was carved was rougher than the rest of the stone. It didn't have that smooth, polished look. I wondered if the stone was defective, or if the person carving it had made a mistake. My father had been pretty good about pinching his pennies, but I tried to imagine the grief-stricken man Annie had described agreeing to use a defective tombstone for his wife's grave if he could get it for half price. No, the rough area of the stone was no accident. It had probably contained her birth and death dates initially, but then my father realized that those dates would be inconsistent with the ages of her "children." He must have had the dates removed and replaced with the inaccurate phrase *Beloved wife and mother*. To keep his secret—our secret—safe.

I wondered how many of the things I'd taken for granted in my life were also part of the carefully created illusion. Is that what we were doing in Shallow Pond? Had we come to this town in the middle of nowhere because no one knew us, no one could question where we'd come from or who our mother really was? Did I actually have family out there some-where? Grandparents? Aunts and uncles? Cousins? I'd always been told that there were no living relatives, but now I realized how unlikely this was. Either my family was the unhealthiest, most ill-fated family of all time or my father had broken off ties with relatives on both sides to keep his secret safe.

The more I thought about it, the more I realized it must be true. It probably wouldn't be that hard to track them down, but what would I do then? How could I explain who I was? I imagined finding my grandparents—no, they wouldn't really be my grandparents. They were more like my parents, though that wasn't quite true either. What would happen if I located them … if I found Susie's parents and showed up on their doorstep, looking like the carbon copy of the daughter they'd lost so many years ago? They would have a heart attack, for sure, but then what? They would want an explanation, and if I told them everything, they could very easily go to the authorities. Those creepy men in the white coats would become more than just the shadowy figures in a bad nightmare.

I reached my hand out and ran my fingers over the carved letters on the cold stone. It was the closest I could get to knowing her, this mysterious woman who was and wasn't the same person I was. She was dead, had been dead for a long time, but in some ways she wasn't. She still lived on in the three of us, more so than someone lived on through their actual children. We weren't simply offspring but younger versions of her. I wished I'd had the chance to know her, that she hadn't died so young… but then, if she hadn't died, I wouldn't exist. It was a weird, dizzying feeling. I took a step back from the stone.

"Babie?"

I jumped at the sound of my name in the quiet cemetery. For one brief moment I thought the voice was in my head, that somehow Susie, alive through my own DNA, our shared DNA, was talking to me from beyond the grave. Then I turned and saw a figure a few rows away. He waved, and I recognized Cameron Schaeffer.

I wondered how long he'd been there. I began to step quickly away from Susie's grave, as though just my presence there would tip him off to the great big secret. As I walked over to Cameron, I saw the headstone in front of him—his father. There were a bunch of different Schaeffers in the surrounding area. Apparently quite a few of them had lived and died in Shallow Pond over the years. Cameron had escaped for a little bit, but now he was back in this town that had claimed the lives of so many of his relatives.

"Your mother?" he asked. I nodded. He pointed toward his father's marker. "Today was his birthday." His eyes were dry, but red as if he had been crying earlier.

I thought of the day I went ice fishing with Cameron. It felt like a million years ago. That was back when my biggest problem had been assuming I was the illegitimate child of Cameron and Annie. If only that was my problem. I'd felt a special bond with Cameron that afternoon, but like everything in my life, it was nothing but a fantasy. My whole life was one big lie, like the blatant *beloved mother* line on Susie's headstone.

"I hate coming here," Cameron said. "I come out here thinking I'll be able to connect with him somehow, but he's not here." I nodded because I didn't know what to say. "Where do you think they are?"

The obvious answer was *in the ground*, but I knew what he meant. Down there, buried in their coffins, those were simply cadavers. They were just the husks left behind after death. What did happen to the people? Did I believe in some sort of afterlife? Was Cameron's dad in heaven? Was Susie? Could she be? Or was she inside of us somehow? Had our creation somehow gone and stolen her away from death, as my father had so desperately hoped?

"Maybe they're just gone," I said. It sounded bleak, so

I said, "Maybe they're finally free." I wished it was true, but I didn't believe it. Cameron nodded, as if he thought this was a valid possibility.

"Hey," he said, as if suddenly snapping out of his grief. "I know it's been a few years since I was a teenager, but this does seem like a weird place to spend an afternoon. Are you one of those goth kids or something?"

"I just needed to think about some things," I said.

"Well, I mean, with the hair and the hanging out in graveyards and all, people might get the wrong impression."

"I don't really care what anyone in this town thinks," I said.

"Amen to that." Cameron laughed. He smiled at me, and I could see how my sister had fallen for him all those years ago. Well, how both my sisters had fallen for him. "It's cold as hell out here, isn't it?" he said.

It was my turn to laugh. It seemed pretty gutsy to refer to hell in a place like this.

"I'm freezing," I admitted.

"Did you walk down here?" he asked. I nodded. "God, you're crazy. But you're a Bunting. It pretty much goes without saying. Come on, I'll give you a lift."

As soon as I got in his car, it hit me. I was sitting beside Cameron just as Gracie did when she went out with him, and as Annie had done before her. I thought about what Annie had said, about people belonging together. Was there some indefinable thing that drew two people together? Was there some pull that existed between us and Cameron Schaeffer? Perhaps he was powerless to resist Gracie. And me? I suddenly shifted in the seat, moving an imperceptible inch or so away from Cameron as he started up the car and cranked up the heater.

Gracie said my father hated Cameron, and now that made sense. How could he not hate Cameron? Because we were not just his daughters—we weren't really his daughters at all. It was like Cameron was dating his wife. The thought was disturbing, and like so many of my thoughts of late, it made me a bit dizzy.

"Are you headed home?" Cameron asked.

"I've got a volunteer thing I have to do. You can drop me off at the municipal building."

"You graduate this year?" he asked as he pulled out of the parking lot.

"Yeah."

"Are you sure you aren't secretly some goth chick? You've got the whole apathetic thing down to a T. Man, when I was your age I couldn't wait to get the hell out of this town. You are going to college, right?"

A week before, I would have known exactly how to answer the question, but now everything was different. "I'm not sure," I said.

"Don't let Gracie talk you out of it," he said. "She thinks she's not smart enough for college, but that's crap."

"It's not that," I said. "I just don't want to get my hopes up." I knew Cameron would hear it as my concern about getting into a school, not my conviction that fate would prevent me from ever leaving this town.

"Jesus. Listen to you. You have to think positively. You won't get anywhere with a negative attitude like that."

"Says the guy who is unemployed and back living with his mother at age twenty-six."

"Ouch." He turned and gave me a smirk to show he wasn't really wounded. Unfortunately, he took his eyes off the road. It was only for a second, but the car ahead of him came to a halt and when he turned back to the road, there wasn't enough time to stop. He swore and slammed on the brakes. They squealed, and we smacked into the car in front of us hard enough to put a dent in its bumper.

We both sat there for a moment, too shocked to breathe. Cameron recovered first. "Babie, are you okay?"

I nodded.

"Crap," he said.

I amended that to double-crap when I saw who stepped out of the car we'd hit. He was off-duty and dressed in jeans and a ski jacket, but I recognized Officer Hantz right away. Apparently I wasn't the only one who recognized him, because Cameron began to curse quietly beneath his breath. He opened his window.

"I think I hit some black ice," he said.

"Cameron," Officer Hantz said, looking into the car. Then he glanced over at me and his expression darkened. "Barbara."

"I was driving Babie over to the municipal building," Cameron said.

Officer Hantz nodded like he didn't entirely believe this, so I added, "I'm volunteering. At the call center."

"Speed limit here is twenty-five," Hantz said.

"I know. Like I said, I think there must have been some ice. I couldn't stop in time."

Hantz glanced at his car with its dented bumper. It wasn't that bad. He seemed to be considering the situation.

"We don't have to report this," he said. "I can send you a bill for the repairs."

"Thank you," Cameron said. "Thank you so much."

"Just slow it down, and watch where you're going. Barbara, I'm headed over to the station anyway. I can drop you off at the call center." It was only another couple of blocks to the municipal building. It seemed silly to get into Officer Hantz's car when we were almost there.

"It's not that far," I said. "Cameron can drive me."

"No," Cameron said. "It's okay. You should ride with Officer Hantz." The two of them stared at each other, and I got the feeling a silent conversation was taking place that I was not privy to.

It was not until I was in Officer Hantz's car that I remembered about Cameron being on the Megan's Law website. Apparently finding out you're a clone and that your whole life has been a lie can make you forget minor details like that. Besides, I'd pretty much come to the conclusion that Cameron's appearance on the website was more of a misunderstanding than anything else. But misunderstanding or not, maybe Officer Hantz didn't trust Cameron.

"Do you spend a lot of time with Cameron Schaeffer?" he asked. He watched Cameron in his rearview mirror and waited for him to drive away.

"No," I said, and then because I thought it would somehow help Cameron's reputation, I said, "He's dating my sister."

"You might want—well—it would probably be better if you didn't spend much time with him."

———————

The call center was quiet.

"Weekday afternoons usually aren't too busy," Danielle told us. "Sometimes people just call to chat. We'll get more calls later on tonight."

Danielle stayed on the line while Meg chatted with an older woman whose husband was terminally ill. It wasn't a domestic violence situation or any sort of crisis, just someone who needed to talk to another human being. Each call was anonymous. I imagined calling the hotline myself. Had they ever had someone call to say they were the product of some genetic experiment and needed reassurance that they were not a complete and total freak of nature? My guess was probably not.

Later in the afternoon, I had my own opportunity to take a call with Danielle listening in.

"I don't know what to do," said the woman on the other end. Her voice was weak and shaky. "It's not that I don't care for him, but I'm not in love with him. Does that make sense?"

"Sure," I said.

"But he says that doesn't make any sense, that I must be confused because if I care for him then I must be in love with him. I told him I need time and space to think about it, but he thinks the only reason I need space is because I have another boyfriend."

"This is your boyfriend?" I asked.

"Ex-boyfriend." She sighed. "He just doesn't seem to understand."

"Has he hurt you?"

"No, nothing like that. But he follows me around wherever I go. If I don't let him in the house, he breaks in."

"Are you at your house right now?"

"Yeah," she said. "But he's not here right now. Not yet, anyway."

"Do you have anywhere you could go?" I asked. "A friend's house or a relative's? We have a shelter if you need a place to stay."

"I guess I could go to my friend's house."

Danielle scribbled something on a notepad and held it up to me.

"It would probably be a good idea to file for a protection from abuse order," I said.

"He isn't abusive," the woman said quickly.

"It doesn't just mean physical abuse. He's harassing you and breaking into your home—that's a form of abuse."

The line went quiet. Was she still there?

"Are you there?" I asked. I didn't hear anything. I looked at Danielle in alarm.

"He says he only does those things because he loves me, because he can't live without me. He thinks I'm being unfair."

Danielle scratched out another note for me.

"Why don't you go and stay at your friend's house to-night? Can you call us back when you get there?"

"Okay," the woman said.

"Then we can talk with you about what is involved in filing a protection order."

"Okay. I'll do that. Thanks."

She hung up. I hung up my own phone and took a deep breath.

"You did a good job," Danielle said to me.

I didn't feel like I'd done a good job, though. I felt shaky. I didn't know anything about this woman's boyfriend, but for some reason the picture that had leaped immediately to my mind was the picture of my father that hung on our living room wall.

This woman's boyfriend had passed the point of love, to something darker and uglier. It was no longer love; it was obsession. I thought of Annie's late-night story. She said we were born of love, but that wasn't really true. We were born of obsession. Just like that woman's boyfriend, my father had been unable to say goodbye, unable to let go. In response, he created us.

———

Meg caught up with me as we were getting ready to leave. I had been doing what I could to avoid her, as much as I could avoid her while being in the same small room as her.

"He loves you, you know," she said.

"Who?" I honestly didn't know who she was talking about.

"Zach. Is there someone else I should know about?"

"No." I paused. "You two really aren't ... ?"

"A couple? Nah, I meant what I said. I'd kind of prefer to not be with a guy who was into someone else. Call me crazy. Anyway, I kind of got back together with my ex."

"I'm not really who he wants," I said. It hurt to say the words out loud, but as I said them I felt sure I was right. I thought of what he'd said in the park. He wanted me to tell him the truth, but if I did, he would only run away screaming.

"Trust me, you are," Meg said. "I could give you a ride over to his place."

I thought of the way it had felt to kiss Zach. I wanted to feel that again—it might just be enough to escape this ugly world for a little while. It was selfish, but I wanted that.

"You know where he lives?"

"It's not like that," she said. "My aunt is his landlady. So, what do you say?"

"Okay," I said.

TWENTY-FIVE

Zach's apartment was over a detached garage on a piece of property at the outskirts of town. Meg's aunt owned the house, which was about a hundred yards away from the garage. Farmland surrounded the rest of the property. Meg offered to wait for me, but I saw that Zach's light was on, and I saw his silhouette pass across the window.

"I'm okay," I said.

I climbed the stairs to Zach's door and stood there, my hand poised to knock, my heart beating about a million miles per second in my chest. I now wished I'd told Meg to wait. I didn't even know what I was doing there. Meg thought Zach was in love with me, but she hadn't been there at the pond. She hadn't seen the way he'd pushed me away and shut me out. I couldn't do this, but I was stranded. It was too far to walk home. I could call for a ride ... in fact, Annie was probably nervous that I wasn't home yet. I should call her anyway. I pulled out my phone.

I hadn't turned it back on after shutting if off for working the call center, and now I powered it up.

The door suddenly opened. Zach stood there looking at me, a puzzled expression on his face.

"How long have you been standing here?" he asked.

"Not long," I said.

"Sorry. I didn't hear you knock."

I didn't bother to tell him that I hadn't yet worked up the courage to actually knock.

"How did you get here, anyway?"

"Meg gave me a ride."

He nodded, as if he'd expected this. "Well, don't just stand there. Come inside."

I stepped into his apartment. I hadn't realized how cold I was until I started to defrost. I glanced around. The place wasn't very big, but it was his own place, and it was bigger than my bedroom.

"I'm sorry things are kind of a mess. I wasn't really expecting company."

I knew what I had to do, but first there was one thing I *wanted* to do. I knew I might never get another chance. I reached up, pulled his face to mine, and kissed him as if we were long-lost lovers reunited after being separated for years. I kissed him as if it was the last time I'd ever kiss a boy— because probably it was. He slid his hand to my waist and pulled me to him. It worked for I don't know how long... I broke free from earth's gravitational pull. I left the whole ugly mess behind. I felt only Zach's lips on mine, the slightly rough texture of the stubble on his cheek. His body pressed against mine was warm and solid. There was no world between the two of us.

Zach pulled away from me long enough to say, "I'm sorry I yelled at you. You don't have to tell me anything you don't want to. I don't care. You don't know how badly I need you."

Then he kissed me, and this time, if it was possible, it was more intense than before. He held me to him and I wrapped my legs around him. He carried me to his couch and we tumbled onto it.

"I want to tell you," I said. "I need to."

Zach lay on top me. He leaned in to kiss me, but I held him back.

"You were right," I said. "I need to be honest with you. I need to tell you everything."

"It doesn't matter," he said. His hand slid beneath my shirt. His body pressed against mine. What was I doing? Why didn't I just shut up? He said he didn't care.

"My sisters and I aren't really sisters," I said. I hated myself for saying it, but I couldn't help it. Once the words started flowing there was no way to turn them off. "We're clones," I continued. "The man I always thought was my father cloned us from the woman I always thought was my mother, because he couldn't handle her death."

Zach mulled this over. "Well, if this is a pissing contest over who has the weirder life story, you win." Then he pushed my restraining hand away and devoured me with kisses.

I pushed him back after a few seconds. "Wait," I said. "Don't you care? Aren't you completely creeped out? I'm a freak."

"So you don't have the usual sperm-meets-egg story, big deal. It's not really that much different than someone who was conceived with fertility treatments."

"It's completely different," I said. "I don't have parents. I was grown in some sort of a laboratory. I'm a copy-and-pasted person, a genetic mutant."

"You certainly look like a human being to me. A very, very attractive human being."

"I'm not joking around."

"And I'm not either," he said. "I need you, Barbara Bunting. You have no idea how badly I need you."

This time, when he kissed me, I didn't even need to escape. There was nothing to escape from. Zach didn't care that I was a clone—and that seemed like undeniable proof that Zach and I belonged together. I couldn't imagine anyone else ever accepting such a confession with the laid-back reaction that Zach had. We belonged together, and Zach was wrong about me not knowing how badly he needed me. I knew, because I needed him as badly as he needed me.

I heard the ringing sound, but I didn't immediately identify it. It sounded like something far away, something I didn't need to worry about.

"It's your phone," Zach said, and I realized he was right. It would be Annie calling to find out where I was. As I pulled the phone out of my pocket, I tried to think of what to tell her, but then I saw it was Jenelle calling. As I clicked to answer, I realized I should have just let it go to voicemail.

"Hey," I said.

"Look, technically I'm not really speaking to you, but

Gracie called me like five times trying to find you, and I guess your phone was turned off or whatever, but they need you back at home." I started to say something but she'd already clicked off.

"What was that?" Zach asked.

"Jenelle," I said. "Something's wrong. I need to go back home."

Zach was propped up on one elbow, looking at me.

"Okay," he said. "I'll drive you. Let me just grab my coat."

———

Every light in the house was on. From the street, the glowing windows seemed to scream like some sort of warning sign. I felt sick. Why couldn't Jenelle have told me more?

"I have to go," I said.

"I'll come with you," Zach said.

"No." The word shot out of my mouth so fast and so loud, I was practically shouting at him. "I mean, it's a family thing. You should go home." I got out of the car and looked back in at him. I'd been so focused on Zach I hadn't even thought of my family, hadn't even bothered to call home, and now who knew what was going on. "I'll call you."

"Barbara, wait!"

I didn't turn back. I shut the door and ran up the front steps. He waited until I was in the house before driving away. I stood inside the door listening to the sound of his car getting farther away from me, trying to catch my breath and ignore the weird aching feeling in my chest.

"Hello?" I called. "Hello?" I didn't hear anything. Where were they?

I searched downstairs, but they weren't there even though all the lights were on. I ran upstairs, but all the bedrooms were empty. Except for my room, all the lights were on up there as well. What the hell? I heard something downstairs. Was that them at the back door? What were they doing outside? I flew down the stairs and into the kitchen. I yanked the door open before I realized who it was.

"Cameron?"

"Babie, hey, long time no see," he said. He gave me that stupid charming smile of his as he stepped into the kitchen.

"Do you know where Gracie and Annie are?" I asked.

"Uh, no. I was actually here to pick up Gracie. We were supposed to go out."

Cameron stood there looking confused. I ignored him. I peered around him, to see if I could see our minivan in the driveway, but the outside floodlights were the only lights that weren't on. I squinted into the darkness, only vaguely aware of how close I was to Cameron until his hand brushed against my face, pushing my hair back behind my ear. I felt the warmth of his breath on my neck.

I pulled away from him, stepping backward until I bumped into the table.

"Babie," he said. "Shit. I'm sorry. I didn't mean to ... "

I didn't have time for this. "Was our car in the driveway?"

"What?"

"The minivan, Cameron? Did you see it in the drive-way?"

"Uh, no. I don't think so. Why?"

"Something's wrong. I don't know where they are."

"What does the note say?" he asked.

"The note?"

He pointed past me, and I turned around to see what I'd missed before. A piece of paper in the center of table. Gracie's scribbled message.

"I need you to take me to University Hospital." I said.

"The hospital?"

"It's Annie," I said. "She collapsed again. Gracie took her to the hospital."

———————

I stared out the window as we rode along in silence. How long ago had they gone to the hospital, I wondered. I should have been there. I should have been there to help Gracie.

"Annie's sick, isn't she?" Cameron said.

"Something's wrong," I said. "I don't know what." But as I spoke the words, I knew exactly what the problem was. I thought of the altered headstone. How old had Susie been when she died? Twenty-six? How had she died? I had a pretty good idea it wasn't a car crash or some random accident. She'd been sick. She'd had something wrong with her. My father had cloned a woman with a terminal illness that had killed her at a young age. We were all walking time bombs.

"That bastard." I whispered the words, but it was quiet in the car and Cameron had no trouble hearing me.

"What?" he asked.

"Nothing," I said. I closed my eyes and tried to will the dark thoughts away. Maybe it was nothing. Maybe what was wrong with Annie was something simple. Maybe she just needed to have her appendix removed or her tonsils or some simple, everyday procedure. But the silence in the car made it difficult to not stray into dark thoughts. I wished Cameron would turn on the radio, anything to distract me from my fears. I turned to ask him, but he spoke before I did.

"I had an affair with one of my students," he said. He spoke softly and I knew not to interrupt him. "She looked a bit like a Bunting; same hair, anyway. I'm not making excuses. There is no excuse. What I did, it was stupid and wrong."

It all made sense. This was how he'd lost his job and wound up back in Shallow Pond. This was why he was on the Megan's Law site.

"I never stopped loving Annie," he said. "I never really got over her dumping me."

"I think she was afraid of becoming obsessed with you."

"Yeah. Obsession, I know all about that. It's an ugly thing."

"My father," I said. "He never really got over losing my mother. It made him into a bit of a monster."

"Yeah. I understand that." Cameron grew silent and I thought he was done, but then he said, "Listen, I want you to know I'm going away. I don't belong back in this town.

It's not good for me to be here. I need to get away, sort some things out."

I nodded. Was it wrong to be jealous of Cameron? He was going to get out of Shallow Pond and I was stuck here. And even if I did make it out, I would only get a few years before the time bomb claimed me. It didn't seem fair.

TWENTY-SIX

We found Gracie in the waiting area. When she saw me, she threw her arms around me and pulled me into an unexpected hug.

"Babie," she said. "I didn't know where you were. I didn't know what to do." She released me and seemed to notice Cameron for the first time.

"Cameron gave me a ride," I said. I wondered if she knew about what Cameron had told me, but then realized that of course she didn't. "How's Annie? Is she okay?"

"It's—they think she can come home in the morning." Gracie shook her head and sat down. "I can't do this."

I thought she meant dealing with Annie being sick; I thought there was some sort of accusation in her words, that she was mad at me for not being there. But then I saw the way she glanced over at Cameron. He looked awkward, like he didn't know what he was doing there. She didn't want to say anything in front of him.

"Have you eaten?" I asked her.

She shook her head. "I'm not hungry."

"You should eat." I turned to Cameron. "Can you go down to the cafeteria and grab her something?"

He looked relieved to have something to do and practically ran out of the room.

"Dr. Feld knows," Gracie said. "He wants to do tests. Not just on Annie, but on you and me too. Babie, I can't do this. I can't be this … this *thing*. I can't handle it."

"We won't let them do any tests we don't consent to," I said. "But you know that she died, and whatever it was that killed her, we must have it too."

"I'm not sick. I'm a perfectly normal person. Look at me! Do I look like a freak?"

I was glad we were alone in the small waiting area, but her voice had grown so loud that I was sure they'd heard it at the nurse's station down the hall. Gracie stood up and began to pace the small room.

"What about Annie?" I asked. "What are they going to do with her?"

"Prod her with needles, scrape off her skin and look at it under a microscope, get her a gig at the local circus sideshow. I don't know—they said something about possible treatments. I can't do this."

Gracie's pacing made it hard not to get freaked out. Annie was always the calm and cool one. Annie was always in charge, but Annie was sick. It shouldn't make a difference, though. If Annie could take charge, then why couldn't I? Other than a few years, there was no difference between Annie and me.

"We'll find a specialist to treat Annie, we'll locate the best

doctor in the country," I said. "Everything's going to be fine."
I forced the shakiness out of my voice as I spoke, trying hard
to be strong so that Gracie didn't break down any more, but
inside I was a wreck.

"No," Gracie said, "it can't be fine. It can't be fine ever
again."

Cameron picked that moment to return from the cafeteria. He was holding a plastic-wrapped sandwich in his hand
and a few bottles of water.

"Tuna okay?" he asked.

"I hate tuna," Gracie said.

"Really?" I said. "I like it." Cameron handed it to me. I
looked over at Gracie. She'd stopped pacing, but she still had
the look of a cornered animal. How was it possible that we
could be clones when we were nothing like each other?

———————

Gracie and I spent the night camped out in the waiting room.
When we took Annie home in the morning, she almost didn't
look sick. She was still too thin and her hair was a mess, but
she looked bright and alert, and even seemed to have energy.
She got into a spirited debate with Gracie over the best route
to take to get back to the highway. It gave me hope, but at the
back of my mind was the nagging feeling that we would be
back at the hospital before long.

Annie confirmed my fears that night at dinner.

"There's no cure," she said, "but the treatments have

come a long way since Susie was sick. The drugs are expensive, but they work."

"What does that mean?" I asked.

"What it means is, I feel great," Annie said.

That wasn't any kind of answer, and she knew it. I looked over at Gracie, but she only sighed and looked away. She'd never really relaxed—she was still on edge, capable of snapping at a moment's notice. It was scary.

"But you're not going to get better," I said.

"I'm fine," Annie said.

"Except not really," I said.

"Shut up! Both of you!" Gracie slammed down her fork. "Am I the only one who isn't cool with becoming some sort of medical pin cushion in the name of science? Did you see the way everyone there was looking at us? We're oddities to them, rare *specimens*."

"Only Dr. Feld knows," Annie said.

"Right, and he doesn't talk to anyone else, I'm sure. Trust me, they know, and if they know, it won't be long before everyone knows. What happens when everyone in Shallow Pond knows?"

"It's possible they could descend on us in an angry mob," Annie said. If you didn't know her better, you might not have seen the smirk on her face. But I didn't think this was the right time for Frankenstein references.

"Maybe it's all a joke to you," Gracie said, "but I've got friends here, a boyfriend. I've got a life. When this rumor gets out, I can kiss all that goodbye."

"If we've made it this far without anyone finding out, then I think your precious little life is safe," Annie said.

"By the way, you're welcome," Gracie snapped. "You would think you'd be a little more grateful that I dragged your sorry ass to some distant hospital, that I gave up my whole night sitting around the hospital being treated like a complete freak."

"I am grateful," Annie said.

"You sure as hell don't act like it," Gracie said. She pushed her chair back from the table and stormed out of the room.

———————

Behind my closed bedroom door, I called Zach. My fingers shook as I pressed the buttons on the phone. Only a day had passed since I'd seen him, but it felt like longer. The world had changed since then.

"My sister was sick," I told him. "She had to be taken to the hospital."

"Oh, God," he said. "Is she all right? Which one?"

"Annie," I said. "And what she has is incurable."

I waited for this to sink in. I waited for him to get it. Zach was a smart guy. I knew it wouldn't take him long.

"Incurable and fatal?" he asked.

"Yes," I said.

"And is this something hereditary? Like, in your genes?"

"Yes," I said again.

"And it's how the original, the one you thought was your mother, died?"

"Yes."

"I don't really know what to say."

"The doctor—he was a friend of my father's, he knows all about us—he wants to do all sorts of tests on us. Gracie is freaking out."

"And you? Are you freaking out?"

"I don't see the point in it."

"Well, that's amazingly rational."

For some reason this struck me as funny. I started to giggle, but the giggle turned into full-blown laughter that I was powerless to hold back.

"Uh-oh, now you *are* freaking out."

"No, I'm not," I managed to choke out between laughs.

"I love your laugh," Zach said. "I love everything about you. I need to see you. I'm coming over."

"No, it's late, and I'm tired. I spent last night trying to sleep in a hospital waiting room. I'll see you tomorrow."

"Tomorrow's not soon enough. I need to see you now. How am I going to live without you?"

He meant, how was he going to live without me tonight, but for some reason that wasn't what I heard. "After I die, you could always clone me," I said.

My laughter vanished. I knew the remark was overly bleak and negative. Zach was so quiet on the other end I wasn't sure if he was really there.

"Okay," he said. "You win. I'll figure out a way to make it through the night without you. I'll see you tomorrow, then?"

"Yeah, tomorrow," I said.

I sat there for a while on my bed with the phone still in

my hand. I tried to understand how in love, how far off the deep end with grief you have to be before thinking that cloning your dead lover is a reasonable solution to your problem. I thought about Cameron Schaeffer and his own battle with romantic obsession. I thought about Annie breaking things off with the boy she loved. She'd said there was someone else.

It wasn't something I wanted to think about, and I tried to think of things to distract myself: school, Zach, whether my blue shirt was in my closet or in the pile of clothes to be washed. But my mind refused to be distracted. A thought wormed its way up from my subconscious; I tried to shake it off as another one of my mistaken theories. It seemed Annie would have told me, but I saw now that she'd tried—she'd dropped clues, and like an idiot I'd missed them.

A good sister would have gone to her, talked to her, offered her belated comfort. But I only lay down on my bed and tried to forget about everything.

TWENTY-SEVEN

There was a hint of spring in the air as I walked to school Monday morning. It wasn't warm out, but it wasn't bitter cold either, and the breeze that blew carried with it the smell of spring. It was like Mother Nature's way of trying to tell me to be more optimistic. But my dark and troubling suspicion haunted my thoughts. I knew it would take more than the sight of a robin and the promise that in a month or so I could go outside without a jacket to lift my spirits.

I heard a car roll up beside me and turned around to see Jenelle. She rolled down the passenger window.

"Want a ride?" she asked.

"I thought you weren't speaking to me," I said.

"Bunting, just get in the car."

I did as she commanded. It was just her in the car. "Where's Shawna?" I asked.

"Home sick. She says it's strep, but I think it's far more serious."

I thought she was taking her candy-striper duties a bit

too seriously. Now she was going around diagnosing people? "What do you think it is?" I asked.

"Broken heart," Jenelle said.

"Broken heart?"

"Bunting, if you ever paid attention to anyone else, then
you'd know that Frank dumped her on Friday."

"What? Why?"

"Apparently he realized he still has feelings for Meg."

I remembered how Meg said something about getting
back together with her ex, and now I remembered that Frank
used to date her before he started going out with Shawna.

"What a scumbag," I said.

"On the plus side, I guess that means Zach is free."

"Oh, he's not free," I said.

Jenelle gave me a look. "That guy sure gets around. Who
is he with now?"

I smiled. Thinking about Zach accomplished all those
things that the warmer weather and the hint of spring in
the air weren't able to. I abandoned my negativity long
enough to picture him. That look in his eyes, the way he
smiled. In my head, I heard the way he said my name and
it was all I could do not to explode with happiness.

Jenelle brought the car to a screeching halt and I snapped
out of my reverie.

"Barbara Bunting, are you and Zach a couple? How come
I am just finding out about this?"

"I'm in love with him," I said. "And you weren't speaking to me, remember."

"Unbelievable," she said. "The other night, when Gracie couldn't find you?"

"I was at his place."

Someone behind us beeped. Jenelle sighed and rolled her eyes, as if they were the ones being annoying when she was the one stopped in the middle of the road, but she did resume driving.

"Oh my God. Who are you and what did you do with Barbara?"

"What?"

"Seriously, Bunting, I don't really recognize you anymore."

She wasn't alone there. I hardly recognized myself either.

"Hey, about the other night, what happened?" Jenelle asked.

"Annie's sick," I said. "She had to go to the hospital. She's home now."

"Again? Sick as in sick-sick?"

"A bit more serious than a broken heart."

"Crap. Hey, I'm sorry. So do you know what's wrong?"

I thought of what a relief it had been to tell Zach everything, but I couldn't tell Jenelle. I wondered if that meant she wasn't really a good friend, but maybe I just knew that she wouldn't understand. She had parents, a normal family. Even without the whole cloning thing, we weren't exactly normal. Zach, the orphan raised by nuns, kind of got the whole abnormal thing.

"They still have some tests they want to do," I told her.

As we pulled into the parking lot, we saw Zach walking up the sidewalk to school.

"Well, there he is, Mr. God's-gift-to-women himself," Jenelle said. She turned and gave me a smile. "Go on."

"No, I'll wait for you," I said. "You've still got to find a parking place."

"Bunting, stop pretending like you don't want to fling yourself at that boy and jump his bones."

"But—"

"Get out of the car," she said. She waved me toward the door, grinning.

"See you later?" I asked.

"Yes, and I want all the details."

I ran after Zach and shouted his name. He spun around, and seeing him made it difficult to breathe. How had I managed to resist him for so long? I didn't think about the fact that we were standing in front of the school while everyone filed in. I didn't think about anything. I ran to him and kissed him. We got some hoots and cheers from our classmates. I pulled myself away from him and blushed in embarrassment.

"Hey," he said. "There's not any chance you'd be up for skipping school again today, is there?"

His eyes had the power to mesmerize me, so I looked away when I said, "We probably shouldn't. I have enough problems in my life. I don't really think getting kicked out of school would improve my situation."

"See, there you go being practical again." He shook his head and laughed, then put his arm around me as we walked into the school.

It was the longest school day I'd ever experienced, and when it finally ended I ran to my locker to dump my books.

"Is there a fire or something?" Jenelle asked when she saw me scrambling to grab what I needed from my locker.

"I'm going out with Zach," I explained.

"Ah, a fire in your pants then."

I'd just shut my locker when I saw Meg running toward me down the hallway.

"Barbara, I'm so glad I caught you," she said.

"What, did you run out of boyfriends to steal?" Jenelle asked. Meg ignored her.

"Danielle had an emergency, and she needed to know if anyone could fill in at the call center. I have a softball scrimmage today but I thought you might be free."

"Why the hell should she save your butt?" Jenelle asked. In that moment I pretty much shared Jenelle's low opinion of Meg. If I'd just moved quicker, I might have gotten out of there before Meg found me.

"Isn't there anyone else who can do it?" I asked.

"There's some conference going on and a lot of the regular volunteers are there."

Did I need to see Zach this afternoon? My brain screamed, *Yes I do!* Would I live without seeing him? My brain screamed, *Absolutely not!* It scared me how much I needed him.

"I can do it," I said.

"You don't have to do that!" Jenelle shouted at me.

"Thank you so much!" Meg said. "I owe you."

"Big time!" Jenelle added.

Zach would be there any minute, and I was afraid that if I saw him I would completely lose my will power. "Do me a favor?" I said to Jenelle. "Explain it to Zach for me?"

"You can tell him yourself," Jenelle said.

"No, I don't think I can."

———————

Danielle was still at the call center when I got there, but she had her coat on and was ready to head out the door.

"Thank you so much for doing this," she said. "The night shift should be here in a couple of hours. I wrote down my cell number in case anything happens, but it's been quiet here all day. Knock on . . . " She looked around for some wooden surface to knock on and settled for a metal desk with a wood-grain-patterned surface.

It was quiet for about an hour and fifty minutes, then my first call came. The voice of the woman on the other end was scratchy and hoarse. I decided she was either a heavy smoker or someone who'd done a whole lot of crying; maybe a little of both.

"I don't know what to do," she said.

"What's wrong?" I asked.

"He's gone. He left. He stuck a note on my windshield while I was at work. The coward couldn't even tell me to my face. It was something about how he couldn't stay in this town, that this wasn't the right place for him. Babie, I don't know what to do."

Hearing my name startled me. I tried to place the scratchy voice on the other end. I played back over what the distraught woman had said, the guy who'd left because this wasn't the right place for him. This wasn't the right place for a lot of people, but Cameron had said he was leaving, that he didn't belong here, and whoever it was knew me well enough to recognize my voice.

"Gracie?" I said.

"He left some stupid note." Now I could hear the familiar voice that was hidden by the scratchiness, the tears.

"He's an idiot," I said. "He doesn't deserve you."

"No," Gracie said. She began sniffling. "I need him. You don't understand. I *need* him."

I heard someone come into the room. I thought it must be one of the night-shift volunteers.

"There's something you need to know about Cameron," I said. "Remember how I said he was on that Megan's Law site?"

"I don't care about that," Gracie sobbed. "That doesn't matter."

"Maybe it's better for both of you if you just let Cameron go."

"But I can't just let him go. I can't handle this anymore. Maybe it's good that he left, before he found out about us, but I don't know how to go on without him."

"What are you saying?"

"How do you go on living when your reason for living is gone?"

"Seriously? Cameron Schaeffer is your reason for living? Do you know how messed up that is?"

"I love him. I love him so much. I just can't handle it anymore."

I heard someone moving around, the rustling of a jacket. It would be okay. I wouldn't have to stay on duty much longer.

"I'm on my way home," I said. "Just sit tight. I'll be there in like ten or fifteen minutes. Just hang on, okay?"

"Why would he leave without me?"

"I'm on my way there," I said as I hung up.

"Do you need a lift?"

I looked up to see not a night shift volunteer, but Officer Hantz.

"Danielle told me you were on your own this afternoon," he continued. "I'm on my way home, so I thought I'd check and see if you needed a ride.

"I have to wait for someone else to take over," I said, "but I think they'll be here any minute."

"Was that your sister on the phone? It sounded pretty serious."

I nodded. "Cameron left town."

"Damn it," Hantz said. "Sorry. He's supposed to check in with us before relocating." He looked at me, and his voice grew soft and serious. "Did something happen? Is there a reason he left?"

"Nothing happened," I said. "He told me about what happened at the school where he worked. He said he wanted to get out of Shallow Pond, get his life straightened out."

Officer Hantz nodded as he considered this. Maybe he also had come to the conclusion that Cameron wasn't really a bad guy.

A few minutes later my relief arrived. Officer Hantz drove me home. As I stepped out of the car, Annie poked her head out the front door.

"Is that your sister?" Officer Hantz asked.

"The older one," I said. "Annie."

"She's pretty."

She was. Being her clone, how could I not have been pleased by such a remark? I nearly thanked him. Hopefully he didn't see me blush. I noticed the worried look on Annie's face, though, and got scared. Something was wrong.

"Thanks for the ride," I said. I wondered if I should ask him to stick around. I didn't. He did stay long enough to give Annie a smile and wave.

She was watching him drive away when I reached the door.

"Gracie called the hotline," I said. "She sounded pretty upset. Cameron left town. He left her some note."

"Apparently it's an epidemic."

"What?"

She handed me a slip of paper. Scribbled in Gracie's handwriting was a note to let us know that she could no longer stay with us. She was going off to find Cameron. She needed to be with him.

"But I was talking to her a few minutes ago. It couldn't have been even twenty minutes ago!" I said. But twenty minutes gave someone enough time to throw clothes and clean underwear into a duffel bag, write a hasty note, and hit the highway. "Did she take the minivan?"

Annie nodded.

Great, she'd taken our only means of transportation. It wasn't like we could chase her down without wheels.

"I can call someone, get them to give us a ride," I said. I looked up the road, but Officer Hantz had already turned the corner. I could call Jenelle, but how much could she do to help us catch Gracie? On the other hand, Zach had a Mustang. That thing had enough horsepower to give our minivan a pretty good chase. "I know someone with a sports car."

"No. Let her go," Annie said.

"What?"

But Annie only shook her head and went back into the house. I followed her inside.

"I'm happy for them," she said. "She loves him. They deserve to be together."

"Aren't you jealous?" I asked.

"No, that was all a long time ago. Gracie's young. She deserves the chance to be free and happy."

"You're not exactly old."

"She's not happy here," Annie said. "This is better for her."

I went over and looked at the picture on the mantle. Susie, the woman who'd started this whole mess. I tried to imagine Gracie out there in the world somewhere, happy and smiling like the woman in the photograph, but another, darker part of me wondered if there was something about how we were raised that made us more prone to obsession. I thought of the crazy-sounding woman I'd spoken to on the phone. The one who turned out to be Gracie. Would finding Cameron make her happy? Or would she simply cling desperately to him, afraid to ever let go?

I knew what it was like to feel that almost magnetic pull, to be lost when you were in the presence of that one person who seemed to have been plucked from the heavens just for you. Only Annie seemed to be free of this burden, but she wasn't really free. For years she'd clung to her memories of Cameron, and I knew that even now she was still in love with him.

"The thing with cloning," Annie said, as if she were reading my tortured thoughts, "is that genetically it creates an exact copy of an individual. But we are more than genetics. There's so much more that goes into making us who we are."

"He never wanted to have children," I said. I knew I was changing the subject. "He only wanted the love of his life back."

"But she was gone," Annie said. "Creating a genetic copy of her is not the same as bringing her back from the grave."

"But we did look like her," I said.

She nodded, and then I knew. I knew for sure. It made sense that she'd become so alarmed when I'd mentioned rape; of course, my theory that the rapist was Cameron was wrong, just like my guess that she and Cameron were my parents was wrong. The rapist was the man we'd called Dad.

"How long did it go on?" I asked quietly.

"It started when I was eighteen. That's how old she was when they met."

"How come you never told anyone?"

"I knew we had to keep a low profile, not rock the boat. If I went to someone about what was going on it would have thrust us into the spotlight. Someone sooner or later would have pieced things together, realized our mother died before any of us were born. I didn't want us to end up in some laboratory somewhere to be studied by scientists."

"Then why didn't you leave? You could have gone to college. You could have run away."

"I couldn't figure out a way to take you and Gracie with me. I couldn't leave you behind. Not with him."

I used to think my sister had stayed in this crappy little town, had become a recluse, all because a boy she'd once loved had broken her heart. I wished I still was under that mistaken impression, because it was a lot easier to deal with than the fact that Annie had sacrificed everything for me and Gracie.

The burden weighed down on me. She'd stayed around while some obsessed, deranged pervert tried to pretend she was the wife he'd lost, just to save me and Gracie from the same fate. It wasn't fair. How could I ever begin to repay her? Now she was sick and probably dying and I felt so weak and helpless. I blinked back the tears that burned my eyes. I wished I could run away from everything, like Gracie did. I wished there was someplace I could go that was far enough to really get away, but I knew that no such place existed.

I turned and was about to head upstairs, lock myself in my room, but Annie caught me before I made it to the stairs and wrapped her arms around me. I lost it. I began to sob helplessly while she patted my hair. It was all backwards. I should have been the one comforting her.

"It's not fair," I said.

"No," she said, "it's not."

TWENTY-EIGHT

For the next week, Annie and I went through the motions of everyday life. I went to school and acted like I was nothing but a normal human being. I wasn't used to having a boyfriend, and though I wasn't intentionally avoiding Zach, I found ways to not hang out with him. I needed to look after Annie—how could I put some guy ahead of my family? Annie, meanwhile, continued to cook and to pretend that she wasn't seriously ill.

Every time the phone rang, I ran to it, expecting it to be Gracie, but it never was. Annie refused to report her missing.

"She could be dead and lying in some ditch somewhere," I said, but somehow I knew she wasn't. She was out there somewhere trying to escape. Maybe she'd found Cameron, maybe she hadn't. "Do you think she'll come back?" I asked.

"Yes," Annie said. "I think she will, eventually."

If anyone deserved to run away with the guy she loved, it was Annie, even if that guy was Cameron Schaeffer. Seeing her moping around the house, and thinking about what she'd told me, drove me crazy.

"You should go out," I told her.

"Go out? Go out where?"

"Anywhere. Go to the movies. Go to the mall."

"Gracie took the car."

"You should go on a date."

"With whom?"

But I knew the perfect person.

Officer Hantz was surprised to see me waiting for him in the police station. He looked a little bit worried.

"I'm actually here about a personal matter," I said.

"Did you want to go into the interview room?" he asked. We stood in the waiting area at the station.

"No, it's okay. I was just wondering if you had a girlfriend or were in a relationship."

His face blushed red and he looked around nervously to see if anyone was listening.

"I, um, ah," he stammered. "Listen, Barbara you're a very lovely girl, but you have to understand that—"

"No, not me!" I said quickly. "It's my sister." He still looked a little bit lost. "The pretty one," I reminded him. It clicked, and a relieved smile appeared on his face.

"For a second there I thought you were, that you—"

"She's free Saturday night," I said. "Can you pick her up at seven?"

"Um, sure," he said, and I got out of there before he had the chance to change his mind.

"You know this is completely backwards," Annie said. "Little sisters are not supposed to fix up their older sisters on blind dates."

We were in her bedroom and she was trying to figure out what she was going to wear on the big date. If I'd known that it was going to take her this long to find a suitable outfit, I would have insisted we start earlier. It was already six thirty, and a pile of discarded clothes lay in a pile beside her bed.

"Well, technically we're not sisters," I said, "and this isn't an entirely blind date. He saw you the other day and said you were pretty."

"What about this?" Annie asked. She stepped out of her closet wearing a badly fitting pair of jeans with a patterned turtleneck.

"Please tell me you're joking," I said.

"What's wrong with this?"

"You look like a soccer mom."

"Well, you thought I was old enough to be your mom," she said.

I thought of that theory. It would have been nice if it were true—Gracie would probably still be home, we could all be nice normal people, and Annie wouldn't be dying of some stupid disease that was going to kill all three of us while we were in the prime of our lives.

"I can't believe you don't have anything decent to wear. I'm going to take a look at this closet." I was pawing through her clothes, trying to find something that didn't make her look completely frumpy, when the doorbell rang. Crap. He was early. I jerked my head up and hit it on the rod. "I'll get the door," I said. "You can not answer it dressed like that."

"Where's my black sweater?" she asked, digging through the pile beside the bed.

I left her there and ran downstairs. I threw open the door, but it wasn't Officer Hantz on the other side. Zach stood there, looking better than it should have been possible for any human being to look.

"Hey stranger," he said.

"Hi," I said back.

"I know you've been acting like I don't exist, but I figured I would push my luck and see if you wanted to go out tonight."

Looking at him standing there, it was hard to believe I'd been managing to block out Zach Faraday's magnetism. Being in his presence seemed to do something to me—I didn't have the willpower to ignore him another second. Thankfully, Annie was going out on a date of her own that night, so I didn't have to feel bad about leaving her all alone.

I heard Annie coming down the stairs behind me. I turned to tell her that it wasn't her date, but she'd frozen in the middle of the staircase. Her skin looked horribly pale, and I could tell it wasn't all due to the black sweater she'd added to her ensemble. She covered her mouth with her hand. She looked absolutely terrified.

She was staring right at Zach, but she seemed not to be seeing him. I glanced over his shoulder to see if there was something going on outside, but I didn't see anything.

"Annie?" I said.

"What? How? Oh God!" she stammered. Was she having some sort of fit? Was she in pain? I couldn't tell what was going on. She shook her head and ran back up the stairs.

"Is she all right?" Zach asked.

I didn't know. "I need to go check on her," I said.

"Maybe now's not a good time, then." There was a defeated look in his eyes, and I felt a pain in my chest.

"I'll be right back," I said.

"I can wait in my car," he offered. He was still standing outside the door. I hadn't gotten around to inviting him in.

"You can wait in here."

He glanced at the empty living room, then up the stairs where Annie had gone. "I'll wait outside."

I shut the door and ran up the stairs after Annie. She was in the bathroom. The door was locked.

"Annie, what's wrong? Are you okay?"

"Is he gone?" Her voice sounded faint and weak from inside the bathroom.

"Who? Zach? He's waiting out in his car."

"Zach? The boy from school that you like?"

"Yeah—what, you thought that was your date? He's kind of young for you, don't you think?" She didn't respond. "Annie, open the door."

"I don't feel well," she said.

"It's just nerves. You haven't been on a date in like forever."

"No, it's my head. I think I'm starting to see things, hallucinate."

I wondered what she'd seen that had freaked her out so much. The doorbell rang. It wouldn't be Zach again. It must be Officer Hantz.

"I have to go answer the door," I said. "I think that's your date."

"Tell him I can't do it," Annie said. "Tell him I'm sick."

"No," I said. "You can come down and tell him yourself."

Officer Hantz was holding a grocery-store bouquet of flowers in his hand when I opened the door. Not being completely overcome with irrational desire as I'd been a few minutes earlier, I remembered my manners and invited him in.

"She's upstairs, just getting ready," I told him.

"I don't know if you're aware of this or not, but there's a young man out on the sidewalk pacing back and forth in front of a Mustang," Officer Hantz said. Apparently Zach had not mastered the skill of waiting patiently. "I'm not sure what you said to him, but I'm hoping your sister goes a little easier on me."

I tried to smile brightly, but I wasn't sure if it was reassuring or not. I was pretty sure that any minute Annie would come downstairs looking like death warmed over and telling Hantz that she was too sick to venture out.

"I'll be right back," I said. I went back upstairs and knocked on the bathroom door. "He brought flowers. You need to at least come down and talk to him."

"Just tell him I'm sick," Annie said.

"No."

I heard the water in the sink running. When she finally

stepped out of the bathroom some color had returned to her face, but she still didn't look that good.

"What was all that about?" I asked.

"I thought I saw someone," she said. She stood in the hallway and stared at the stairs. "I'm afraid to go downstairs."

"I'll walk with you."

We walked down the stairs together, Annie taking them one at a time like an invalid. She gripped my arm when we reached the bottom of the stairs. Officer Hantz was standing by the mantel looking at the picture of Susie. He turned around when he heard us. Annie's grip tightened on my arm, but before I could cry out in pain, she released it and I felt her relax. Officer Hantz smiled at her.

"That must be your mother," he said pointing at the photo. "She looks just like you."

"Yes," Annie said with a smile. "You'll have to excuse me, I haven't been feeling well."

"Oh. I'm sorry. We could go out another night if you're not up for it."

"No," I said a little too loudly for our small living room. "She's fine. She needs to get out of the house."

"Have you eaten?" Officer Hantz asked. "We could just grab something to eat if you wanted."

"I'd like that," Annie said.

A few minutes later I watched them walking down to Officer Hantz's car and caught a glimpse of Zach, now seated behind the wheel of his car. I really shouldn't have kept my distance from him.

I threw on my jacket and ran down to the street. I yanked open the passenger door of his car and got in.

"Let's go to the diner," I said.

"Sure," he said.

TWENTY-NINE

"You've been so chilly to me this week," Zach said when our food arrived. We'd barely spoken on the ride over, and other than exchanging a word here and there, we'd said nothing to each other since sitting down in the diner.

"Yeah, I've had stuff on my mind," I said.

"So that means you avoid me?" he asked. "I don't understand why you can't just talk to me. I thought we had something, and I thought that if you were upset, you would talk to me about it instead of trying to pretend I don't exist."

"My sister left town," I said.

"Gracie?"

"Yeah."

"Well, see, that wasn't so hard, was it? Talking to me, telling me stuff."

I shook my head. I tried to focus all my attention on the grilled cheese sandwich on my plate. If I looked at Zach I was pretty sure I'd lose the ability to speak entirely.

"It's more complicated than that," I said.

"It's not complicated at all."

I put down my sandwich and looked at him. He was gorgeous. If I had the chance to play God and design a perfect-looking guy, I would have created someone who looked just like Zach. His eyes met mine and I felt my pulse quicken.

"Why do you like me?" I asked.

"What kind of question is that?"

"I'm serious. Why do you like me? Why me and not someone else?"

"Because you're smart and you're pretty. You're independent. You don't care what anyone else thinks. Because no one else makes me feel the way you do."

I replayed his last sentence in my head: *Because no one else makes me feel the way you do.* Did he feel it too, then?

"When I'm around you, I become someone else," I said. But no, that wasn't quite it. "I don't recognize myself around you. I lose control."

"Is that such a bad thing?" he asked.

"It's scary," I said.

"No, what's scary is thinking you could walk away from me—that I could lose you."

"You're not being realistic. We don't know each other that well. Besides, we have our whole lives ahead of us."

"The reason we don't know each other that well is because you keep yourself closed off," Zach said. His brow furrowed in anger, and it was something about that wrinkled forehead and the dark look he gave me that made me gasp out loud and drop my sandwich onto my plate as I turned away from him. For a moment there, he hadn't looked at all like Zach.

When I looked back at him he was smiling at me, and he looked like Zach again—but no, I could see it. It flickered in and out, but if I squinted and pictured Zach looking older, I could see it.

"Oh my God," I said.

"What?" he asked. He turned around and looked behind him as if there might be someone back there, but there wasn't. He was the one I suddenly couldn't take my eyes off of, and not because of his incredible good looks. In fact, I was beginning to doubt that he really was good-looking.

Annie had thought she was hallucinating, and I'd thought she was freaking out from a bad case of nerves, but she wasn't hallucinating. I could see it too. I now understood why she'd been so scared that she'd locked herself in the bathroom. Zach bore a striking resemblance to our not-quite father. It wasn't surprising that Annie had seen it before I did—she'd spent more time with him, too much time. Plus, she'd known him longer, known him when he was a bit younger. Most of my mental images of my father came from unreliable childhood memories and what few snapshots we had of him. Of course there were only a few of these—*he* had been the one who was usually behind the camera, not Susie, since she'd died before we were ever created.

"Are you all right?" Zach asked.

"I'm not sure," I said.

For a moment I wondered if I was overreacting. Maybe the stress of everything—Annie being sick, Gracie leaving, the three of us being something other than normal—had taken its toll on me. I could be hallucinating. I looked at

Zach, and it was like I was looking into the eyes of my father. How could I have never seen it before?

It all made sense, too. Zach had been left on the steps of a convent. He'd never known who his parents were—and that was because, like me, he didn't *have* parents, not in the traditional sense. He was the product of some mad scientist's stupid experiment. Who would do a thing like this? Why would they do it?

As these questions spun through my mind, they must have written themselves on my face because Zach said, "You're starting to freak me out."

"I'm starting to get freaked out," I said.

I realized something else. All these years, Zach's life had been financed by a mysterious secret benefactor. Not only that, but for no apparent reason this same benefactor had arranged for him to move to Shallow Pond. That was no accident. Of all the towns in the country, to be sent to Shallow Pond—which was already home to three more clones than your average American town—could be nothing but pure manipulation. Everything I felt about Zach—the way it seemed he'd been sent just for me—that wasn't just a feeling. That was real. This wasn't the work of the fates of the universe. Zach's benefactor wanted him to move to Shallow Pond so that he could meet me and we could fall in love, just like our clones had thirty-some years before.

My stomach churned uncomfortably and I felt hot and dizzy. Suddenly everything was too close. I needed space and fresh air.

"I'll be right back," I said. I ran out of the diner and into the parking lot. It was chilly outside, and I'd left my jacket back in the booth, but I didn't care. The cold air felt good.

We were like chess pieces in someone's weird and twisted game, or puppets dancing at the pull of a string. I began playing back events from my life to see if they had really been the way I remembered them or if they, too, had been orchestrated by some demented puppet master. Who was this puppet master? Obviously, one and the same as Zach's benefactor. Perhaps before he'd died, my father had set up some sort of trust fund and given some attorney or someone specific instructions on providing for the alleged orphan boy. Perhaps Dr. Feld was involved in some way—but no, he hadn't known about my father's death.

I thought about how strange that was. Surely someone so close to my father would have heard the news of his death. Annie had handled all the arrangements, and Annie had known about Dr. Feld; she'd made us take her to University Hospital specifically to see him. So why wouldn't she have contacted him when our father died?

I knew there was only one answer that made any sense. I played back the events of his death. There had been a short service at the funeral home. Besides us, some of the other folks from around town had been there, but not friends of my father's. He really hadn't had any; it was just folks who knew Annie or Gracie. I think my teacher showed up. There hadn't been any viewing, of course, just the urn containing his ashes on display at the front of the room, next to the most recent photo we had of him. I thought of Susie's grave in Shallow Pond's cemetery. Why would he choose to be cremated instead of being laid to rest beside the love of his life?

"I thought you might be cold out here," Zach said. He walked over and handed me my jacket. "Was it something I said?"

I shook my head and thought about how Zach said I didn't share things with him. Maybe that was instinct on my part.

"Remember how my sister freaked out before?" I asked.

"Hard to forget."

"I think maybe I understand why. Do you think you could drive me home?"

"Sure, fine." His shoulders slumped as he walked toward his car. I stood there for a moment watching him, then jogged to catch up.

"Zach!" I called, even though I was only a step or two behind him. "I'm crazy about you!" His eyes brightened. "It's just I'm not sure why I am, and I'm scared about why I am."

"Is that supposed to make sense?"

"I'm sorry. I can't explain right now."

Just the porch light was on when Zach pulled up to the curb. I figured Annie must still be out, which made sense. The night was young. I should still have been out too. "Pull into the driveway," I said. "It's okay. Gracie took the minivan with her when she left."

"I'm not worried about the minivan," Zach said. "I'm worried about you."

"I'm fine," I said. "I just need to check something. Wait here. I'll be right back."

I ran into the house and went straight to the small room my father had used for an office. After he died, we'd kept the room closed, using it for boxes of Christmas decorations and other odds and ends. I'd never liked the room, maybe because I'd always associated it with my grumpy father. I went straight to the desk, which still had some papers on top. What I wanted to find was a death certificate. That would make it all official. But the papers on the desk were mostly copies of old utility bills and tax papers. I opened the drawers, surprised to find them empty. Most people don't clean out their desks before they die, but I figured maybe Annie did after he died—though why leave other papers on top of the desk? I looked around the room to see if there was some other place a death certificate might be lurking. Instead, my eyes fell on the urn.

It was an ugly thing, in black and gold, probably the cheapest model the funeral parlor offered. No sense spending any more than was necessary on the death of an unpleasant man. Unless the urn hadn't even come from the funeral home. Perhaps it had been bought on the clearance shelf at Wal-Mart. Perhaps it didn't contain ashes at all. I yanked the lid off and peeked inside, but saw immediately that it was two-thirds full of ashes. I quickly replaced the lid, uncomfortable staring at my dead father reduced to a pile of ash. It was strange to think that a full-grown person took up so little space after cremation.

I was about to walk out of the room, to give up, when a nagging feeling made me go back to the urn. Part of me resisted the idea, creeped out at the thought of looking at what remained of my father. I bit my lip as I lifted the lid again and forced myself to look at the contents.

Ashes. But as I stared, I saw it—a piece of ash that was bigger than the others, too big. I held my breath and reached my hand into the urn. The large piece of ash was a piece of paper. I stared at the type on it. Random letters that had once been part of long-lost words, and something else: *$300 OBO*. I was looking at what remained from a page of newspaper classified ads.

There could be a reasonable explanation. Maybe my father had a newspaper with him when he was cremated, or perhaps just a page from a newspaper that he'd clipped out and shoved into his pocket, and even though the high heat of the cremation furnace had reduced the rest of him to ash it had somehow left behind this scrap of fragile paper.

I knew what I needed to do. I sucked in my breath and held it again as I reached into the urn and this time scooped a handful of ash in my hand. I stared at it as I let it drift through my fingers. At first, I saw only gray ashes, but as I stared I caught glimpses of a few letters here, a number there, everything in black no-nonsense newspaper type. The urn did not contain human remains, just newspaper remains. It confirmed what I'd already figured out. He was still alive.

I sank down to the floor and rested my head against the wall. The urn fell from my hand, spilling its newspaper ash across the floor. Annie had known this whole time, of course. She was the one who'd made him leave. The other night I'd asked her why she hadn't simply run away, but she was smarter than that. She'd figured out a better solution. She'd made him go away, and had him fake his death so that no one would ever try to find him. She must have blackmailed him into leaving. She certainly had enough information to do so.

For a moment I wondered how this changed anything. The man I'd barely known who'd turned out to not be my father after all wasn't dead as I'd believed. He was alive, probably living under an assumed name somewhere out there in the world. Did this really make any difference to me? The more I thought about it, the more I realized what I needed to do.

I jumped up and went back over to the desk. I rummaged through the papers there, but it was the same pile of old bills. I glanced around at the room again, but I knew what I was looking for wasn't here. Annie wouldn't have put it here. She would have hidden it someplace safe.

I ran upstairs to her room. I didn't know where to begin. I opened the drawers of her dresser, digging through her clothes, but there was nothing buried beneath them. I pawed quickly through the books on her bookshelf. I glanced under her bed, where shoes and a herd of dust bunnies had taken up residence. I lifted up her mattress—and was rewarded with the sight of a small envelope.

Tucked inside was a piece of paper with a name and address scrawled in a shaky hand. *Donald Haley.* Could that be his new name? If it wasn't, then I had no idea who it was. I'd never heard her mention anyone by that name before. He apparently lived in Dunmore, PA.

In my room, I fired up my computer while I threw some things into my backpack. I plugged the address into Mapquest. It was about two hours away. Doable, I figured.

I threw my backpack into the back of Zach's car and sat down in the passenger seat, clutching the envelope with the name and address on it, along with the Mapquest directions.

"Are you running away from home?" Zach asked.

"No, we're going to find your benefactor," I said.

"What are you talking about?"

"Just drive," I told him.

"You're doing it again," he said. "You're shutting me out."

"I'll explain along the way."

THIRTY

We'd been on the road for a little more than half an hour without speaking. I was thinking through what I'd say when we got there. Zach mostly watched the road, but every few minutes he would turn and glare at me. Finally, he pulled off the highway into a truck stop parking lot. He killed the engine and turned to face me.

"I'm going to run in and use the facilities, and then, when I get back in the car, we're going to turn around and drive home."

"Do you really consider Shallow Pond home?" I asked. "You don't even know why you're living there."

"I'm okay with not knowing who my benefactor is," Zach said. "Obviously, he or she doesn't want me to know, and that's fine with me. I'm not going to drive through the night just to find someone who doesn't even want to be found."

He got out of the car and slammed the door after him. I weighed my options. I could tell him what I knew, but I suspected that would make him want to hightail it back to Shallow Pond even faster.

My phone rang. I assumed it was Annie calling. I realized I'd never left her a note. I felt only slightly bad; it wasn't exactly like she'd done such a good job of sharing information with me over the years. But when I looked at the number, I realized I didn't recognize it. In an instant, I knew it had to be Gracie.

"Hello?" I said into the phone.

"Barbara? Where are you?"

"Officer Hantz?" I couldn't imagine why he was calling. With everything that had happened, I'd forgotten that he was out on a date with my sister. Wait, if he was on a date with Annie, what was he doing calling me?

"I had to take Annie to the hospital. She collapsed." For an officer of the law, he sounded panicked and nervous. "Barbara, you need to come here immediately. Do you have someone who can give you a ride?"

Zach unlocked his door and got in. He saw I was on the phone and silently mouthed the words, "Who is it?" I waved him away.

"What seems to be wrong with her?" I hoped Officer Hantz was overreacting. He probably wasn't used to his date collapsing on him. It was unfair of me to get him to take her out without telling him she was sick.

"She had some sort of seizure," Officer Hantz said. "She's in a coma."

I felt like I had just plunged into a tub of ice water. For a moment I forgot how to speak.

"Barbara?"

"I'll be there as soon as I can," I said.

I felt numb and drained. I clicked off my phone and stared out at the truck stop's glowing sign.

"What's going on?" Zach asked.

"It's Annie," I said. "She's at the hospital. She's in a coma."

"What? Was she in an accident?"

"No, it's the disease. She collapsed."

"Which hospital?" Zach asked as he started the car. "I'll drive you there."

I looked down at the papers still clutched in my hand. The overhead lights at the truck stop shone down into the car like a spotlight, illuminating the scrawled handwriting on the front of the envelope.

"We need to go to Dunmore first," I told Zach.

"Your sister's in the hospital."

"And *he's* the one who put her there." I waved the envelope in his face.

Zach grabbed me by the wrist, his hand tight around me. His face was inches from mine. I stared into his eyes and could feel my heart speed up, but this time I felt something else as well, a sickening sense of revulsion.

"How did my benefactor put Annie in the hospital?"

"Because your benefactor and the man I used to think was my father are one and the same person."

"I thought your father was dead."

"Until an hour or so ago, so did I. Zach, we're alike."

"What's that supposed to mean?" Zach released my wrist. He popped the car into gear and stepped too hard on the gas, but he bypassed the entrance to the highway that would take us back toward Shallow Pond and instead turned onto the ramp toward Dunmore. "Who is Donald Haley?"

"He made me," I said, "and he made you."

"How do you know?"

"Because you're his clone."

"And you know this because ... ?"

"Because you look like him. That's why my sister freaked out when she saw you before."

"This is a bit much to believe," Zach said.

"Yeah, I know. I've been there before, believe me."

"Just give me a moment to think about this." Zach held up his hand to silence me. He didn't take his eyes off the road, but I saw his brow furrow as he considered what I'd told him. A few minutes later he said, "Why would he do something like that?"

"That's one of the things I plan on asking him."

"We're the same age, which means he must have created us at the same time, right? He leaves me on the steps of a convent until he has me move to Shallow Pond."

"We're like puppets," I said. I rested my head on the window. The cool of the glass helped to chase away the new wave of nausea that washed over me.

"I don't like this," Zach said. "I don't like any of this."

THIRTY-ONE

"Wake up. This is the exit."

My eyes shot open. I'd dozed off, but now we were almost there. A thin drizzle had begun to fall. The wipers squeaked as they dragged back and forth across the windshield. I sat up and helped Zach find where to turn as we squinted at the street signs. It was late, and I realized that Donald would probably be asleep. It wasn't like I was worried about inconveniencing him, but now I worried that he might not hear us at the door or that he might be the sort of person inclined to greet a midnight visitor with a shotgun in his hand.

Zach rolled slowly down the road while I read off the numbers on the doors. "This must be it," I said. We were in front of a shabby-looking triplex, its front porch crowded with old furniture and bits of trash. Zach found a parking spot and the two of us stared at the house for several minutes.

Suddenly Zach began to laugh. I turned to stare at him and he got his laughter under control, wiping the tears out of his eyes.

"What's so funny?" I asked.

"It's just that all these years, I've tried to picture my benefactor. Who it was, where they lived, that sort of thing. I always pictured someone who was wealthy, who lived in some big old mansion. Maybe they had a tennis court and a pool, maybe they kept champagne and caviar in their refrigerator. Whatever it was, I knew it had to be someplace pretty swank." He gestured at the shabby house. "Turns out he lives in some dump."

"I guess he hasn't figured out a way to turn his hobby of cloning people into a cash cow," I said.

"Well, or maybe he's spent all his money supporting us over the years and he doesn't have much left. My car is nicer than every single one parked on this block."

"Hang on—are you siding with him?"

"No, but I don't think he's the selfish bastard you seem to think he is, that's all."

I got out of the car and slammed the door after me. Almost immediately I saw someone's light come on across the way. Apparently this was the sort of neighborhood where a slammed door late at night was enough to get the neighbors out of bed. Zach followed me up the stairs to Donald's front door.

"We probably should have called first," Zach said.

"And give him the chance to run and hide? I don't think so."

I yanked on the handle of the storm door, but it was locked. So I pounded angrily on the aluminum frame, loud enough to rouse a few neighborhood dogs. Someone in a neighboring building yelled at me—or perhaps the dogs—to shut up. Finally, I heard someone on the other side of the door fumbling with a chain. The door creaked open, and we found ourselves staring at each other through the storm door.

I'd always remembered my father as looking sort of old, but he looked even older now. His hair had gone completely white. It was a mess on top of his head. There was the beginning of a patchy beard on his face. The robe that he wore was so filthy, I doubted it had ever seen the inside of a washing machine. His tired eyes suddenly brightened as he recognized me. He unlocked the storm door.

"Susie!" he cried out, lunging toward me with his arms outstretched. I dodged away, and Zach was suddenly between us with a murderous look in his eyes.

"Don't touch her," Zach said.

Donald stared at Zach, and then a smile stretched across his face. He'd realized who Zach was. I wondered if it was the first time he'd seen Zach since he was an infant.

"Look at you two," Donald said. "Have you come all the way from Shallow Pond? What are you doing here? I have so many questions."

"You have questions?" I said, incredulous. "What right do you have to have questions?"

I looked around. I was pretty sure that more lights in the neighborhood had come on. The dogs were still busy alerting everyone to our presence.

"We're only here because we need your help," Zach said.

"Let me guess. You're in love and you want to be married right away. Wait, you're not pregnant, are you?"

"Annie's in the hospital," I said. "She's dying. She's in a coma."

His face fell. He shook his head, as if trying to shake my words right out of it. Then he glanced past us, as if just then noticing the barking dogs and the lights.

"You better come inside," he said.

His place looked worse inside than outside. The room we stepped into was strewn with boxes and piles of crap. Pizza boxes and used dishes littered the floor like this was a stereotypical college dorm room, not the home of a grown man. He led us through the messy room and into a kitchen, which was just as bad, but at least there were chairs. He invited us to sit down, and we did. He didn't sit. Instead he paced back and forth across the small room.

"She shouldn't be sick," he said. He looked puzzled. He ran his fingers through his messy hair. "I'm pretty sure I fixed all that. Are you sure she's sick?"

"She's in a coma!" I yelled. I hadn't meant for my voice to come out so loud, but I had a hard time being civil to this man. "You need to help her."

"What am I going to do?" he asked. He waved his hands in the air helplessly. "I'm not a physician."

"You made her!" I screamed at him. I looked at Zach for backup, but Zach was too busy staring at Donald. He seemed mesmerized. Well, how could he not have been? It was like looking at a future version of himself. "How could you do this?" I went on. "How could you just play around with people without even knowing what you were doing?"

"I knew exactly what I was doing," Donald said. "I'd

performed numerous successful experiments using animals. I had no doubt everything would be fine. Of course, at first I couldn't figure out how to clone a male, but eventually I conquered that obstacle as well."

"Stop it!" I ordered. "We're not science experiments. We're people!" I stood up from the table. I didn't want to stay there anymore. I didn't want to talk to this loathsome man. "Zach, come on. We're leaving."

"Leaving?" Donald repeated. "But you just got here."

I yanked on the sleeve of Zach's jacket and he staggered to his feet. I pushed my way past Donald's old refrigerator, and noticed the old and faded picture there. Susie. I could tell by the style of clothes that it was her and not Annie, but otherwise there was no clear difference between them.

"She's at University Hospital," I said to Donald, "and if you have even a shred of humanity in you, you'll go there and figure out a way to fix her."

He reached out a hand as if to stroke my face, and Zach shifted his weight beside me as if preparing to strike.

"What I need right now is for you to be the father you always pretended to be," I said. I could feel tears streaming down my face, and I hated myself for showing weakness in front of him. I turned and ran out of the house, Zach close behind me.

Thirty-Two

It was around two a.m. when Zach dropped me off at the emergency room and went to park the car. The place looked deserted, and the woman on duty at the desk told me that she couldn't admit any visitors at this hour.

"But it's my sister," I said. "She's in a coma."

"I'm sorry," she said.

Someone stirred on a couch by the doors, and as he removed the blanket covering him and stood up, I realized it was Officer Hantz. He looked exhausted.

"How is she?" I asked. He shook his head.

"Nobody seems to know anything, or they aren't telling me. She's still in a coma."

Zach stepped through the doors, and maybe it was the fact that he looked tired or the poor hospital lighting, but he looked so much like a younger version of Donald that it was a little creepy. Who was I kidding? It was very creepy. The whole thing was creepy.

I introduced Zach and Officer Hantz, and our sleepy-looking group found seats in the waiting area.

"She seemed fine," Officer Hantz said. "We went to that Italian place, the one just past the bowling alley. We were getting ready to leave and she said something about feeling dizzy; then she just passed out. I have no idea why, and nobody will tell me anything."

"She's sick," I said. "She has been for a little while, but I thought she was doing better. I guess not. It's sort of a hereditary kind of thing."

We spent what was left of the night in a half-awake, half-asleep state in the uncomfortable waiting-room chairs. Visiting hours began at nine the next morning, but Officer Hantz had to be back for his shift. So it was just Zach and me there when one of the hospital's volunteers said I would be allowed to go up and see Annie. It was a family-only thing, so I would have to go up by myself.

"You're practically family," I said to Zach, in a voice too quiet for anyone to overhear. "I mean, you're the clone of the man I used to think was my father. That's got to count for something, right?"

He didn't bother to answer my question. "Are you going to be okay?" he asked. "Visiting her alone?"

"I think, with all I've been through in the past few weeks, visiting a comatose hospital patient will be like child's play."

"Okay," Zach said. "But after this, I'm taking you home to get some sleep."

It wasn't child's play. When I first saw Annie lying in that bed, I gasped. She was so thin and pale, she already looked dead. There were a bunch of tubes that snaked from her body to various devices in the room. One looked like it was measuring her heartbeat, and I took its steady rhythm as a sign that she was still alive.

A nurse came into the room and began checking on each of the machines. She changed out an IV bag.

"You're her sister?" she asked. I nodded. "I could tell. You two look a lot alike."

Never heard that one before. I kept my mouth shut. She was just trying to be nice.

"Is she going to wake up?" I asked.

"I don't know. You know that she's pretty sick." I nodded again. "You can talk to her. We don't really know if she can hear you, but sometimes it seems to help if you talk to them."

I waited until the nurse left the room, then pulled up a chair so that I was sitting beside the bed, as close to Annie's head as I could get. Then I talked. I told her all about Zach, how crazy I'd been about him, and then how I realized our meeting was engineered and not some twist of fate. I explained how I wasn't sure what I felt about him anymore. Without mentioning Donald or the fact that I knew he was still alive, I told her that we were going to figure out a way to fix all this, that she was going to get better. Then I told her about how sweet Officer Hantz was, staying all night in the waiting room even though they wouldn't let him up to visit her, even though he had to be at work in the morning. She needed to get better, I told her, because she had a sweet, handsome guy who wanted to take her out again. I talked until my voice grew hoarse, then lay my head down on the bed beside her. I shut my eyes and silently counted to fifty, promising myself that when I opened my eyes, Annie would open hers as well.

When I reached fifty and opened my eyes, Annie's remained closed. I sighed and pushed my chair a few inches back from the bed.

"How was she doing before this?"

I half-expected it to be Donald, but when I looked up it was Dr. Feld. He gave me a lopsided smile that wasn't at all reassuring.

"She seemed to be doing okay," I said. "But things have been stressful. Our other sister ran off."

"When you have a chance, I think we need to sit down and have a conversation. There are some things I need to tell you about."

I thought of when we'd first brought Annie to the hospital, when she'd asked to speak with the doctor alone. He must still think I was in the dark.

"I know about the cloning thing," I said, "if that's what you want to talk about."

His eyes grew large and he looked into the hallway to make sure no one had heard me.

"I tracked him down," I continued. "Joseph. He goes by Donald now. He should be getting in touch with you. He's going to figure out a way to fix her."

"I see," Dr. Feld said. He patted his belly as he considered this. "Of course, we will do whatever we can, but you need to understand that Annie is very sick."

I told him I understood, but the truth was, I didn't. I

didn't understand how someone who'd gone through as many bad things as Annie had should also have to have her life ripped from her at such a young age. It wasn't fair—and I clung to the hope that she had to get better, if only to make up for all the suffering she'd patiently endured.

————————

Someone who worked at the Italian restaurant where Annie had collapsed knew Shawna's mother, and, in typical small-town fashion, the news of Annie's coma spread quickly through the town. When Zach drove me home Sunday afternoon, Jenelle and Shawna were waiting for me on the front steps.

"My mom wants you to stay at our place," Jenelle said.

"I'm fine here," I said, but the truth was, being in our house alone spooked me out. Other than for a few hours here and there, I'd never been home on my own before.

A half-hearted debate ensued in which Jenelle, Shawna, and Zach insisted that I should stay with Jenelle, and I offered up increasingly feeble protests. In the end they won, and agreed to help me pack up some things to bring with me.

Annie's room was in a sorry state from the ransacking it had received at my hands the previous evening. Shawna even wondered if a robbery had occurred, but I assured her that it was fine. I packed a suitcase with clothes and grabbed all my school things, though the idea of going to school the next day seemed out of the question. When I grabbed my pile of school books, my scholarship letter fluttered to the ground. Jenelle picked it up, but before I could grab it from her hands, she read what it said.

"This is fantastic! Bunting, why didn't you tell us about this?"

"What is it?" Shawna asked.

"It's nothing," I said. I saw Zach standing awkwardly in the hallway and felt the need to keep the news from him. Fat chance of that with Jenelle around.

"She's getting a full college scholarship," Jenelle said.

"Awesome!" Shawna threw her arms around me, nearly suffocating me with her embrace. I saw Zach watching from the hallway.

"It's just an offer," I said. "It doesn't mean anything. I haven't signed anything yet."

My nonchalance did little to dim the enthusiasm of my two friends. Zach's look was penetrating and accusatory.

"I'm not sure I'm going to be able to go," I said, but nobody seemed to be listening to me.

We went back downstairs and were about to head outside when Jenelle gasped, and I turned around to see that she was looking into my father's old office. I'd left the door open, and I saw what she saw—the urn tipped over on the ground, the ashes scattered across the floor.

"Somebody has been here," Jenelle said. She quickly shut the door to block the view. "Bunting, you do not need to go in there."

"What is it?" Shawna asked.

"It's not what you think," I said. I knew that explaining further would mean telling them that my father's death had been faked, and I couldn't think of any way to explain that without telling them everything. For a moment, I toyed with the idea of confessing the whole thing. I imagined the look of horror on their faces. I could see how the story would spread through the town. I imagined a Frankenstein-like revolt by the residents of Shallow Pond, in which they attempted to exorcise their little town of its demons. I imagined that the next time I came back to this house, it would be burned to the ground.

So I kept my mouth shut, and we filed silently out of the house.

Thirty-Three

I went to school each day and sleep-walked through my classes. Even though I was staying with Jenelle, and even though I saw Jenelle and Shawna as well as Zach every day, I felt more alone than I'd ever felt in my life. Jenelle's mom drove me to the hospital each afternoon. The rides were long and silent, and then I went and sat in the room with my silent sister. Sometimes I told her about my day, but mostly I sat there listening to the whir of the machines, making deals with God about when she would open her eyes. But God never held up his end of the bargain.

One afternoon I stepped into her hospital room and found that I wasn't alone. The unruly white hair had been combed since I'd last seen it, and the dirty old bathrobe had been exchanged for old but respectable-looking clothes. He sat in one of the chairs at the end of her bed, and he looked up at me when I came in. His eyes were bloodshot and his face had the puffy look of someone who's been crying. That look in his eyes scared me. I looked quickly at the machines, but they all seemed to be chugging along just fine. Annie was still alive.

"You have to understand," he said. "I never wanted any of this."

"What were you thinking? Cloning some woman who had a disease that killed her?"

"I thought I'd fixed that," he said. He rubbed his face and sighed. "We had a dog, a golden retriever, who had a genetically inherited issue. Hip dysplasia is a common occurrence with large purebred dogs."

"Rose, Tulip, or Crocus?" I asked.

"No, this was their model, Daisy. I cloned her, but I used a procedure to fix the hip dysplasia in the process. The three cloned dogs never had any hip issues."

"The dogs were clones," I said. Of course—it made sense now. I couldn't believe I hadn't seen it before.

"Yeah. And they were fine. So I thought the three of you would be fine. No one was supposed to get sick."

A part of me wanted to trust this man, wanted to believe he wasn't just some selfish jerk, but there was too much ugliness to easily ignore it.

"Why do it at all?" I asked. "I just don't understand."

"Because I had the means to give her another chance," Donald said. "It wasn't fair what happened to her, and I wanted to make it up to her, let her live her life all over again."

To hear him say it, he was some sort of selfless saint, but I didn't believe it. "You didn't do it for her," I said. "She was dead. You couldn't bring her back to life just by making some"—I glanced at the hallway to make sure no one was listening—"*copy* of her. Instead, you've forced someone else to go through the same torture all over again." I waved my hand at my comatose sister.

"I didn't mean for this to happen."

"You didn't do this for her," I repeated. "It was never about Susie. If it was really about her, you would have simply let her die and not tried to play God. You did it for yourself, because you couldn't deal with losing her."

"It's not something you could ever understand," he said.

"But why *three* of us?" I asked. "Four, if you count Zach. Why do this to four people? What gives you the right?"

My voice had grown loud enough to attract the attention of one of the nurses, who poked her head in to ask if we were doing all right.

"We're fine," I said. When the nurse left, I turned back to Donald. "You made this mess, and you're going to fix it." Then I stormed out of the room and down to the hospital lobby, to pretend to work on homework for a while until I could visit Annie alone.

As I pulled a notebook out of my backpack, I saw the acceptance letter I'd shoved inside for safekeeping. I sat in the chair, folding and unfolding the letter. How could I go off to college with my sister in a coma? A morbid part of my brain thought that if Annie were to die, there would be nothing holding me in Shallow Pond, that it would make sense to go to school. But the more I thought about that, the less sense it made. Why spend four years at college when it was pretty much guaranteed that I only had a short time left to live?

Donald came by and took a seat opposite me without asking my permission. I shoved the letter into my backpack.

"You're so much like her," he said. "I mean, not just looks, but you act just like her."

"You don't even know me," I told him.

"What was that paper?" he asked.

"College scholarship," I said. He started laughing and I grew annoyed. How dare he laugh at me?

"Sorry," he said when he saw the look on my face. "It's just that Susie was awarded a scholarship too, a partial scholarship, but it meant we would have had to separate. The school that gave her the scholarship was three hundred miles away. She didn't want to be apart. I tried to talk her into accepting it, although I wasn't too crazy either about us being apart for that long."

"Well, see, I'm not like her," I said. In that moment I'd made up my mind. "I'm going to accept the scholarship. There's nothing to hold me back."

"That's good," he said. He did look surprised, and I thought he was going to say something about Annie, the only reason in the world I'd ever stay in Shallow Pond, but he said, "What about Zach?"

It was my turn to laugh. "He's just some guy who goes to my school," I said. "Some guy whose life is as messed up as mine."

Saying it made it real. I wasn't obsessed with Zach. I felt surprised that I ever had been.

———

A few days later, almost two weeks after Annie first entered the coma, I was called out of class and asked to report to the main office. I took my time walking there. My heart was in my throat, and I wasn't sure I wanted to find out why I'd been called out of class. When I got there I saw Jenelle's mother waiting for me and felt my legs grow weak. She saw the look on my face.

"Barbara, she's awake," she said.

The relief took its time making its way through my body.

The ride to the hospital had never felt so long. I was desperate to get there, worried that every second counted, that at any moment Annie would slip back into a coma and I would lose the chance to see her.

But we made it in time, and when I walked into her room Annie was sitting up in bed. She looked awful, but she was clearly awake. I ran to her and hugged her. Tears ran uncontrollably down my face.

"Hey," Annie said, "knock that off. You're getting me all wet."

I straightened up and smiled at her. My tears melted into laughs of relief. Annie just shook her head at me like I was crazy.

"They said I've been in a coma for twelve days," Annie said.

"You have," I said. "It was scary."

"I can't remember anything." She shook her head again. "The last thing I can remember was thinking I'd seen Dad's ghost at our door."

I didn't want to talk about any of that, not now. I needed

her to get better, and that wasn't going to happen if we focused on unpleasant things.

"I've decided to accept the scholarship," I told her.

"That's good, Babie. I'm glad. I don't want to see you make the same mistakes I made. My whole life has been one mistake after another. I'm going to leave this life with nothing but regrets to show for my time."

"Don't talk like that!" I shouted. "You're not going anywhere. You're going to have plenty of time to make up for your mistakes."

She sighed and turned away from me. She thought I was being foolishly optimistic, but I wasn't. Donald had figured out how to make us, and he could figure out how to fix us.

"Get out of Shallow Pond while you're still young," Annie said.

"I'd spend my whole life here if it meant living to a ripe old age," I said. "But it doesn't matter. We're both going to live our lives the way we want to. You'll see."

She sighed again and made a big deal out of adjusting her blankets and pillow. I itched to explain things, to let her know about the secret weapon in my arsenal, but I knew I couldn't tell her without upsetting her, and that was something I didn't want to do just yet.

But then he walked into the room. Annie recoiled, gasping with fright and maybe confusion too. I spun around quickly and saw that Donald looked surprised. Perhaps no one had told him that Annie was awake.

"Get out of here," I hissed, and he backed slowly out of the room.

"It's happening again," Annie said. "I'm seeing things. I don't know what to do."

"You're not seeing things," I explained. "There's some stuff I need to tell you." I sat down in one of the chairs and slowly told her about Zach, about realizing that he must be a clone of our father. I told her about finding the fake ashes, and then the address in her room, and then about going to track down the man who'd gotten us all into this mess.

"What have you done? Why would you do that?" Annie moaned. "He can't be trusted. Never allow yourself to be alone with him."

"He's going to figure out a way to make you better," I said. "That's why he's here."

I sat with Annie until the nurses forced me to leave so she could get some rest. Donald sprang on me as I headed down the hallway. I jumped back, recalling what Annie had said about trusting him. His icy blue eyes were bright and manic-looking. The normally bustling hallway seemed way too empty.

"Have you eaten yet?" he asked. "Come have some dinner with me in the cafeteria. There's something I want to talk to you about."

"My ride's waiting," I said. "I have to go."

He looked annoyed at this, but I didn't care. I didn't want to be anywhere near this man. I continued to back slowly away, heading in the direction of the nurses' station.

"I've got good news and bad news," he said. "The good news is I've figured out how to fix her. How to fix Annie."

I stopped backing up. He had my full attention now.

"Then what's the bad news?"

"The bad news is I won't be able to do it without your help."

"How is that bad news? Of course I'm going to help."

"Well, it means you aren't going to be able to accept that college scholarship. You'll have to stay here during the treatments, and it could take as long as a year."

I thought of how he seemed to want me to be an exact duplicate of Susie, how he couldn't understand why I didn't want to stay with Zach, how he'd assumed I too would not make use of my college scholarship. And I remembered what Annie had said, that I shouldn't trust him. Had he actually figured out a way to fix Annie, or was this all some trick—a trick that would keep me around so that I could become his new Susie?

THIRTY-FOUR

At lunch, Todd Jameson asked Shawna to the prom, which meant that of the three of us, I was the only one without a date. But it didn't matter. How could I possibly be worried about the prom when my sister was in a hospital bed, pretty much on the verge of death? Maybe I had the power to save her, or maybe the man behind my utterly messed-up life was just feeding me more of his twisted lies. But could I take that chance and be the one responsible for hammering that last nail into Annie's coffin? I didn't feel like I had a choice in the matter. I was stuck in Shallow Pond for at least another year, perhaps for all eternity.

But there was a prom coming up and I was supposed to be all excited about it. In fact, judging by the reactions of my friends, I was supposed to be freaking out that I didn't yet have a date. We still had more than a month to go before the big day, but by the way Jenelle and Shawna were acting it seemed like the fate of the entire world hung in the balance.

"I don't understand why Zach hasn't asked you yet,"

Jenelle said for what must have been the fiftieth time. The school day was over and they were both waiting for me at my locker. Either I was moving too slowly or Shawna had to pee—she was dancing around and hopping from foot to foot, which couldn't have been easy in her platform sandals.

"It's not like we're a *thing* thing," I said.

"I don't know what that means," Jenelle said.

"It's just that it's kind of complicated. I can't explain."

"You never can." Jenelle sighed. "Look, anyone can see he's crazy about you. He's probably scared to ask you to the prom because he thinks you're going to say no. Guys hate rejection."

"You say that like there's someone out there who likes rejection."

"Boy alert, eleven o'clock," Shawna said.

"Two o'clock," Jenelle and I corrected her in unison, when we saw Zach walking toward me.

"It's about time," Jenelle said. "Okay, catch you later. Call if you need a ride." The two of them scurried away so that I could talk to Zach alone.

I was still seeing Zach every day at school. We said hi to each other as we passed in the halls or grumbled about our English teacher and her doddering ways, but mostly we didn't talk. We hadn't spent any actual time together since the night we'd tracked down Donald.

"I hear your sister's doing better," Zach said.

"Yeah, well, as good as can be expected," I said. I heard the bitter edge to my voice and tried to compensate for it by saying, "She's awake now, which is nice."

"I feel like you've been avoiding me," he said.

"I see you all the time."

"You know what I mean."

I couldn't meet his eyes, not because I was afraid he'd see through me, but because I was afraid of what I would feel. What if I looked into those eyes and I lost it? What if there was still some undeniable physical pull between us if I gave it a chance? We were made for each other, after all, and I remembered how I'd always lost control whenever I was with Zach.

He reached a hand out to grab my backpack, and I shied away. "Come to the pond with me," he said.

"I should get to the hospital," I said, but the truth was I wasn't sure if I was going to the hospital. I wasn't ready to give Donald an answer yet.

"I'll drive you over," he said. "But first we need to talk."

The surface of the pond still looked frozen, but there was water around the edges and I could tell the ice wasn't all that thick. It would all be gone soon. The weather was warm and the ground muddy, with only patches of dirty snow here and there. Even though the coming of spring should have been a happy thing, I felt sad inside.

I walked up to the edge of the pond. A breeze blew across it, carrying the cold off the ice. It felt like someone had opened a freezer door. I shivered, and Zach put his arm around my shoulders. I stiffened, but I didn't pull away from him.

"He's staying at a motel out near the university," Zach said.

"Who?"

"Your father."

"He's not my father." The angry tone of my words surprised me.

"I went to see him," Zach said. "We talked for a while. I know you don't like him, and I can't say that I blame you, but he isn't evil."

"You don't know what he did to Annie," I said.

"Actually, I do. He told me."

"It was incest."

"You yourself said he's not your father," Zach said.

I glared at him. "Well, it's morally wrong, abusive. And you still think he's a good guy?"

"I didn't say that. He's got problems, Barbara. He was too much in love with Susie and never was able to get over losing her."

"So, that makes what he did all right? Lots of people lose people they love and they don't go around creating clones."

"If he hadn't, then neither of us would be here. Doesn't that sort of freak you out?"

"This whole thing freaks me out!" I screamed. "I wish that I wasn't here. I wish that I'd never been created by some mad scientist who couldn't just join a support group or something." I removed Zach's arm from my shoulder and stormed back to his car. I didn't get in, though. I could see my reflection in the passenger-side window and it was like looking at Annie. I felt hot tears stinging my eyes. I thought of Annie in that stupid hospital bed and was reminded of how unfair her whole life had been. Donald was probably lying about being able to fix her—he probably didn't have a clue. But it didn't matter. If there was even a tiny little chance that I could somehow save my sister, I had to do it.

"I'm not accepting that scholarship," I said.

"What?"

I wasn't sure if Zach hadn't heard me because I'd spoken so softly or if he was incredulous that I would turn down a free ride to college.

"I'm staying here in Shallow Pond," I said. "I'm not going to college in the fall."

"Listen," Zach said. "If this is about me, there's something I think you should know."

His response was so much like Donald's that I couldn't help myself. I spun around and shouted, "What is it with you two? Do you really think I'd stay in this crappy town because of some dumb boy? Do you really think I am that pathetic?"

Zach staggered a few steps backward, as if I'd physically taken a swing at him. I yanked open the car door and got in, slamming the door after me. A few seconds later Zach got in on the driver's side.

"I'm not staying in Shallow Pond," Zach said. I wanted to tell him how that had no bearing one way or another on my plans, but he stopped me before I could say anything. "I always felt like I could never know entirely who I was because of that big, unanswered question about my origin," he continued. "I imagined all the time what they must have been like, my parents. I figured that some day I'd find them, and then my whole life would come together and I'd finally understand who I really was. But now that I've found out where I came from, I'm still as lost as ever, maybe more so. I think I need to go somewhere, take some time to think things over to make sense of it all."

"Are you going back to the convent?" I asked.

"No, not there. I don't really know where I'm going. I'm going to get in my car and drive, go as far as I can, or to wherever feels like a good place to stop for a while."

I imagined Zach out there, driving down some endless highway against the backdrop of a clear blue sky. I was jealous. Why did he get to leave while I had to stay?

"It sounds nice," I said.

"The thing is," Zach said, "I'm going pretty soon. I made some arrangements to take final exams early. Donald helped me with that, actually, and, well..." He looked down at his feet. For the first time, I saw a Zach who was entirely different from the boy I'd known. He looked nervous and unsure of himself. He looked the way a teenage guy was supposed to look, and it was oddly reassuring.

I smiled at him, in spite of myself. Maybe I'd fallen for Zach simply because I was biologically programmed to. Maybe he only became interested in me because it was embedded somewhere in his DNA. But a part of me wondered whether, if we'd been different people, kids who'd led perfectly normal lives, who didn't have some weird past life controlling our present life, we could have found each other and fallen in love anyway. I felt so cheated by the whole stupid thing.

"Look, it's not anything against you," Zach said. "I

like you, but at the same time, I feel like…" He hesitated, and I jumped in.

"You feel like you don't know whether you like me because of who I am, or because years ago our clones fell in love with each other."

"Yeah," he said. "I guess I'm being stupid. It probably all sounds like some excuse."

"It's not stupid," I said. "As soon as I realized who you were, what you were, I knew I couldn't trust my feelings."

"It sucks," Zach said. "It really sucks."

"Yeah," I agreed. "But remember, I just wanted to be friends anyway."

This got him to crack a smile and even let out a short chuckle. I held my hand out to him.

"Friends?" I asked.

"Friends," he agreed, and shook it.

EPILOGUE

The feeling stole up on me at unexpected moments. It was a weird hollow feeling, like a small chunk of me was missing. Like I'd misplaced a little bit of myself somewhere along the way. As suddenly as it appeared it would vanish, but it never really went away, not completely. I missed him.

In the months after Zach left, I would catch glimpses of him in Mr. K's, only to find upon closer inspection that it wasn't Zach Faraday but a middle-aged woman or a ten-year-old boy or some other completely random person. My heart quickened at the sound of roaring engines, but they always turned out to be motorcycles or souped-up Hyundai's. It was never Zach. Zach was gone.

I knew from the start that I should have kept my distance from him, but the universe had other plans. Even though we were literally made for each other, even though our meeting was completely engineered, I suspect that if Zach had never set foot in Shallow Pond, sooner or later our paths would have crossed, because destiny is a powerful thing. Actually, it's this thought that keeps me going some days. I'm convinced that one day, maybe a long time from now, I'll run into Zach Faraday again—not through the deliberate machinations of a disturbed man, but through random chance. And then who knows. Maybe when that happens, things could be different.

Of course, saying all that makes me sound like some heartbroken, obsessed freak, and I'm not. I mean, most of the time I don't even think about Zach Faraday. He's a little blip, a phantom pain that shows up in my life—a life that has veered so far off course, sometimes I have a hard time remembering who I am.

Because Annie and I share the same DNA, and because I hadn't yet gotten sick, Donald was able to use my blood samples to create a patch that could repair Annie's damaged DNA. It was a lengthy process, and I had to provide fresh blood samples every other week. Within just a few weeks, Annie started to get better. I watched her daily, sometimes hourly, for signs of improvement. In the back of my mind was the thought that I'd put my entire life on hold for what might turn out to be no reason at all, but I tried my best to block out all pessimistic thinking. Slowly, I began to see real improvement, and it gave me a glimmer of hope.

Annie got well enough to continue her treatments as an outpatient. Two months after she first began the treatments, she felt good enough to attempt a second date with Officer Hantz, and he was brave enough to agree to it. On their third date they attended my high school graduation.

When I phoned the college to explain why I wouldn't be accepting their offer of a full scholarship (well, I left out a few details, like the fact that my sick sister and I were actually clones), they offered to hold my place and the scholarship until the following year. Maybe that's how I was able to get through the year, how I was able to force myself every other week to go to the hospital to meet with Donald and have my blood drawn. I made it a condition of Annie's treatments that all procedures were to be administered by Dr. Feld or a nurse; Donald was to have no contact with Annie.

Even though I'd already fulfilled my volunteer hours, I continued to put in time over at the women's support hotline. It gave me something to do, and sometimes it was nice to be able to talk to someone new. Sometimes women called just to have someone to chat with, and I understood it completely. We discussed clothes, the weather, movies. One evening when I returned from a shift at the call center, Annie told me that years before, she'd called the hotline.

"It gave me the courage to do what I needed to do," she said.

"They told you how to get Donald to leave?" I asked.

"No, but they told me to be strong, and they convinced me to do something I probably should have done much sooner."

I never found out what happened to a lot of the women I spoke to, but I liked to think that talking to me had helped them find their own inner strength.

In the fall, Officer Hantz learned that Cameron had registered as a sex offender in a town in northeastern Pennsylvania near the New Jersey border. We didn't know for sure whether Gracie was with him, but it was worth a shot. At Christmas

I sent her a card, with a note explaining everything that had happened since she'd left. We didn't receive a response.

With the blood samples he'd taken from me, Donald had also been working on creating a serum that would repair the problems in my DNA as well as in Gracie's, if we ever found her, before we became sick. He was working on a way to alter some of his notes, hiding the fact that his discoveries were based on research with human clones, in order to create a cure for others with the same disorder. I sent another note about this to the address Officer Hantz had given me.

In the spring, Gracie, Cameron, and their child—a baby girl named Lisa—showed up in Shallow Pond. The baby was adorable, and I'm happy to say she looks nothing at all like Gracie. Gracie and I received our treatments at the same time; as far as Cameron knew, it was because we'd all tested positive for the same hereditary disease—which was, technically, true. For a little while, with Gracie, Cameron, and Lisa staying at the house, it was sort of like old times. I was worried that seeing Gracie and Cameron together might open old wounds for Annie, but she didn't seem affected; maybe it helped that she and Officer Hantz—who now insisted I call him Steve—had gotten engaged on Valentine's Day.

"How are you doing?" Cameron asked one morning as the two of us sat eating breakfast together. Everyone else was still asleep upstairs.

"Okay," I said. "I have a college scholarship for next fall."

"That's great. You know, Gracie's planning on taking some classes at a community college."

While a part of me felt that Gracie was wrong to keep

Cameron in the dark about the cloning, more and more I was coming to realize that it didn't matter. While it's true we're clones, it doesn't have to have any bearing on who we are or what we do with our lives. We share the same DNA and we all look alike, but we're unique individuals.

"Is it weird being back here?" I asked Cameron. "Surrounded by Buntings?"

"A little unsettling," he admitted, "but now that I've spent so much time with Gracie, you all look so different to me."

I laughed at this, and he did too. But I think he was serious about this, even though I'd let my hair go back to strawberry-blond and was once again looking like a younger version of Gracie and Annie.

In the end, we all left Shallow Pond. After her treatments, Gracie returned to her home with Cameron and Lisa. Annie and Steve Hantz got married in September, and when he accepted a job with the Hershey police department, they bought a house there. Of course I finally left Shallow Pond too, a year late, to go to college. I didn't bother to stay in touch with Donald, but the hospital knows where to reach him if we ever need to.

I think about Zach sometimes. My past and where I came from is something I can never entirely escape, but at least I'm not alone. I have Annie and Gracie. Zach has no one other than Donald, the man who remotely controlled his life for so many years. I think about that day I first saw Zach Faraday walking down the hall at school and how hard it was to take my eyes off of him. I wonder what would have happened to us if we'd never learned the truth about our origins. Would we have unwittingly followed the path that Susie and Donald followed all those years before? Or could we have found our own path, lived our own lives, and still have been happy together?

I don't know the answers to these questions, but it doesn't matter. That's all part of the past, and with each step I take away from Shallow Pond, I put a little bit more distance between myself and the past. I used to live with one foot in the future, desperate to get out of town and get on with my life, and we know how well that worked out. So I'm trying to remain right here in the present for a little while.

I'm more interested in now, anyway. Not having to worry about the past or the future frees up my mind to think about things. For years, long before learning how very much alike my sisters and I are, I would worry about growing up and turning out to be like either one of them. And it was an unfounded fear. Of course, we do have quite a lot in common, but that doesn't make us carbon copies, despite what our DNA says. Little by little, I'm beginning to understand who I am. I'm not Susie or Annie or Gracie. I am Barbara.

Brittany Ortman

About the Author

Alissa Grosso is the author of two previous young adult novels, *Popular* and *Ferocity Summer*. She lives in Bucks County, Pennsylvania, and can be found online at alissagrosso.com.